MAGICAL MATE

BOOK FOUR OF THE WESTWOOD PACK

F.D. FAIR

Foundations Book Publishing
4209 Lakeland Drive, #398, Flowood, MS 39232
www.FoundationsBooks.net

Magical Mate
Book 4
The Westwood Pack

ISBN: 978-1-64583-111-2

Copyright © 2023 by FD Fair
Cover by Dawné Dominique Copyright 2023
Book Formatting by Bella Roccaforte

Published in the United States of America
Worldwide Electronic & Digital Rights
Worldwide English Language Print Rights

Chapter One

11 years ago – Sarah

It's just another day in the life of a mage's daughter. Some days I feel so suffocated by the need to be the perfect daughter, which is setting me up to be the perfect wife for some man that my father will choose for me. I don't even get a choice in who I marry or have children with. It's all arranged like we're back in the Middle Ages.

The only time I feel even slightly happy is when I'm at school. I wish that I could stay there forever, especially in English class. Not only can I get lost in fantastical stories my father has banned from our house, for fear they'll 'fill my head with ideas'–as if that's a bad thing–but my teacher, Mrs. Jones, is amazing. She's always making up excuses for me to stay at school longer, knowing a little of the customs of our coven—or what she thinks of as a 'community'.

Though she only started teaching here a few years before I got into grade nine, she's had the opportunity to teach quite a few of the girls from our coven and has picked up on the misogyny within. She doesn't agree with any of it: the pairing at eighteen, the roles of the women to be homemakers, or the fact that the men in our coven are completely set in their ways, believing that women should be 'rarely seen and not heard' and should stay 'barefoot and pregnant in the kitchen' for most of their lives. I, for one, would rather die than live that life, but I know that's exactly what will happen if I try to leave. I've seen it happen.

One girl, Miranda, who was a few years older than me, decided that this life wasn't for her and ran. The search for her took weeks, but when they finally found her, she was dragged back to our coven, kicking and screaming. I must've been about fourteen at the time and had to watch as she was brought in front of the entire coven, tied to a pole, and left there to rot. We were ordered not to give her any food or water or risk being tied up there with her. I still remember the day I tried:

I glance outside and see Miranda still tied to that pole, people walking around her, not even glancing her way as if she were just an ordinary lawn ornament rather than a person. It makes me sick to my stomach. I grab a bottle of water, slipping it into my pocket before making my way outside. I sit on the deck behind our house, watching and waiting for a lull in the number of people around so that I can bring it to her.

Looking at her breaks my heart. Her wrists are bloody and raw from the rope binding them, her eyes have large black bags under them, but the worst, I think, is her lips. Her lips are cracked and raw, though no blood is dripping out. It's been two days, and I know she can't last much longer without water.

I look to the left and right, not seeing anyone and decide that this is my chance. I rush over to her, unscrewing the cap as I go.

"Pst. Miranda," I say, lifting her chin with one hand and getting ready to pour the water with the other.

"Sarah?" She croaks, and I nod.

"Here. Drink," I tell her, bringing the bottle up to her mouth, but she shakes her head no, clamping her lips shut.

"Leave me," she says, and I scoff.

"Don't be like that, just drink."

She looks me in the eyes, pleading with me. "Please just leave me. You're only delaying the inevitable. But promise me: if you get the chance to leave without them finding you, do it," she says just before her head slumps down, and she passes out once more. This time, though, her breaths are shallow, too shallow. I place my hand on her foot, knowing that these could be her last moments and don't want her to be alone. I sit there, just touching her leg for hours before she takes her final shaky breath, and I cry. I place a soft kiss on her head, not knowing what else to do, and run back into the house.

That's the first time I realized exactly what kind of people mages were. They aren't people at all. They're monsters. Even Miranda's parents did nothing to help her. If it weren't for me, she would've taken her last breaths alone, tied up in the middle of the yard connecting the houses, soaked in her own blood, sweat, and pee. What kind of person lets that happen? A pang of sadness flows through me. It's been four years since then, and soon I will have to make the same decision to stay or run.

I shake my head to clear the thoughts, trying to focus on the present. Today is Friday. The day Mrs. Jones always lets me stay after school to 'help' her with grading the papers from the grade nine and ten students and anything else she needs, knowing that I'll be stuck with my father for the entirety of Saturday and Sunday.

Classes seem to fly by, and next thing I know, I'm walking into her class. She doesn't have any papers on her desk, so I'm assuming today will be just sitting and talking. Although I love this time with her, sometimes I wish we could just grade papers. She always asks questions I can't answer and tries to make suggestions that I know won't work to get me out of this situation.

"Hi, Mrs. Jones," I say as I enter the classroom.

"Oh, Sarah. I'm so glad you're here. Sit down. I want to talk to you about something," she says excitedly, gesturing to the chair opposite her.

I sit down nervously, feeling like this is a serious conversation and not just our normal chit-chat. I hope it's not her telling me I can't help her anymore. I don't have long until I graduate and then I won't have any more escapes. I need to make as much of this time as I can. Or worse, this is another suggestion on how I can get out of my predestined life.

"So, I've entered that short story you submitted the other day into a contest at the University of Toronto on your behalf, because I knew you wouldn't, and guess what?" she asks me, and I can't help the pang of anxiety that begins making its way through my body. She knows why I wouldn't have submitted it: my father will never allow me to go away to a university. I'll be lucky if my future husband allows me to take community college courses, or even get a job. But again, that's highly doubtful. In their minds, women already have jobs: cooking, cleaning, and birthing children. There is nothing else for us to do.

I shrug my shoulders at her question because I don't trust my voice not to give away the complete and utter terror I'm experiencing right now.

"They offered you pre-admittance and a full scholarship to get your English degree!" she half-shouts.

"Wha... What?" I stumble over the words. A full scholarship? Just because of one story?

"I've been telling you for years that your writing is amazing. Heck, you could do my job for me with the knowledge you have now! Imagine what you could achieve with a university degree," she continues.

"But Mrs. Jones, you know I can't go away to school. That's why I didn't apply anywhere," I whisper.

"Yes, I know. And I've been thinking about that. I want you to move in with me when you turn eighteen. Being an adult, you can make your own choice of where to live, and we'll get you enrolled and off to the University. Just because the other girls in your dad's little cult," I give her a pointed look; she knows I dislike that word, "sorry, *community* are happy to get married off and play house-wife, doesn't mean you have to. You have options. Besides, you know you would be absolutely miserable with your life if you stay," she adds on the last bit with a pointed look of her own.

Letting out a sigh, I know she's right. I will be completely miserable, but I also will be alive, and I'm pretty fond of living.

"I'll think about it," I tell her, gathering my stuff up. Usually, I'm dragging my feet to stay longer, but right now I can't. She gives me too much hope for a different life, a life that I could actually live. A life that is so completely unattainable to me that it might as well be on the moon. My father will never let me go.

"Okay, they need an answer by next Friday or they are giving the spot to the runner-up," she says, grasping onto my arms. "You deserve so much more out of life than they have planned for you. Please think about it. I will do anything in my power to help you," she finishes, wrapping her arms around me tightly in a hug. This is a first. I don't think I've had a hug ever in my life. Even when I was small and craved affection from my father, he never hugged me. I got a pat on the head and was sent to run off and play.

Reluctantly, I wrap my arms around her middle, relishing in the warm feeling spreading throughout my body. I let a tear or two slip out of my eyes. I rarely cry anymore, especially not from happiness. I'm always being told to suck it up or to stop crying because, as my father says, 'it's not befitting of a woman to cry in front of people,' and that she should 'reserve all of her tears or complaints about life for her alone time.'

Thinking of all the rules and restrictions I have placed on me makes a few more tears slip out. But when Mrs. Jones rubs my back, it's as if a dam has broken, and I can't stop the sobs that come out. So I cry. I cry for the dream of a life I know I'll never have, for the future I'm going to hate. And then I cry more for any future children that I will have because they'll be resigned to the same fate. We stand there embracing each other for a long while before my tears finally stop flowing. I know my eyes must be red and puffy, but as I step back, Mrs. Jones just wipes my cheeks off with a smile.

"A good cry always helps me," she says with a soft look, and I can't help but wish that I could take her up on her offer to help me carve a new life for myself. But I know what she doesn't. Not only would they punish me, but they would punish her, too. After all, even though she may be a teacher and not in our coven, she is still a woman, acting above her station by even suggesting that she would help me.

"Thank you, Mrs. Jones," I tell her as I break out of our hug and finish gathering my things.

"Anytime, Sarah," she replies, but I'm already walking out of the door.

I take the long way home to give myself time to think. I wonder if I can figure out a way to attend the University? Surely, there has to be some sort of reasoning I could use to get them to allow me. I could say I am willing to go to the University to be a teacher in order to homeschool the kids in the coven. They're always complaining about the curriculum taught in public schools and the fact that we're taught about women's empowerment. The fact that they have an entire course dedicated to women's studies is just the cherry on top.

The more I think about it, the more my mood lifts; I might actually be able to get away with it. But then I'll be forced to actually go through with teaching the younger generations, and there is no way that I'll be comfortable showing young girls that it's okay to live like this.

I'm still trying to come up with ways to convince my father to let me go to school when I arrive at home. "Hi, Father," I say, walking through the door. He's sitting on the couch in his spot, the same as every other day.

"Sarah. How was school?" he asks. It's the same every day. He asks me how school was, and I tell him it was good on my way to begin preparing his dinner. Today though, I'm going to try. What's the worst that's going to happen? He's going to punish me? I've taken the whip before, not often since my father is more of a yell-and-scream type of man, and I'm sure I'll take it again at some point. But it will be worth it if he says yes.

"It was good. Can I talk to you for a minute?" I ask shyly while continuing to look into his eyes. I normally keep eye contact to a minimum because, once again, I'm not at the same 'level' as him since I'm a woman.

I can tell by the look on his face that he's shocked that I'm asking, or maybe it's the eye contact. I fully expect him to get pissed and shoot me down instantly, but to my surprise, he nods and gestures to the loveseat opposite of him.

Before I lose my nerve, I put my bag down and take a seat. "They offered me a scholarship to the University of Toronto today," and he goes to speak, so I quickly add, "Please, just listen before you turn it down." Reluctantly, he agrees, skepticism written all over his face.

"Well, I was thinking: if I were to attend the University and get my teaching degree, I would be able to homeschool all future children for the coven so we wouldn't have to send them to public schools," I let the words spill out, hoping that he sees merit in my proposal.

He raises his hand and rubs his chin, the way he always does when he's mulling over something.

"I'll consider it. But we need to talk with your future husband first. You turn eighteen next week, so ultimately the decision will be his," he says, and I let my shoulders slump. There's no way that any of the mage boys he's introduced me to will allow it. "You'll be meeting him tomorrow," he adds on.

"I thought I had met all the boys already?"

"Apparently, they've already been matched," he says with a snarl, as if it's a personal affront to him that they didn't pick me, but I don't mind. "A new man just moved here from Halifax with his son, who just turned eighteen. He is looking for a wife. I have a good feeling about this one," he states, waving his hand dismissively at me. I guess he's done with the conversation, so I get up and swiftly head to the kitchen to make his dinner. I put more effort into tonight's dinner, hoping that it will help with my plea.

The next morning, I wake up with a smile on my face for the first time in as long as I can remember. Even though my father had not given me a straight *yes* as an answer, he didn't give me a flat-out *no* either. That's a win in my book. Hopefully, whoever this future husband is will be progressive enough to allow it. The thought of him not allowing me to do anything makes a frown appear instead. How do the wives live like this their entire lives, this constant worrying over whether a man will allow them to do something? I've grown up living with my father that way, and while I knew I'd be given to a man to do the same, I can't help but want more for myself. Maybe I've been spending too much time with Mrs. Jones...

I give my head a shake to clear the negative thoughts. I don't want to ruin the good mood that I woke up in. I have hope for the first time in my life, and I'll be damned if I let anything ruin it. I shower and get ready for the day, quickly heading downstairs to get started on my chores. If I can show that I'll be a fitting wife in the future, maybe he'll be more likely to agree. Especially if I prove that I can still keep up with the household while attending school.

The entire house is sparkling and smells like a bakery. I may have gone a little overboard for a light luncheon meeting, but I really want to impress this man. After all, he holds the key to my entire future. I just hope he's not like the rest of the mage men I've already met. Maybe his old coven was different.

Just before one o'clock, the doorbell rings; my father answers, greeting our guests loudly. I wait in the kitchen, knowing that if I were to make an appearance prior to being called for, all of my hard work could be spoiled.

"Sarah, would you join us in the sitting room with drinks please?" my father calls for me. I grab the already loaded tray with glasses and iced tea, making my way into the room. The first thing I notice is the older man with salt and pepper hair sitting on the love seat. I never believed that someone's face could look evil, but looking at this man, I quickly realize I was wrong. He has sharp features with a large pointy nose and eyebrows that point down toward each other. Ugh, I suppress a shudder. Goddess, I hope his son doesn't look like that.

As if sensing my thoughts, his son turns from his spot on the lazy boy to take me in. As his eyes roam my body, I notice the look of desire that passes over his face with a cruel grin. There goes hoping he's not like his father. He's almost the spitting image, although his nose is a little more proportionate to his face. Without my permission, my head tilts slightly to the side, hoping that he will look better at a different angle. Nope.

"Ah, there you are, Sarah. Come, meet our guests. This is Michael. His brother is the leader of the coven in Halifax. And this is his son, Joe," he gestures to each as I place the tray on the table and pass out the glasses.

"It's very nice to meet you," I say quietly to both, keeping my eyes low, as is the custom for mage women to do. Well, really, we aren't mages; we're witches, as our souls are not tainted, but because our magic is linked to the covens, we can not be called as such. We're not permitted to even use magic. Though I know some like me use it in secret, as much as we can access through our tethers. The more magic a woman has, the stronger the tether is, draining it out of her and supplying it directly to their father when they're younger and then eventually their husband. Luckily, I have a very small amount of magic, so my tether is so weak I'm able to still perform a few spells that help me with studying or chores. When my father isn't home, of course.

"She looks nice enough, doesn't she, Joe?" Michael says, as if I'm not in the same room.

"Sure does, Father. And by the smells coming from the kitchen, she can cook, too," Joe adds in a voice filled with desire, making my skin crawl.

My father's chest puffs out as if he's just been given the compliment. "Oh, she does. It will be a hardship to pair her off, but it would be a great honor for her to have a husband as prestigious as your son," he says, obviously kissing this man's ass.

"And her hips look to be good and wide, perfect for bearing sons," Michael states, looking me up and down before adding, "When does she turn eighteen, again?"

"Next week, but she doesn't graduate high school until June," my father explains, but Michael waves his hand.

"School is no bother. She can graduate early or drop out. My son needs an heir, and we hope to start as soon as possible," Michael states while taking a drink.

I suck in a breath, sharing a small look of panic with my father. "Actually, I was thinking that Sarah is a smart enough girl that if the coven were to send her to get her teaching degree, we could start our own small school just for the girls so they wouldn't have to be subjected to the new way of teaching poisoning their minds," my father says, his face scrunched up in disgust when mentioning the so called 'new way' of teaching.

Michael seems to ponder this for a moment, sharing a look

with his son. I hold my breath and watch with my head down as Joe shakes his head no. "I don't think that's wise. The colleges and universities in this country are even more polluted with women thinking they have the same rights as men. If she were to attend, there is no telling what they would fill her mind with."

"No, I think if she's smart enough to teach, she could do it without a degree. After all, there are women all over the world homeschooling their children without degrees," Michael finishes, and I watch as my father nods in agreement.

My chin trembles slightly at the thought. There goes my life. Not only will I not be attending any post secondary education, but I'll be dropping out of high school and having children right away.

The rest of the afternoon goes by smoothly, with me playing my part, only speaking when spoken to and basically pretending to be a statue in the room. I listen and learn more about the man that I'm to marry. If I thought my father was cruel, this man would blow him out of the water.

Once they leave and I finish cleaning up, I approach my father in the living room. "Father?" I start and he turns, gesturing for me to continue.

"May I go for a walk?" I ask demurely. "The day is so nice, I would like to get some fresh air. I already have supper in the oven and will be back before it's ready."

"As long as you're back before it's ready," he relents, going back to reading his newspaper.

I hurry out the door and jog my way to Mrs. Jones' house. It's at least a fifteen-minute walk. I need to make it there and back in less than forty-five minutes, but I need her help.

I'm covered in sweat by the time I get there. I'm not out of shape, but I'm also not a very active person. Running is not high on my priority list.

I knock on the door quickly, praying that she's home. "Sarah? Is everything okay?" she says, opening the door.

"Sorry to bother you, Mrs. Jones, but I need to ask for your help," she opens the door wider, allowing me to enter.

"Of course," she says, leading me to the kitchen. "Want some water?"

"Please," I say and guzzle the water when she hands it to me.

"What do you need?" she asks.

"Well, first, thank you for trying, but I won't be able to attend the University." She looks saddened by this statement.

"But I do need your help. I met with the man my father has paired me with, and he wants me to start having children right away. I can't put a child through this life, but I also can't actively prevent it on my own," I say, and she nods.

"How can I help with that?" she asks, her brows scrunching up in confusion.

"I need you to get me birth control. But it can't be in my name. I know this is a big thing to ask of you, and I wish I had other means, but you're my only hope," I plead with her.

"Of course, I will," she says without hesitation.

I rush around the kitchen island and engulf her in a hug. "Thank you," I whisper.

We talk for a few minutes longer, making plans for her to attend the doctor's Monday after work in order to obtain birth control for me. With renewed hope that at least I won't have to bring a child into this life, I rush back home and continue with dinner. If I'm resigned to a loveless marriage controlled by a man, at least I won't have to watch as he is cruel to any children we would have.

Chapter Two

Sebastyn—Nineteenth Birthday

"Come on, birthday boy!" My sister, Skarlyt, calls out from the living room of our family home.

"Coming. Hold your horses! Geez," I call back from my room with a chuckle.

"Well, it's not my birthday," she says. "If you want to be late for your own birthday party, suit yourself. I'm leaving in five."

I take one last look at myself in the mirror, ruffling up my straight black hair a little bit before walking out of the room. "Let's go. Gosh, Skar, why do you take so long to get ready?" She scoffs at me and rolls her eyes.

We walk out the front door, both of us calling upon our air magic to lift us into the sky. I call a strong gust to blow me in the direction of Supernatural, the downtown bar owned by Skarlyt's friend Trevan. It's the only place where us supes can go and be ourselves. It was a huge scandal when Trev left his Fae Court to come live in the human world full time and open a bar, of all things. After all, his parents are high up in the hierarchy and had to pretty much disown him. Now, he is allowed to visit and would be welcomed back, but he would have to cut all ties with his friends here which, according to him, is something he will never do. The little that he's told me about his court, I completely understand why he made the decision he did.

As the wind whips at my back, pushing me faster and faster, I raise my hands and direct the magic to swirl me around. Flying is my favorite thing to do, especially because we don't get to do it often. I can almost hear my mother now 'Sebastyn, just because we have magic, doesn't mean we should use it all the time. We need to respect our magic, not abuse it.' She believes in doing things the mundane way; although, I've caught her a few times using her magic to help with the housework or cooking. I thought about calling her a hypocrite, but then I thought about her life and how the other moms all have a partner to help her, and I stopped myself, choosing instead to take on more chores myself.

"Sebastyn, we need to be careful," Skarlyt warns, looking below us for humans. I just push myself higher, using the clouds to conceal me. Skarlyt follows.

"Slow down, Seb!" she calls, speeding up and trying to catch up to me, but she won't be able to. My dominant element is air where hers is earth.

I spin in circles flying high until I'm high enough that even other supernaturals wouldn't be able to see and wait for her to catch up.

"Sebastyn," she scolds. "You're being reckless."

I wave her off. "Come on, Skar. Be my 'fun big sister' instead of the 'responsible High Priestess in waiting.' And fun killer. You've been spending too much time with Alaric, and he's rubbing off on you."

She looks taken back for a moment. "I'm not..." she begins, but I raise a brow and she blows out a breath. "Fine, maybe I am being a fun killer. But someone needs to be responsible, and we both know that won't be you."

I fly closer to her, grabbing onto her hands. "Remember all the fun we used to have when we snuck away from Mom to practice our magic?"

"Of course I do, but things are different now..." she begins, but I cut her off.

"You're right. We're older and have responsibilities to the coven, but that doesn't mean we should stop living. Mom is an amazing woman, and she's fantastic at keeping the coven and us safe, especially since Dad died, but she's lost herself. She doesn't know how to have fun anymore." I turn to look at her.

She sighs. "You're right. She's scared. Rightfully so."

"I know that. Believe me I do. But we can't live our lives in fear of what may happen. If we do that, it's not really living." She wipes a stray tear from her eye Our father was an incredible man, and an even better witch, more powerful than even our mother, and that's saying something.

He had come across a group of human hunters in the woods. Normally, he would've steered clear of them, but one of them had fallen down a ravine and badly broken his leg. The other four were in the process of trying to figure out how to get help when my dad made himself known. He healed the man right there and then with his magic, something we're not supposed to do, but he did it anyway. When he got home and told us the story, my mom chewed him out something good, but he said he believed they were honorable men and wouldn't do anything. That ended up being his downfall: he believed in a world that doesn't exist, a world of good people who do what's right. And as sad as it is to admit, that world *will* never exist.

It took almost three months for those hunters to find him, and when they did, they weren't alone. Other than a letter floating down from the sky with the words 'I'm sorry I was wrong. Stay away from the hunters. I love you' scribbled on it, we haven't heard from him since. If it weren't for the fact that my mom felt the bond break, we wouldn't know if he was alive or dead.

Even understanding her reasoning for wanting to conceal our powers, we can't live like this forever. We're not being true to ourselves.

I wrap my sister in a hug. "I didn't mean to make you cry, Skar."

She hugs me back tightly, letting her air magic fall, trusting me to hold her up. "I know. And I know you're right. It's just hard."

"Okay. Enough with the serious stuff. Who all's going to be there tonight?" I question. She wipes her face and strengthens her air magic, floating away from me.

"Everyone, I think. Alaric, Darren, Heyden, Josh, Matt, and obviously Trev and me," she says with a smile.

"No Opal?" Her face drops once again, and I inwardly curse. I didn't mean to bring her up; I know it's a sore spot lately.

She shakes her head. "Probably not. It's weird; she's been travelling for almost a year now, and Matt says she's different when he talks to her."

My brows furrow in confusion. "Different? Different how?"

"I don't know. He just said 'different.' I guess we'll find out whenever she gets back."

I nod my head but in the pit of my stomach, a worrying feeling begins to settle. Opal was one of my sister's best friends and her brother Matt was one of mine. She's like family. She was part of our group, all of us, always together. Then after her birthday, she up and left, saying she needed to go 'find herself,' whatever that means. She checks in with Matt often, but I don't dare bring her up to him. He's already having a very hard time with her gone. They were closer than siblings, closer than even Skarlyt and I.

As the first of the buildings come into view, Skarlyt and I hold hands and whisper our spell.

"Cover of darkness, hide us well. Let no one see that which is contained by this spell." Almost instantly I can feel the pulsing of

the barrier keeping us unseen by those underneath us as we fly toward the glowing lights of Supernatural.

I see our friends waiting in the back patio area, and Skarlyt and I float down. As soon as we release our hands, the spell dissipates.

Darren jumps seeing us just appear, placing a hand on his chest. "Gods! I hate when you do that." I just chuckle, slapping him on the back.

"You'll get used to it."

He shakes his head and grumbles under his breath. "Probably not."

I laugh and make my rounds, saying hi to each of my close friends. I didn't want a huge spectacle for my birthday this year and only invited those closest to me.

I look around the space: a pool table is to the left, surrounded by bar height tables and chairs, to the right is a foosball table, small dance floor with a laptop and speakers hooked up to it. Above one of the tables on this side is a large banner with 'Happy Birthday, Seb.'

Skarlyt sees me looking at it and chuckles. "We couldn't fit your entire name on it."

"It is a pretty long name," I say before joining in on her chuckles.

The next hour or so involves me having the time of my life, dancing, eating, and playing pool with the friends I consider family.

"Hey, buddy. You having a good time?" Matt says, stepping up and clapping me on the back.

"Hell yeah. This is the best night of my life," I tell him, my words slurring just a little from the extreme amount of faery wine I've had.

"Thus far." He adds and I bob my head.

"Thus far." I agree. Then, because the alcohol has lowered my ability to keep my mouth shut, I ask, "Have you heard from Opal lately?"

His face gets a strange expression on it; it's not quite happiness, not sadness either, but a mix of both. He nods. "Yeah, actually. That's why I came over here. She's coming out tonight..."

"That's great!" I interrupt but instead of smiling like I am, he's frowning. "It's not great?" I ask, raising a brow.

He lets out a sigh. "I don't know. But I need to warn you."

I step back, even more confused now. "Warn me? About what?"

"Opal..." He begins as a beautiful blonde Barbie-looking woman walks out of the back door.

"Seb!" She exclaims, running over to me and wrapping her arms around my neck. I hug her back, looking at Matt over her shoulder.

He mouths 'Opal' with a flick of his head toward the woman, and I push the woman back, getting a good look at her. Her face is caked with make-up, her lips painted a deep red with cat-like eyes, and blonde hair falls in waves over her shoulders which are sporting straps of her skin-tight, red dress.

"Opal?" I ask. She sort of looks like Opal, but our Opal doesn't wear make-up. She always made fun of the women who seem to put too much effort into their appearance. The amount of make-up on her face hides the natural beauty underneath.

"Who else?" She says, playfully smacking me on the chest. "I couldn't miss your big day," she tells me with a grin.

I go to release her, but she snuggles right into my side like she was meant to be there. Anyone else would be ecstatic to have a beautiful woman running her hands over their chest, but not me. It feels... *wrong*.

I look down at her, but not as far down as usual due to the insanely high shoes she's wearing. "What happened to you?" I question softly.

A flicker of sadness falls across her face before that fake smile is back on. "Nothing, silly. I realized who my mate is."

"Who?" I ask with a smile, stepping back to be able to look at her straight on.

She steps back up to me, melting her body into mine. "You, of course. Don't you feel it?"

I search inside myself for that feeling of attraction or lust that would give me a clue if she was right, but I find nothing. Not a single flare of desire when I think of Opal. "No. I don't," I admit, and her face falls momentarily again, a pang of hurt crossing it before that fake mask of hers hides it again. The way she's smiling at me is almost predatory.

"Don't worry. You will," she whispers, and I'm stuck wondering if that is a promise or a threat.

The next little bit of my night is spent trying and failing to get away from Opal. She's glued to my side, always touching me, rubbing herself on me. When she tried to reach up and kiss my lips, I turned my head to give her my cheek, something I never thought I'd do, especially to Opal. She's always been beautiful, and before I would have loved nothing more than to have her as my mate. But this woman... She is not Opal. She's someone else.

Finally, she declares she needs to pee and heads to the washroom. I make a beeline for Matt. "What is that?" I demand.

He turns to look at me and sighs. Not bothering to ask what I mean, he knows exactly what I'm talking about. "That's what I wanted to warn you about. She's obsessed, Seb. Dangerously so. She got back earlier today, ranting and raving about how you two are mates and that she's going to do whatever it takes to make you hers. The way she talks about it..." I watch as he shudders.

"What can we do? Because that..." I point in the direction she went, "is not Opal."

"I know. But it is. Mom did a spell to make sure because of how strange she's acting, but it is. She's just..." He says, looking over at the door to outside. I turn to see what he's looking at and watch my sister step in front of Opal, trying to get her attention. Opal curls her upper lip up in a sneer, shoulder checking my sister in order to make her way to me. I share a sad look with Skarlyt.

"What the fuck was that?" I demand as she gets closer.

Her steps falter momentarily. "What was what?" she asks, almost sweetly, and I catch a glimpse of the old her, but only for a second.

"You just snarled at my sister and shoulder checked her."

She waves her hand in the air, brushing me off. "Oh, that was nothing. Just a conversation between two old friends."

She goes to step back into my side, but I raise my arms, holding her away. "That's not what it looked like to me," I challenge. "If you aren't going to be nice to our friends, you can leave," I tell her, putting the emphasis on the word 'our' because that's what they are... or *were*, I guess.

She pushes my hands off her shoulders, stepping right up to me with a sneer on her face. "You can try to make me leave, but I'll just keep coming back, *mate,*" she whispers it so low that only I can hear her, and the way she says it makes fear bloom in my stomach. She steps back, plastering that fake smile back on her face. "Don't worry, Seb. I'll be nice."

What the fuck? I mean, what the actual fuck is going on here? I look at my friends strewn throughout the room, searching out Darren. One look at his face, and I know he's been watching and listening to everything. He has a mixture of confusion and rage. He meets my eyes and gestures to Opal, silently asking if I want him to get rid of her. The two of us are so close, we're able to speak without words, and I shake my head. For some reason, I think that might be the wrong thing to do. For now, anyway...

Chapter Three

Sarah–Six Years Ago

I open my eyes, feeling like a fog has been lifted from my head for the first time in years and look around me. I'm in my bedroom, the room Joe and I share with our king size bed, cherry wood dresser, and walk-in closet. As I think of Joe, a strange feeling comes over me. And not one I remember feeling before. Well, not about him, anyway.

As if sensing me being awake, the phone rings. I reach onto the bedside table and pick up the portable landline. "Hello?"

"Good morning, my beautiful wife," Joe coos over the phone. My stomach drops, dread settling in. What is this about? I shake my head trying to clear the strange feelings.

"Sarah, are you there?" He says after a minute of me silently trying to figure out what's wrong with me.

"Yeah. Sorry. I just have a headache." The lie flows easily off my tongue.

"Okay. Anyway, just wanted to get you to prepare a guest room for my return. I'll be bringing someone with me."

I know better than to ask who, but I can't stop myself. It's like someone else has taken over my body. "Who?"

I can hear the snarl through the phone, as if I were looking directly at him. "None of your concern. Just do as I say," he says. A shudder rolls through my body before I hang up, leaving me staring at the phone in concern. What is wrong with me today?

I throw the blankets off and hop out of bed, stretching my muscles in preparation for a day of laundry, cooking, and cleaning. Normally, I'm happy to do these things, but not today. My face falls into a frown from not understanding these new feelings flowing through me. I shake myself out, then head into the shower, get dressed, and walk to the kitchen to make some tea. As I open the tin, finding it empty, I remember. I ran out of tea the other day, and, with Joe gone, I haven't been able to replace it. I had meant to bring it up to him today, but my head feels weird, different.

I go through the motions of making myself some regular tea and pop a couple Tylenol as I take the first sip. What is wrong with me? I try to think about the past week, to see if I can find the cause of this feeling. Everything has been business as usual. Joe's gone for the week, as is typical, and will be home tomorrow for the weekend. I've spent my days cooking, cleaning, and reading in the garden to pass the time, but as I think about Joe, new feelings replace the love I always feel for him: hate, disgust, regret. That can't be right. I close my eyes, running our past through my brain.

I remember feeling reluctance at marrying him for some reason but can't put my finger on why. Must've just been cold feet. Fast forward to our wedding day. That was the day I realized how in love with Joe I was. I don't know what changed my mind from before, but from that moment on, I was head over heels in love with the man. Even when he got in his moods, I brushed it off, knowing–believing–that it had nothing to do with me.

Our sex life was great. Or was it? I skip the reel to each time we've been intimate- every Friday, Saturday, and Sunday for the last six years-and watch myself moan at the right times, convulse at others, but I can feel the undeniable truth. It may have been great for him, but it wasn't for me, no matter how hard I pretended it was.

I shake my head, thinking more of my past with Joe, and with each second that passes, the uneasiness grows. All of a sudden, it's like something snaps, and I collapse on the floor from all the feelings bombarding me: I'm not happy. I'm not in love. I hate Joe. I hate my life. This is not the life I wanted for myself. I wanted to run away. I wanted to go away to school, to have a life of my own.

I begin to get angry at myself, wondering how, why I have been such a compliant wife for the last six years. Then it dawns on me: the tea...

Every day since the week before our wedding, I've drunk the special tea Joe has given me, saying it is full of supplements to help me get pregnant. At first I didn't want to drink it, but after arguing with my father—and hoping that the birth control pills would counteract it anyway—I drank it. Not too long after that, I stopped taking the pills, instead hoping and praying to the gods above that I would get pregnant. Never once did I stop to wonder why I all of a sudden wanted the one thing I said I never would.

I shakily stand up and rush to Joe's office, the one room in the house that I'm not allowed to go in, and throw open the doors. The only explanation for these feelings is that I was spelled to feel them. I find his grimoire on the desk, laying open. I walk over and read the name of the spell: *'Unconditional Love.'* What. The. Fuck?

I continue reading.

Will create feelings of unconditional love toward the spell caster. Repeat the spell over any loose-leaf tea and have the intended recipient drink daily.
In times of trouble, you will be there.
In times of need, you will be there.

Obedience, loyalty, and love.
Bound to me you will be.
As long as I live, so mote it be.

What the actual fuck? He spelled me to love him? I quickly turn the page searching for a reversal but find none. What I do find though is a protection spell for myself so that the tea won't affect me any more. Strange, this book doesn't ask for sacrifices or blood. All the spells either have simple herbs as ingredients or words. The magic that the mages use always contains some sort of blood, be it another's or their own. Weird. I flip the book closed, holding my finger between the pages to look at the front. I expected to see the skull symbol on the front—as is on all mage grimoires I've seen—but on the front of this is a crescent moon, with silver stars strewn throughout. A witch grimoire. Maybe from his family before they were tainted?

No matter. I flip back to my page and recite the spell.

Mother Moon protect me
from those who wish me to change.
In my hour of need I beseech thee.
Protect my body from feeling that which is not
my own.
As I will so mote it be.

As soon as the spell is finished, a tingling sensation flows through my body, almost as if I can feel the spell settling into my pores.

I set the book back in the same position I found it before

heading out of the room. Although I may be myself again, I know that the second Joe realizes the tea isn't working, things will get bad. I've been lucky to have had six years with no beatings, something I didn't think I would get, but now I'm going to have to work on my acting skills or that's going to change.

For the first time in six years, I pull the hidden box from the back of the closet, ripping open a pack of birth control and swallowing a pill down. I have at least a three-year supply saved in here since I never told Mrs. Jones I didn't need them anymore. Like clockwork, they showed up month after month until she moved away a couple of years ago. I could've thrown them away or flushed them down the toilet, but for some reason, each time the package showed up, I placed them in a box, hiding them in my closet. Maybe I subconsciously knew that I would need them again one day.

I get to work quickly, throwing the laundry in and cleaning the room before sitting down to make myself something to eat when there is a knock at the door. I'm not expecting anyone.

I rush over to the door, ripping it open to find Phoebe standing on the porch. "Hey," she greets me.

"Hi," I respond, clamping my lips closed. I have the urge to tell her everything, spill my guts and come clean about how I'm feeling. If anyone were to understand, it would be her, but then it would put her in a bad spot. I don't know what is so special about her, other than her being insanely gorgeous with a heart of gold and the best friend anyone could ask for, but I know if I were to cause issues between her and Tanner, or if she were to stick up for me with Joe, it would be bad, like really, really bad. Besides, she doesn't know anything about magic.

"Come on in," I say quickly when I realize she's still standing out on the porch.

She steps inside, and I immediately notice the lack of children. "Where are the boys?" I ask.

"Tanner wanted to take them fishing." Her face scrunches up showing me what she thinks of that idea. "I should be grateful right? That he wants to take them out and do things with them. But I can't get rid of the gnawing feeling in my gut that they're in danger." She's right, though I can't tell her that. Anything that Tanner is doing or teaching those boys is probably dangerous. Be it for them or others, I don't know. That's why I'll never understand how Tanner got his hooks into Phoebe. She's so sweet and kind, and he's... Well, he's a monster who preys on the weak. Even through the fog of the last six years, I can see that with every look he gives her or the boys. Most men would've been happy to have two handsome, strong boys to carry on their name, but not Tanner. No, he wanted girls. He was so upset when they found out they were having boys that he came over and completely destroyed my house. Furniture was tossed, holes were punched in the walls, and he even set a small fire in my kitchen causing thousands of dollars worth of damage. I didn't care though. As long as he was taking out his anger here, he was far away from her.

"I'm sure they're fine," I tell her, placing my hand on her shoulder in a show of support, and she nods, though I can tell by the pinching of her eyebrows she doesn't believe me. I don't believe me either, if I'm honest.

We walk through to the kitchen where she sits down at the table, putting her head in her hands as I make us some coffee. I know this exact scenario has happened quite a few times over the years, but where normally I am cheery and tell her that everything will be okay, I can't find the strength to do that. Because if I'm being honest, I don't think it will. Not for her, not for me.

I hand her the coffee, and as I watch as she twirls her wedding rings around, I look down at my own. I know they're tethers. All mage women's rings are. We're not allowed to practice magic, and we live to serve our masters, I mean 'husbands,' giving them our magic in return for them providing for us. I inwardly snort, not wanting to disturb Phoebe's inner dialogue. Sometimes a woman just needs to be in her own head for a minute or two without someone interrupting. But as I glance down at her rings, I can't help but wonder if hers are tethers, too. I look up at her face, trying to see... Well, I don't know what I'm trying to see. It's not like she'd be wearing a big sign that says, 'I'm supernatural.' She could be; though I doubt it, considering she's never brought anything magical up to me, and I would like to think she would.

"Phoebe?" I probe, and she looks up, her eyes glazed over with unshed tears.

"I can't shake the feeling," she says.

"That something bad is going to happen?" I ask, and she nods. Though I don't believe it myself, I force the words out of my mouth, "It will be okay." She gives me a slight smile, not believing me either, but she's trying to.

Goddess above, please help my friend and keep her boys safe. I send up a silent prayer hoping that she is listening and willing to help.

The next few years are a blur of beatings. I tried, I truly did, to pretend to still love Joe, to still be under his spell, but it was hard and the small slips in my demeanor gave me away. Now, the good days are only when he is gone, but even those are few and far between because he 'can't trust me anymore.' The bad...well, the bad take up the rest. The degrading remarks, the smacks, the orders. Phoebe and I got close, and she convinced me that it would be okay to ask Joe if I could get a job to help bring money in. I was stupid and foolish to have ever thought it was a good idea. That was the night, he tied me to the same post as Miranda and whipped me for what felt like hours. No one stopped him. Not one. They all stood and watched like obedient little robots. Even those I considered friends.

But something inside me broke with each lash. Slap! There went my will. Slap! There went my desire for a different life. Slap! There went my hope..

Since then, I keep my eyes on the floor, my house clean, and my husband satisfied. All so that I won't end up tied to that post again. I can't. I won't. I'll be the good little mouse he wants me to be, and I'll die this way.

The only silver lining is that I called Mrs. Jones after finding her number online and asked her to continue sending birth control. At least I'll never carry his child. His bloodline will die with him, as it should.

Chapter Four

Present—Sarah

I'm standing in the shadows watching everyone having a great time at the mating ceremony of Sophia and Darren. Everyone except me. As much as I want to join in their revelry, I can't. The pit of anxiety that is constantly lingering in my gut prevents me from doing anything remotely fun. That is, unless I'm holding Aurora. She has something about her; no matter how stressed and anxious I am, she makes me feel like I'm Wonder Woman and that I can take on the world.

Out of the corner of my eye, I see a beautiful woman with long sandy blonde hair, high cheekbones, olive skin, and bright green eyes. She looks identical to the only picture of my mother that I have, but when I turn to look, she's gone. It's been happening more and more lately. I see her everywhere: at the lake, in the forest, even in my dreams. I'm concerned that I might finally be having that mental breakdown I've been expecting for years.

For as long as I can remember, I've dreamed about myself as a young girl, dancing and twirling in a forest with my mother. It always felt more like a memory than a dream. A single happy memory from a childhood that I hardly remember. When I have the dreams, which is more often than not lately, I wake with a sense of longing for the woman I've never met and I'm not even sure is real.

The one time I asked my father about her when I was younger, he lost his shit. He always did that when I did or said anything that made him think of my mother, going on about how I killed her coming into this world and I should be grateful for the life he had given me. It was always on the tip of my tongue to ask 'what life?' But I knew then, and I know even better now, what would happen if I were to speak out of turn.

Even after leaving the coven, I've logged in to check my emails and voicemails randomly to see if my dad was concerned about where I've been. A sliver of hope resting inside me that he actually does love me. Instead, I've received about a thousand nasty messages from just about every member of the coven, calling me every name you can think of, blaming me for Joe's death. The one message I did receive from him basically told me that, if I didn't come back and marry one of the widowed men, I would be disowned... As if I would care about that. Although, the fact that I still check the messages shows that I must care at least a little.

"Do you want to dance?" I'm ripped from my train of thought by Skarlyt's brother, Sebastyn. He's spoken to me, but I'm always too shy to respond. That doesn't mean I haven't appreciated him from afar though: his toned, tanned, slender body, paired with his bright blue eyes, straight midnight black hair. And don't even get me started on the tattoos you can see poking up out of his shirt and down his arms. He's by far the sexiest man I've ever seen, and he's asking me to dance. As much as my body is screaming "*Yes*" and my pussy is throbbing with need for this man, I shake my head *no* and shrink back into the shadows.

I watch as his entire body deflates at my rejection. "Maybe another time," he says, lifting my hand and bringing it to his lips, pressing a featherlight kiss to it. I'm sure a blush spreads across my

30

face at his act, as I can feel my cheeks grow hot. Damn it, this man is dangerous. My heart hammers in my chest as tingles spread throughout my body, and I'm one second away from telling him I changed my mind. I open my mouth to tell him when a feminine hand touches his shoulder.

"Seb, come dance with me." One of the more beautiful witches coos at him, going as far to grab his hand and drag him away from me. All I want to do is pull him behind me and claw her eyes out for daring to touch him, but I don't. I lower my gaze and watch as he's pulled out onto the dance floor with another woman. A beautiful woman at that. Her long blonde hair falls in waves, shining in the moonlight, her red lips painted perfectly like the rest of her face are just the cherry on top of her perfect body. She has large breasts that sit high and perky with an hourglass waist and big hips, covered only by the skin tight dress she's wearing. She's everything I'm not. He looks my way more than once, but when I see her grinding her ass all over him, I decide I'm done with torturing myself over a man that is obviously way out of my league and turn to walk away. Maybe one day...

I walk out to the dock to get some distance for myself, sitting down to watch as the moon and stars dance in the lake's reflection. Ever since Phoebe brought me here, I feel such a sense of rightness, and I wish that I could be a different person and as outgoing and sure of myself as the other women around here. But the years of conditioning by my father and Joe are proving very difficult to break.

As I'm sitting and contemplating my new life, Samara walks up. "Sarah, do you think we could talk for a minute?" I turn to look at her, shocked. I didn't know that she had any desire to talk to me. I've caught her watching me, and sometimes the looks that she gives me aren't all that friendly. I knew it was only a matter of time before Sophia asked her to have a talk with me. Sophia and I have grown so close, and with Samara being her best friend, it's the logical thing.

"Sure, but I didn't think you liked me all that much?" I ask.

She lets out a deep sigh. "It's not that I don't like you; it's just that you're a mage. I've watched my whole life how the mages have treated Sophia, and it's created a deep hatred for them within me. It's really hard to get past that. But Sophia says that you're different, and I admit that I've been watching you to see if she's right. You do seem so much different, and I just thought that maybe we should sit down and listen to each other's stories before we make up our minds."

"Okay," I tell her, and she comes and sits on the end of the dock with me, both of our legs dangling close to the water but not touching. We sit there in a comfortable silence, and I wonder who's going to start first. I had already told Sophia my story about how I grew up, but I haven't really told any of the others. I feel ashamed that I allowed myself to be treated that way for so long, especially after watching all these women here who are strong and capable and free. I feel like I don't fit in, like I don't belong. And if I don't belong here, then I'm not really sure where I do belong. Because I sure as fuck do not belong in Morpeth.

"I'll go first," she says, and I breathe out a sigh of relief. As comfortable as I felt sharing my story with Sophia, I don't know if I will feel as comfortable with Samara. Not yet...

"I met Sophia when we were in first grade. She was always a little different from everyone else. Always standing on the outside watching, looking in. I could tell that she wanted a friend, that she wanted to run and play like all the others. But the more I watched, the more I realized that she couldn't. There were kids that were all friends and hung out in the same group. Their parents were friends, so they were automatically friends. You know what I mean?" she asks, and I nod, knowing exactly what mage children are like, especially the boys.

"Anyway, the more that I watched her, the more that I had this pull toward her. Like she needed my help and protection. Until finally one day I walked up to her and said, 'Hey do you want to play?' She tucked her head down into her shoulders and shook her head *no*. But I didn't give up. It took me almost two weeks to try and get her to just play on the jungle gym with me at recess. And when she did, she was always watching out of the corner of her eye to see if those kids were watching her. The times that they were watching her, she would sit down in the middle of the grass, even if we were playing tag or soccer, and just start picking up flowers or picking up the grass. At first it hurt. I thought she didn't want to be seen with me, whether it was the color of my skin, or just me. I didn't know then that she was trying to protect me. I just didn't realize what was going on.

"When we were eleven years old, in sixth grade, Sophia brought me home to meet her family. Her dad took one look at me and sent me packing. He didn't give a reason, just, 'Nope, you need to go.' I thought he smelled funny, but I was so young, and my lion hadn't made her appearance yet, so I didn't recognize him for what he was. The next week Sophia went on a 'vacation' with her family, or that's what she told everyone. When she came back to school, she was so different. So dejected. I watched and noticed as she moved in certain ways she would wince in pain. All she told me was that her dad taught her a lesson. I wanted right then to go and rip out his throat, because without telling me, I knew that he had hurt Sophia. She begged and pleaded with me not to. She told me about the one time that child protective services actually came, and at first, it seemed like they were going to help. But after they talked to her dad, something happened, and they accused Sophia of lying.

"I went to my parents after that. I grew up in a large Pride, and like most shifters, women and children are protected, cherished, and loved. They thought they could help at first by just talking to

Sophia's dad. I remember the day that my parents went to talk to him, and my dad came home in a fit of anger, mumbling under his breath about the dumb mages. It was then that we started to gather evidence. We took rotations. We took pictures and videos. My parents brought it to the police, to a lawyer, to the crown attorney. No one did anything. They said all that the pictures showed was a father disciplining his daughter. So finally, when Sophia and I were about to turn eighteen, my parents had made a plan. We were going to get Sophia away. We were going to gather other supernaturals in the area to help us fight them. To help us fight for Sophia's freedom.

"It was a few days before the plan was set to be put in motion, and I was sitting at home in the kitchen with my parents going over last-minute details," she takes a deep breath to steady herself, tears brimming in her eyes lit up by the moon.

"When the first siren went up, announcing a threat, I didn't believe it. But my parents did, and they sent me down the hatch under our kitchen table and told me to run. They told me not to come back. They said, 'If we don't meet you in two days' time, you need to go to our lawyer.' I sat down at the end of the tunnel at the edge of the forest for two days. I was tired, hungry, and I was thirsty. Luckily, I let my lion out to eat and drink. She always tried to go back to our family's home though, so I had to take control back.

"After the two days, despite my parents' wishes, I returned to our family home to find nothing but ash. They burned everything. I found what I think were the ashes of my parents and had a small burial. They killed everyone: men, women, children, even babies in their cribs. They didn't leave a single person alive," she pauses, looking up at the moon and wiping the tears that fell from her eyes.

"After that, I lived in the hunting cabin behind Sophia's house. I would go to the city to get supplies and resources. It turns out my parents left me a hefty amount. I had my lawyer run it through multiple different accounts and change my name so that they wouldn't find me. And for the next ten years, I did everything I could to protect Sophia by keeping in the shadows, all the time trying to convince her to leave. But she never would. And I'm sure that she has told you the rest," as she finishes, tears aren't only streaming down her face, but mine as well. And now I understand the looks out of the corner of her eyes. How could she not hate all mages?

"I'm so sorry, Samara. I couldn't imagine having to watch and not be able to do anything for someone you love. And as much as I'd like to say that not all mages are like that, the truth is they are."

She looks surprised at my statement, but schools her features quickly. "From what Sophia says, you're not like that, so that can't be true."

I sigh. "I guess, but then I have never truly felt like a mage. I haven't told anybody this, but I've always had these dreams. Well, not like dreams, more like memories. It's always the same. I'm running and spinning in circles in the forest, much like this one, and in a clearing with beautiful wildflowers. And there's a woman. A woman with sandy blonde hair, olive skin, and bright green eyes, laughing, singing, waving her hands, the flowers growing up to reach them. Even without words, she makes me feel loved. Wanted. Good. Something I've yet to feel outside of the dream.

"My dad was much like Sophia's, except he rarely hurt me physically. He knew that if he really wanted to hurt me, all he needed to do was not allow me to go to school. School was the only time that I felt happy. It wasn't because of the other kids. My teachers were my friends. By high school I had become friends with my English teacher. She was amazing. The type of woman that you aspire to be: strong, confident, compassionate, and caring. She knew some of what goes on in our coven, *their* coven," I correct myself. "She actually called it a cult on multiple occasions," I let off a little chuckle at the memory. I always disliked it when she used that word, but now, being here with these amazing people, I'm able to see that's exactly what it is.

"She knew that when I turned eighteen, they would pair me with a man for the rest of my life. She got me accepted to the University to be a teacher. She even offered for me to live with her so I could get away from my family. Obviously, that didn't happen. My father arranged the match with an evil man. I haven't even told Sophia this, but my husband Joe was Devin's nephew. I'm so scared that if I tell her, she'll hate me forever," Samara goes to say something, probably to tell me that Sophia wouldn't care, but I raise my hand to stop her.

"Please, just let me get this out. Joe was an evil man. Almost as bad as his best friend, Tanner, Phoebe's ex-husband. He was controlling, abusive, everything that you would expect from a mage, and because my dad didn't 'teach me lessons' the same way that Devin taught Sophia, Joe felt that it was his duty to make up for lost time. I can't tell you how many times I wanted to run away, or wanted to die, just to escape. But I was a coward on all accounts.

"He placed a spell on me for a long time making me believe I was in love with him. It was during that time that I met Phoebe, and I was ecstatic. I thought I'd finally found a friend Joe would approve of that I could talk to. I confided in her about my desire to work. It was my only complaint back then, completely and utterly under the control of the spell. She didn't understand why I couldn't if I wanted to. Truthfully, it wasn't that I wanted to work; I just wanted to get out of the house and talk to other people. In the Mage culture, that's a big no-no. It was after one of our conversations, and after I broke the love spell Joe had placed on me, that she convinced me to finally broach the subject with Joe. I made him an amazing meal and had it ready on the table when he got home. I was a mix of nervous and excited about the prospect. Phoebe had convinced me that I had all the reasons why I should work outside the home; I could bring extra money into the home, and I would still be able to do my wifely duties. But Joe didn't see it that way. Joe felt that I wasn't doing the one job that I was supposed to: give him a child. We never got pregnant. Not for lack of him trying though. What he didn't know is that the same English teacher who tried to help me get out had helped me get birth control. I took it religiously. I never wanted to bring a child into a life with that man as their father. Luckily even while spelled, while I had stopped taking the pills, I didn't get pregnant.

"When I called Phoebe because Joe went missing, I could hear the sadness in her voice at the prospect of upsetting me. She didn't realize that day was the happiest day of my life. I was going to be free. Free to live my own life. When she offered for me to come stay here, I was so reluctant. It's so hard to imagine a life where a man and a woman could be partners rather than servant and master. But after watching all the couples around here, I see that it is possible. And it terrifies me.

"I know you don't think I'm like other mages. And I guess I'm not. But I'm not like the rest of you either. I'm not strong, I'm not confident, and I surely don't have a true mate out there waiting for me. And if by some miracle I do, I'm sure he's not going to want me." Before I can continue, Samara's arms wrap around me, pulling me toward her, cocooning me, and I let the dam break. I let every moment of pain come out. All my frustrations and desires to be a different person come out in my tears.

"You are different. And you are strong. You're here, aren't you? In a safe place surrounded by people who care about you and will help you become whoever and whatever you want to be. If you haven't realized it by now, we're one big family here. You may have been Phoebe's friend first, and then Sophia's. Now you have me. You'll never have to feel unwanted or not part of a group ever again. You belong here with us. You may not feel strong right now, and that's okay. We can be strong for you until you're ready. That's what family is for," as she finishes, she pulls back to look at my eyes, wiping the tears off my cheeks. I can see the honesty there. She really means that.

"Thank you," I can't say anything else through the emotion that's clogging my throat. But I know I have one thing now that I have never had: hope.

Chapter Five

Sebastyn

As Opal pulls me away from Sarah, I can't help but look back. I watch as an angry expression crosses her face before being replaced by sadness. I want to replace that frown with a smile so badly. Doesn't she realize how beautiful she is? When I left to go meet her, while Joe was being detained and our friends were getting ready to 'take care of him,' I felt an instant pull toward her at the mere mention of her name, though it didn't compare to what I felt when I saw her for the first time.

I teleport into the picnic area of Pittock Conservation Area to await Phoebe's friend Sarah. I was expecting her to be here already, but when I step out of the trees at the Husky Trail parking area, there is no one. I hear a car rolling across the gravel and slip back into the tree line. I don't know why I'm hiding, or better question, why I feel the need to be here for this woman. But I don't need to wonder for long. As she pulls up, I watch her through the windshield. She's gorgeous. She has beautiful olive skin, chestnut brown hair, and a face even the goddesses would envy.
She reluctantly opens her car door and gets out. Goddess. That's

what she is. My heart is hammering in my chest. Not only is her face beautiful, but she has curves on her body that I can't help but want to explore every inch of. She looks around, confused and worried, with her eyebrows pinched together. As she moves to sit on the bench, placing her head in her hands, I know I can't hide anymore. I need to talk to this woman. The overwhelming urge to protect, comfort, and cherish her for the rest of her life consumes me, leaving me wondering what the fuck that's all about?

As I step out of the shadows, I say, "Hi, I'm Sebastyn. Are you Sarah?"

She jumps in fear. Her eyes widen as she takes in my face, quickly dropping to the tattoos on my neck. I know I look a little rough. Being covered in tattoos, I've gotten used to people being scared or wary around me. She tries to hide the fact that her eyes begin to roam my body, not in fear, though, like I expected. There's lust shining through her eyes. As if she senses that I'm still standing there looking at her, she raises her eyes back to mine. Her cheeks redden at getting caught staring, before she dips her head, acknowledging that she is Sarah. Goddess, that pink tinge to her already olive skin just makes her look even more gorgeous.

"Do you mind if I sit here with you?" I ask, and she scoots over closer to the edge, making room for me. I watch her body language as I go to sit down, and she stiffens, like she's afraid of what I might do. Maybe I should've gotten the full story from Phoebe. This woman is reacting as an abused animal would. I move around the other side of the picnic table to sit on the bench, allowing a healthy distance between us in order to put her at ease. It seems to help to have the tabletop between us, and she slowly relaxes. "I know I look a little rough, but I promise you're safe with me. I would never hurt you," I tell her. She doesn't say anything back. I'm not sure if it's out of fear or if she's just shy, but it doesn't stop me from continuing to talk.

"I heard you and Phoebe are friends." Again, she says nothing. She

just nods in agreement. *"Do you want to know what to expect?"* I ask, and her eyes shoot up to meet mine. Again, she nods. *"Okay, first I need to ask, were you mates?"* Her eyes widen in shock, and she finally speaks.

"I don't think so." Oh my goddess. Her voice is so beautiful. I want to close my eyes and listen to her speak about anything, everything. I want to know, no, I need to know absolutely everything about this woman. The good, the bad, and all that's in between.

"Okay, well, when you two got married or cemented your bond, did your magic mark each other?" She shakes her head no so I continue. *"That's good. You might not feel anything then. Even if your magic marked each other, it's unlikely you would feel anything other than something very minor. Your magic probably sensed the evil in him. It's amazing how our magic almost has its own intuition."* She looks back down at her hands, playing with the white outline on her ring finger from where her wedding rings probably used to reside. I really hope I'm not making her uncomfortable with this conversation, but I can't stop.

"Phoebe says you've been married for ten years. Do you have any children?" She shakes her head no at my question, but I watch her shoulders tense up. Maybe that's a sore subject for her.

 I decide that I don't want to make her feel uncomfortable, so I promptly change the subject. *"Why don't I drive your car and you can ride in the passenger seat, and that way we can leave now and be there in a few hours."* As much as I'd love to be able to spend the entire day just sitting here and talking to her, she seems very uncomfortable and I hope that being close to Phoebe, or at least on the way to see her, will help open her up more. I'm not sure what happened in her past that made her so timid and shy, but I do know that this woman has me wrapped around her finger. I would brave the depths of Hell for her, and she has only said four words to me. For real, what the fuck is going on with me?

She agrees, and we begin to make our way back to Parry Sound. I *try to make small talk in the car, you know, about the weather or different things, but nothing I say ever really truly engages her. I don't think she's said more than four or five words in a sentence to me since we began, and I just want more. I want to hear her laugh. I bet her laugh is beautiful.*

As we get closer to Parry Sound, I stop talking and let her watch out the window. She looks like a kid in a candy shop. Everything is new and shiny. She gasps as she sees different animals walking by. Finally, when we're getting closer and closer to pack land, she speaks.

"What's Phoebe's mate like?"

I'm surprised by the question, but I answer anyway. "Alaric?" I turn, looking at her, and she inclines her head, her eyes meeting mine briefly before dropping back down. It's almost as if she's submitting to me and anger flows through me. This goddess should never submit to anyone. I take a few breaths to calm myself before I answer. "He's the alpha of the Westwood pack. He's fair and just, and he genuinely cares about everyone. I'm best friends with his younger brother, Darren. Growing up, he was always there for us. When we needed someone or something, he was the one we would turn to. He searched for his mate for so long that he feared that he'd never find her. Now that Phoebe is here, he's different." I turn and look at her, seeing her eyes widen with fear. "Not bad different. Before, he was always duty driven, nothing came above the needs of the pack. Not even his own. I used to call him the fun killer because everything was always about what people would think. Now he lets loose, is more care free. He still takes care of the pack, but his priorities shifted, and now Phoebe and the kids are his entire world. You can see in his eyes how much he loves her. They sparkle every time she walks into the room." She nods when I look over, but goes back to staring out the window, leaving me wishing I would've given her a shorter answer so that she would ask more questions.

I'm brought out of my memory by Opal grinding her ass against me. "Seb, when are we going to cement the mate bond?" she questions.

I sigh as she spins around to face me. "Opal. You know we aren't mates." I've told her time and time again that I don't feel anything for her. She is either stupid or just doesn't care, which is the complete opposite of the Opal I grew up with.

"You know that's not true. I love you. I've always loved you. We are perfect for each other. Can't you see that?" she tells me while running her fingers down my face. I hate when she does that. Her persistence and delusion of us being mates is one of the reasons why I took to traveling.

I turn and walk away from her without saying anything, heading straight for Darren. "You sure I can't come with you on your honeymoon?" I ask.

Darren laughs, "Opal putting the moves on you again?"

"Always. I wish she'd just give up. I don't feel anything for her. There is no way she's my mate," I say with a sigh.

"She's never going to believe that. Look at her. She's pining over you even though you literally just left her standing in the middle of the dance floor," Darren says pointing at her. Ugh, he's right, she's still standing there looking at me like a lost puppy. She's beautiful. There is no doubt about that, but she's also crazy. Downright certifiable.

"Why don't you come for the second week when you bring Trev and Samara? Oh, you can bring Sarah too," Sophia pipes up.

I'm surprised by her statement but mull it over quickly. "I think I should be able to do that." Then I will be able to spend some quality time with Sarah. It's a win-win to get away from Opal and spend time with the woman that is consuming my thoughts. What can go wrong?

"Hey," Samara says, walking up with Trev, looking like she has been crying.

"What's wrong?" Sophia asks, immediately rushing to her side.

"Oh nothing. Sarah and I just had that talk you have been wanting us to have. I wanted to ask if you would be okay with her coming with us to see you the second week of your honeymoon? I think she needs to get away from here, even if it's for a little while," Samara asks, as if she is a mind reader.

"That makes me so happy," Sophia says, pulling Samara into an embrace, and I look at Darren in confusion. He mouths 'I'll tell you later' to me, and I dip my head in agreement. Sophia steps back. "We were actually just talking about that. Seb is going to bring you all for the second week." And they start talking about all the things we're going to do. I take that opportunity to snag Darren by the arm, pulling him off to the side.

"What's up, man?" he asks.

"What's up with that?" I ask.

"Oh, well, Samara has a huge problem with mages because of everything. When she found out that Sarah was a mage, she was leery, but Sophia convinced her to talk to her before jumping to conclusions, and I guess that's what just happened." I bob my head in acknowledgment but seethe internally at the implication of what would happen if Samara didn't like her story.

"Speaking of Sophia and Sarah... You know how you felt that pull to Sophia, and it turned out that you were mates?" He nods his head but creases his brow in confusion, waiting for me to continue. "Well, that's how I feel about Sarah. I can't explain it. She consumes my thoughts both day and night. I end up watching her like some creepy stalker when I see her out. I can hardly focus on anything," I blow out a breath. "I need your help. She seems so uncomfortable whenever I'm around her. I don't know how to get her to even have a conversation with me. I tried asking her to dance, but she turned me down instantly." I run my hand through my hair as I begin pacing.

"Okay," Darren says. I stop my pacing, turning to look at him.

"We'll figure it out. But we might need to bring Sophia and Samara in on it. Based on what Sophia has told me about Sarah, she's had it rough, and her view on men and relationships isn't good." He walks up and clasps me on the shoulder. "But if you're mates, you need to trust in Mother Moon that everything will work out. There has to be a reason she was brought into your life now," he finishes, and I admit that I feel a bit better knowing that they are going to help.

"Hey girls, want to come over here for a sec?" Darren calls out to Samara and Sophia. I turn and give him my best 'what the fuck' look. I guess we're doing this now.

"What's up?" Samara asks.

"Seb wants to ask for our help with something. Go ahead, Seb," Darren says, and I shoot another look his way. This time though, my look promises payback. I thought he would talk to Sophia in private, then she would talk to Samara. Not put me on the spot and make me ask.

I force myself to calm my nerves. "I think Sarah is my mate." The words rush out and both girls look shocked at first, before getting giant smiles on their faces.

"Oh, Mother! That is so amazing! Does she know?" they ask at the same time.

"No. At least I don't think so. She always seems so uncomfortable when I'm around so I try to give her space," I begin my pacing again. "Is that the right thing to do? Or should I be trying harder to talk to her? Or should I just leave it alone and trust in the Mother that everything will work out?"

"Woah, Seb. Calm down," Sophia says as she comes and places her hands on my shoulders. "Sarah has been through a lot. I'm not going to tell you her story because it's not my place, but I will say this. Her view of men is not good. She hasn't had a lot of positive interactions with any man in her life. With that said, you just need to prove to her that you are different. It's little things like asking how her day was and genuinely wanting to hear about it, even if she only says two words. It's being present, not disappearing, showing her that you are here and want to know her, without having something to gain."

"But I do have something to gain," I say.

"Yeah, but you wanting to be her mate, to cherish and love her for the rest of her life, is a different kind of gain than someone who just wants her for sex, or to do their cooking and cleaning. That is what you want, right?" With a dip of my head, she continues. "Good, she's had enough of men like that. You just need to show her that you're different. I'm not going to lie and say that it's going to be easy, because it's not. Sarah needs to build herself up before she can even consider having a mate. The men in her life have done an amazing job of making her feel worthless."

"She's not worthless," I spit out through ground teeth.

Sophia chuckles. "I know that. You know that. Everyone in this pack and coven can see that. But it's not about us being able to see it. She has to see it herself."

I nod. "Okay. Will you help me figure out what to do?"

"You don't really need our help, Seb. Just be you. Show her that you're different, and don't try to be someone else. Don't be fake. If she's your mate like you think she is, she will already feel the pull toward you. Just use that," Samara adds.

"Okay. Be myself. Show her I'm different. I can do that," I say out loud. Not sure if I'm telling them or myself, but I've got it. I can do this.

"She's sitting on the dock by herself right now," Samara says with a smirk.

"Thanks," I respond, already walking toward the dock. No time like the present. I snag a bottle of wine from the table and head to the dock.

Chapter Six

Sarah

I'm still sitting on the dock, thinking about the conversation with Samara and marveling at how much better I feel after talking to her. Though both Phoebe and Sophia have told me time and time again that I'm not alone, that I belong here, that I've finally found my family, it has been hard to believe. But with Samara, there's something about her, and I don't think she would tell me that if she didn't truly believe it, especially with me being a mage. I'm still trying to make sense of the new feelings spurring inside of me when Sebastyn comes and stands next to me.

"Is it okay if I join you?" he asks. Why the fuck does he want to join me sitting on the dock when he could be wherever with that blonde Barbie? Just thinking about her makes my blood boil. I can't explain it, but my heart thinks it has a claim on this man. Maybe it's because he was the first person I saw after Joe went missing, or maybe it's because he's giving me positive attention and I'm not used to it. In the past, the only time a man would give me any type of attention was when they wanted something, though Sebastyn doesn't give me that vibe. Like Samara, there's just something about him.

"Sure," I say, still looking out at the water. My body starts buzzing as he sits next to me, our shoulders barely separated. I watch out of the corner of my eye as he pulls out a bottle of wine and takes a swig.

"Would you like a drink?" he asks, offering it to me. I think about it for a minute, before deciding a small drink wouldn't hurt.

"Thanks," I say, taking the bottle from his hands. Our fingers brush against each other, sending tingles down my arm and straight to my clit. What I wouldn't give for those fingers to brush up against somewhere else, but I know that's not possible. A man like that will never look at a woman like me in that way, a woman who is too damaged to have a conversation with a man without thinking that he's going to yell, scream, or hit her. As I take a drink from the bottle and the warmth spreads down my chest, I let out a small moan. It tastes so good. I've never particularly liked the taste of wine, but this one is fruity. Wonder what kind it is. I look at the bottle, unable to find a label. Maybe I should ask...

I risk a small glance in Sebastyn's direction and see the heat in his gaze as he stares at me. A shudder flows through me, remembering when Joe used to look at me like that and what would happen after. I shake my head, clearing those thoughts. Sebastyn doesn't seem like the type of man to take advantage. No. If he wanted someone to go to bed with, that blonde bimbo seemed willing enough for both of us. I can't deny that I'm happy he's here with me rather than her, even if I don't fully understand it.

I lower the bottle and offer it back to him, never losing eye contact. I dart my tongue out of my mouth to lick my suddenly very dry lips, and watch as his eyes drop down. If I didn't know better, I would think he wants to kiss me. But I do know better, so I quickly turn back to the water.

Seb clears his throat. "So, I was talking with Darren, Sophia, Samara, and Trev, and we were wondering if you would like to join us in the Amazon for the second week of their honeymoon?"

The way he asks is almost like he's worried about my answer, but again, that can't be right. Why would he care?

I turn to look at his face again, and I'm surprised to see the vulnerability there. He genuinely does look worried about what my answer will be. I snag the bottle from him once more, taking a bigger swig this time before I answer.

"Why?" I planned to say *sure*, but the question just kind of popped out of my mouth.

"I just thought, or *we* thought that you might enjoy it. Samara, Sophia, and Darren have never been out of Canada before, and we assumed you haven't either and might want to join us," he says with a shrug, trying to make it seem like he's indifferent, but I caught the 'I thought' part at the beginning of his statement.

"Okay," I say, taking another small drink of wine. Already my body is buzzing. I have never been a big drinker, so this wine is going straight to my head.

We sit there staring at each other once more, and I feel like I'm getting lost in his bright blue eyes. My tongue darts out once again to lick my lips.

"I really want to kiss you, Sarah," he says as his eyes follow the path of my tongue.

"Why?" I ask again instead of saying the 'yes, yes, yes!' that my body is screaming. My brows crease in confusion once again at how words seem to pop out of my mouth instinctively, rather than what I'm thinking.

"Because you're the most beautiful woman I've ever seen," he says, and my brows shoot up in surprise.

Despite my head warning me this is a bad idea, that men only ever want to use me, I give a small nod, and he moves in closer, placing his hands on either side of my face. He's an inch away, and he stops to look into my eyes. He must be satisfied that I haven't changed my mind because he closes the distance. The first brush of his lips is featherlight, and I close my eyes. I snake my arms up around his neck, pressing my lips to his even harder. He licks at the seam asking permission, and I grant it, pushing my tongue out to dance with his. Mmm, he tastes sweeter than honey. I'm not sure if it's my overactive libido or the wine, but my body presses closer to his while my hands begin to run through his hair.

He abruptly pulls away and I get a sense of loss, missing the feel of him. "I'm sorry," he says, and a strike of pain slices through my heart. I knew that I wasn't good enough for someone like him. I turn back toward the water, trying to hide the tears that are shining in my eyes and incline my head, not trusting my voice.

"Hey, look at me," he says, attempting to turn me to face him. I hold my ground. I don't want him to see how pathetic I am, crying over a kiss.

Not taking the hint, he hops into what must be the freezing water so he can look up at my face. "I'm not sorry I kissed you. That was the best moment of my life so far. I'm sorry because I don't want to rush you into something, and I'm worried that the wine is lowering your inhibitions. I don't want you to wake up in the morning and think I took advantage of you.

"I want to get to know each other. I want to be the last face you see before you fall asleep and the first one when you wake. I want to be the first person you run to when you're excited, celebrate with you when you're happy, and hold you when you cry.

"I can't explain why I feel this, but I do, and it's real. I know you're not ready, and that's okay. I just want a chance to get to know you, and for you to get to know me." His voice is shaking by the end, and his lips are turning a slight blue from the cold as I stare at him after his declaration.

I want to ask why again, but I manage to stop myself this time. "Okay, as long as you get out of the water," I tell him, and he chuckles as he hops back up onto the dock. He goes in for a hug, and I use my hands to push him away, not wanting to get wet as well.

He looks down at himself, realizing that. "I'll be right back," he says, and he blinks away, leaving me reeling. Did that really just happen?

"There you are!" I jump, hearing Skarlyt's voice sounding behind me.

"I just needed some time away, if you know what I mean," I tell her, and she nods.

"I get it. But I was looking for you because we were hoping you'd come stay at the coven for the week, see if we can unlock your full powers, and hopefully you can find your place," she says.

"Sure," I say excitedly. For the first time in a long time, I'm genuinely excited about something. This night just went from amazing to perfect. "Thank you."

She waves her hand at me. "You never need to thank me," she crouches next to me, wrapping me in a hug. "You're not alone anymore." I hug her back, letting those words seep into my soul. She steps back with a grin. "I'll pick you up in the morning. You're going to love the coven!"

Seb blinks back beside me as Skarlyt is walking away. "What did I miss?" he asks with confusion showing on his face, watching his sister leave.

"She invited me to come meet with the coven this week," I say, and he grins.

"I think you'll like it." If they're anything like Skarlyt and Sebastyn, I have absolutely no doubt that I will.

We spend the next hour talking. Actually talking. I tell him my story and he listens, rubbing my back at times and giving me a hug at the end.

"You'll never have to feel alone again. I promise." He kisses me on the forehead. That's the third time tonight I've been told that. Maybe a few more times and I'll actually believe it.

"What about you? What's your story?" I question him. Of

course, I've heard little bits here and there about him, or more specifically, the pranks he likes to play on Darren.

"I've had a good life. I feel bad for saying that after the tale you just told me, but it's the truth. I have a mother who loves me and a sister who drives me crazy but would do anything for me. My father died when I was young, but from what I remember, he was amazing and loved us more than anything. Oh and I have a best friend who I love to annoy the shit out of," he laughs at the last statement.

"If that's true, why did you travel so much?" I watch as he takes in a deep breath, looking out at the water before he answers.

"Well, first, I've always wanted to travel and thought that I could help our coven by traveling around the world, finding others to share our knowledge with, and I did. I spent the majority of my time in Egypt, where I learned so much of our history that was lost, like how to teleport.

"But the other reason I went traveling was the pressure I was under to find my mate. As the coven leader's son, it seems like every woman within age has thrown themselves at me. Most of the time, when I've said I was not interested and there was no way we could be mates, they left me alone. However, there is one in particular who just doesn't seem to take *no* for an answer.

"Most people think that as a man, having women throwing themselves at me should be flattering, or that I shouldn't be complaining, but it borders on sexual harassment. The amount of times I have had my junk grabbed or neck kissed without my permission is enormous, and rather than feel flattered, it makes me feel violated." I'm surprised by his admission. It is not very often that a man would admit to feeling violated by a woman's sexual advances. Especially with women as beautiful as the ones I've seen in the coven.

"So you haven't met your mate yet?" I ask, trying and utterly failing to keep the hope out of my voice. Why I care so much, I don't know, but when he admitted to wanting more with me, I didn't tell him, but I feel the exact same way.

He turns his head so that he's looking right into my eyes. "Actually, I think I have," as he says the words, my entire body deflates. Of course, he's met his mate. Look at him. He's gorgeous. Sure, the number of tattoos on his body may turn some people off, but to me, it just makes him even more attractive. I would love nothing more than to explore every inch of him to try to find the one spot not covered in ink, but if he's met his mate, then the chances of being able to do that just flew right out of the window.

"Wait. Why did you kiss me if you met your mate?" I'm getting a little upset now, realizing that he just built up my hope. He told me everything I've always dreamed of hearing from a man, and then told me he met his mate. I opened myself up to a man for the first time in my life only to be crushed minutes later. I don't wait for an answer. I get up and start walking toward the little cottage I've been staying in.

"Wait, Sarah," he yells, running after me. I consider continuing to walk, but the pleading in his voice has me stopping and turning to face him.

"What?" I bark out.

"I was talking about you," he exclaims.

"What about me?" I spit back.

"That I think you're my mate," he says, grabbing my hands.

My eyes widen in shock. That can't be true? Can it? "How do you know?" I whisper to him.

"Because I've never felt this pull toward anyone. It started as soon as Phoebe said your name, before we even met. I had this urge to find you and keep you safe.

"Of course, the only way to know for sure is for us to have sex." I suck in a breath at that. My brain isn't ready for that, even if my body sure as hell is. Luckily, he continues. "But I know you're not ready for that. So, for now, I'd like to spend time together. Get to know one another. Let things happen the way they should. For me though, you should know that I'm already all in. There is no way that I would immediately have such strong feelings toward you if you aren't my mate."

"Sebastyn." I'm lost on what to say. As much as I would love to tell him that I feel the same, that I want nothing more than to find out for sure if we are mates, I know I'm not there yet. Years of conditioning has me questioning everything. I know he is saying how he feels, but my head is running through every word, trying to find the lie. There is no way that a man like that would ever be paired up with me. I'm nothing. I can't even perform any magic, not that I've tried in years.

"It's okay, Sarah. You don't have to say anything back. I just wanted you to know where I stand. I didn't want to lie or keep my suspicions from you. I want to start whatever this is the right way. No secrets." He pauses, and I nod, loving the sound of that. "I know it's going to take a while for you to trust in what I'm saying, and that's okay," he stops talking, moving his hands up to my face. "But you know that everything your dad or Joe ever said about you not being enough was a lie. Right? Just from the little that I know of you shows me that you're a good woman, with a heart of gold, and you're absolutely the most gorgeous woman I've ever seen." I look down, not used to being complimented, and he brushes my hair out of my face, raising it back up to look at him. "You may not believe me now, but I'm going to make sure I tell you every day until you do." He leans in and presses a light kiss to my lips. My body melts into his as if this is where I'm meant to be. This is home. My heart and body know, and now I just have to work on reprogramming my brain.

"Let me walk you home," he says, taking my hand in his and walking toward the little cottage Phoebe is allowing me to stay in. It's secluded, far enough away from everyone that I feel safe but still close enough to Phoebe that she would be there in seconds if something were to happen. Once we step onto the porch, he gives my hand a soft kiss, before striding away with a promise to see me tomorrow.

I head inside and watch through the window as he walks away. Holy shit. Did that just happen? I place my hand over my heart and lean back onto the wall, sinking down. This is just a dream. It has to be. That would never have happened to me in real life. I need to figure out how to never wake up. I pinch myself to prove that it's real and feel the sting of pain. Nope, not a dream.

I need to talk to someone. I jump up and start pacing, going back and forth between the door and the kitchen. Do I go talk to Phoebe about it? No, I can't. She has Aurora, and I don't want to wake her up. Do I go talk to Sophia about it? No, it's her mating night, and she lives on the outskirts of pack land. What about Samara? She's right next door, but it's her mating night as well. I guess I could go see if the lights are on or not.

I quickly make my way next door and walk up to the porch. I notice that there are lights on, but I have to strain to hear if there is movement inside. The last thing I want to do is bother them if they are consummating their mating. I begin pacing once again and just as I go to step off the porch and head back to my cottage, Samara throws open the door. "Are you just going to pace on the porch like some creeper or are you going to knock?" she asks with a chuckle.

I turn around quickly. "Sorry. I didn't mean to bother you," I whisper, feeling extremely bad for interrupting their night. What was I thinking coming to talk to her on the night of their mating? Way to go, Sarah. You did it again! Stupid.

"Hey. It's okay. You obviously need to talk. I'm glad you came to me. Come, sit," Samara comes and grabs my shoulders gently.

We head up the porch and sit on the bench in silence. My brain is going a million miles a minute with the anxiety of upsetting her when we just became friends. She snaps me out of it by grasping my chin and forcing my eyes to meet hers. "Calm down.

Deep breaths. Is everything okay? Did something happen?" The concern in her gaze cuts me deep. Other than Phoebe and Sophia, I've never had someone look at me like I mattered before. Seb doesn't count because behind his concern was lust, and I still can't fathom why he feels the way he does.

"No, nothing happened... Well... Something did happen, but it's not bad like you think," I begin, and she gestures for me to continue. "Sebastyn thinks he's my mate," I blurt out. Instead of being shocked, she gets a big smile and nods. "You knew?"

She nods again and a pang of hurt slices through me. Is this why they invited me on their trip? Because they wanted to play matchmaker? It isn't because they wanted me to come with them. It was so that Seb wasn't the fifth wheel. Of course that's why.

"It's not whatever you're thinking right now," she grips my shoulders.

"It's not that you guys invited me to the Amazon with you, so that Sebastyn isn't a fifth wheel?" I ask accusingly.

"What? No. Of course not. I brought it up to Sophia before I found out Seb's feelings. I thought you would enjoy coming with us," I search her eyes and voice for evidence of a lie and find nothing.

"Really?" I can't help the anxiety that laces my question. It's becoming increasingly difficult for me to hide my insecurities. Before, I didn't have to worry about it because I wasn't talking to anyone, but now that I've made friends, I can't help but worry all the time.

"Of course. Listen, Sarah. I know your story, and I've been around Sophia long enough to understand some of what you went through. I promise you that you never have to worry about me doing anything without your best interest in mind. I know you're not ready to have a mate, and I would never try to force something on you that you're not ready for.

"But you're not alone anymore. If anyone does anything that

upsets you or makes you feel anything other than happy, including me--no, especially me—you can tell me. Okay?" My anxiety tamps down with her words. I've always had to worry about everyone else's wants or needs before my own, so it's going to take some getting used to, but I see the sincerity in her eyes and realize that she means what she says.

I nod, and she claps her hands together. "Now tell me what happened with Seb." We talk for an hour or so about Sebastyn and the coven, and she tells me that she will come with me to meet with them. I used to think Phoebe was my only real friend, but I think I've finally found more friends who seem to genuinely care about me like she does, and it feels amazing.

Chapter Seven

Sebastyn

I wake up with a huge smile on my face: just another night filled with dreams of a beautiful brunette with olive skin and bright green eyes, the same as I have had every morning since the day I met her. But this morning is different. This morning, I have the memory of last night and the taste of Sarah still on my lips.

To say that what happened on the dock was unexpected would be the understatement of the century. I considered the possibility that I would get Sarah to open up, perhaps say more than two words, but getting her entire story and a couple of kisses was a complete surprise, an extremely pleasant and arousing surprise. I had to force myself to slow down and remember that she wasn't ready; my body was ready to claim her right there and then. Any doubts I had about her being my mate vanished with the tingles that came with every touch of our skin. Seeing the hurt on her face when I pulled away almost killed me, though. Then the anger in her gaze when she thought that I was just toying with her because I was mated to someone else sent crippling guilt and pain through my heart. Luckily, I was able to rectify it, but I'll never forget how it felt seeing that pain on her face and knowing that I was the one who put it there.

Hearing her story of how that asshole Joe treated her made me wish I could bring him back from the dead and kill him all over again. How dare he make this beautiful, kind-hearted woman feel like anything less than absolutely perfect? Hell. When she told me about how he reacted to her simply wanting a job, I had to hold back my anger. All she wanted was to get out of the house during the day. What could be so wrong with that?

Then there was her father. Holy shit, do I want to track him down and beat the ever-loving fuck out of him. How could he not see that she was meant for more than just being a wife and mother? How could a father not stand up for his daughter and allow her to be treated like dirt for years? I know it's the way of the mages, but it makes me sick. And on top of that, to send her a message demanding that she return and be married off once again to another sick fuck. I swear to the Mother he better wish we never come face to face because I will not show him any sort of mercy.

I get dressed quickly, chuckling at myself, remembering my plan for Darren before he goes on his honeymoon. I know he is going to be so pissed at me, but after his stunt last night, it's more than deserved. I rush back to the kitchen, grabbing the little blue pill I purchased from a guy at Supernatural. He assured me that Darren will be rocking a very large boner for the next twelve hours. I crush it up and set it aside while I make the smoothie.

After pouring out Darren's smoothie and adding in the crushed pill, I quickly set to making another one, sans pill for Sophia. I have no idea how Viagra would affect a woman, but I'm sure it wouldn't be pleasant and she's not on my hit list. If anything, this little prank benefits her greatly.

Once I'm satisfied with Sophia and Darren's smoothies, I teleport over to their house to take them to the Amazon.

"Hey, guys," I say as I pop into their kitchen, causing Darren to jump two feet into the air and Sophia to fold over in laughter.

"Seb! What have I told you about popping in here?" Darren attempts to berate me.

"Not to," I say back, attempting to look ashamed. "But I brought you breakfast smoothies to make up for it." I hand him his smoothie and Sophia hers, attempting to hide my snickers.

"Thanks, Seb. That was so sweet," Sophia coos, taking a big drink and moaning in delight.

Darren takes a drink. "It is good. But it doesn't change the fact that you're not supposed to pop in here anymore."

"Yeah, yeah. I got it. I'll try to remember next time. Are you ready?" I ask, noticing that Darren has already drunk half of his smoothie and really want to be on the way before it kicks in. I do not want to be anywhere near him when it does. I walk over and grab each of their packs in a hand, carrying them over.

"What's the rush?" Darren asks, taking another drink.

"Sarah is heading over to the coven today, and I'd really like to be there," I tell him, thinking on my feet. It's not a lie. I do really want to be there, but I also know my sister, and she won't be heading over until this afternoon. Skarlyt loves her sleep, and with my nephew being the bundle of joy that he is, he loves to wake her up multiple times a night.

Darren nods before downing the rest of his smoothie, with Sophia following suit. They grab their bags and I teleport with Darren first, arriving at the small village on the edge of the Amazon forest where they have rented huts for the week. Since I came here once during my travels, I was able to pop them right in the middle of the village rather than them having to take a flight. I sneak a peek down at Darren's pants to see if the little pill is starting to kick in or not, and after seeing the slight bulge there, I chuckle to myself once again. Oh, man, he's going to be so pissed, and I'm not going to be here to listen to his yelling. It's the perfect prank.

I teleport back for Sophia, arriving with her in front of a furious-looking Darren with a lot larger bulge in his pants. "Sebastyn... what did you do?" he growls, seeing my smirk.

"Why do you think I did anything?" I ask, trying to look and sound as innocent as I possibly can. He doesn't answer, he just growls at me again and takes a pained step toward me. "Why, Darren? Is something wrong?" I ask again, not bothering to hide my laugh as I walk backwards.

"Sebastyn! I'm going to get you back for this," he growls out, and Sophia moves to his side, seeming to notice the bulge for the first time. I wasn't sure how she would react, but she looks at me with wide eyes before busting out laughing so hard tears are falling down her cheeks.

Darren's growl gets louder, and I take that as my cue to leave. I'm laughing when I land in the middle of my mom's living room.

"What did you do now, Sebastyn Moon?" my mom's voice rings out from the kitchen.

It takes me a minute to compose myself enough to answer. "Why would you assume I did anything?" I ask, walking over to sit at the breakfast bar, grabbing for the plate of pancakes she has stacked.

"Because the only time you laugh like that is after you pull a prank on poor Darren. He's on his honeymoon. You better not have done anything to that boy to ruin his trip," she berates me.

"Course not, Mom," I say between bites. I don't know what she makes these pancakes out of, but I've never been able to recreate them, no matter how I've tried. She once told me that I would never be able to because the secret ingredient is a mother's love. More like a mother's magic I wanted to tell her, but I kept my mouth shut not wanting another lecture on magic usage.

"For your sake, I hope so, because if you ruin his week with his mate, he's going to get you back worse." That statement sobers my good mood. I did just ask for his help with Sarah. Shit, what if he does something to fuck it up for me? No, he would never. Right? Besides, how upset could he really be at needing to be locked in the bedroom with his mate for a few hours?

"Save some for your sister and the girls. They'll be here soon," she says and, as if on cue, the door opens. I straighten up, expecting Skarlyt and Sarah. Instead, Opal walks through the door.

"Oh, Seb, baby, there you are," she exclaims, coming up and rubbing herself on me. I try to back away, but because of the stool and island, there's nowhere for me to go.

"For the last time, Opal, we are not mates," I spit out with more force than I've ever used on her. I have to give her credit, other than a moment of shock, she continues with her game.

"Oh, baby, you don't really mean that. We both know we are, and the sooner you realize that the better," she leans in for a kiss. Because I have nowhere to go and would never physically hurt a woman, I'm trapped; there is nothing I can do but let it happen. As soon as her lips make contact with mine, I hear a sharp inhale of breath and Opal pulls back, allowing me to see Sarah standing at the door with tears brimming in her eyes. Fuck.

"Sarah," I start, but she shakes her head and walks back out the door. Skarlyt goes after her, but Samara stays put, looking murderous. Opal, the fucking psycho she is, looks between the door and me with a sick smile on her face like she just won the lottery. Obviously knowing exactly what she just did, she must've seen Sarah and I last night.

I push her away from me as gently as possible and begin for the door. Opal grabs onto my arm, "Where are you going, Seb baby?"

Now, I'm livid. I turn to face Opal and through clenched teeth I say, "For the last time, Opal, you are not my mate. You will never be my mate. I would die a happy man if I never saw your face again." Tears begin to brim in her eyes, and I walk away but I can't find it in myself to care.

"You don't mean that," she says, following me, but Samara steps between us with a menacing growl.

"You better listen to what he just said because he may not hurt a woman, but I will have absolutely no problem teaching you a lesson about personal space. In fact, my lion is demanding it," Samara's eyes flash gold with her statement, and Opal has the intelligence to look terrified as she runs out of the house.

Samara then faces me, her eyes still gold. "Talk."

"I promise, Samara, I don't want her. I never have. Ask anyone. I only want Sarah. Please. You have to help me fix this." I'm not sure if it's the fact that unshed tears are lingering in my eyes, or she hears the truth in my words, but she seems satisfied with whatever it is because her eyes go back to normal as she nods.

"I swear to the Mother, Sebastyn. I don't care whose son, brother, or best friend you are, if you hurt that woman, I'll tear you apart." Now it's my turn to be terrified.

"I would never do anything intentionally to hurt her," I plead, berating myself once again for being the one to put that look of hurt on Sarah's face.

"Thank the Mother," my mom says, coming up to hug me. "I've been so worried that vile woman is your mate. She's very convincing. Obviously she's wrong, and this Sarah is. Am I right?" she asks, looking between me and Samara.

I incline my head. "I'm pretty sure. But I don't know how I'm going to fix this. With her past, I don't know how I'm going to prove that I'm different, now."

"I'm going to help you. But don't make me regret this," Samara says, clasping me on the shoulder.

"So what do I do?" I ask.

She sits at the island and starts shoving food in her mouth.

"First, we give her a few minutes with your sister. Hopefully, Skarlyt will tell her how crazy that bitch is so that Sarah will actually listen when you talk. Then after a little while, we go find her and you plead your case."

I take a seat at the island next to her and try to finish my food, but all of a sudden, I'm not all that hungry.

"So this Sarah, tell me about her," my mom says, coming to stand at the island and leaning her elbows on it.

"I'm sure Skarlyt has mentioned her," I respond, not exactly knowing what to say.

My mom waves her hand, "Sure she did. But I want to hear it from you."

Samara looks at me between bites, paying close attention to what I say. "She's incredible. Beautiful, funny, heart of gold. She wouldn't hurt a fly."

My mom smiles with me. "And what about her past? You mentioned it earlier. What's the deal with that?"

Once again, Samara eyes me warily. "That's her story to tell. All you need to know is that she's been hurt a lot by everyone in her life. She needs love and patience," I tell my mom adamantly. Both women smile, obviously approving of my choice in words.

"And you, dear, must be Samara," my mom says, turning toward her.

Samara swallows her food quickly, wiping her mouth on a napkin. "Yes, ma'am. That's me."

My mom waves her hand once again and I chuckle knowing what she's going to say. "None of that *ma'am* stuff. You can call me Constance."

We spend the next ten minutes with Samara telling us her life story. There were things about Sophia's past even I didn't know, and now I feel kinda bad for the prank, but then I think, she's probably benefiting from it and feel a bit better.

Chapter Eight

Sarah

I wake up in the morning, and my entire body is buzzing, remembering my night with Sebastyn. He's so different from any other man that I've ever met. Not only is he the most amazing kisser, but he also listened and seemed to genuinely care about everything that I said. I move my fingers over my lips, remembering the taste of him. Goddess, what I wouldn't give for a repeat. And if he's right, I will get one or a thousand. If we're truly mates, I will be able to get as many as I want, for the rest of our lives.

As upset and hurt as I was at him last night for pushing me away while we were kissing, I am glad that we didn't go any farther. I didn't realize how much wine I had actually had to drink until this morning, when my head began pounding.

After drinking my coffee and taking some Tylenol, I begin to feel better, just in time for both Skarlyt and Samara to knock on my door.

"Ready to go?" Skarlyt asks. I put my mug in the sink and walk toward them.

"Yup," I say and we walk out the door as one. Skarlyt teleports

Samara first, then me, to the edge of the coven, giving us a quick tour as we make our way to her mom's house. It's set up like the pack, with more greenhouses and gardens. Each house has solar panels on the roof and beautiful flower gardens out front.

As we walk up to the biggest house on the road, I'm awestruck at the serenity of this place. I feel a sense of familiarity with it, like I've been here before. I run into the back of Samara as she stops abruptly in the doorway. I'm just about to say something to her when I realize why she's stopped. Looking around her, I suck in a breath, seeing that same blonde bimbo from the other night, with her lips pressed to Seb's. My Seb.

"Sarah," he says as she steps back with an evil smile. I simply shake my head at him, turning and walking back out the door. I don't know where I'm going, but I know that I can't stay here. I walk with tears falling out of my eyes, weaving around houses, through the forest until I come to a clearing... And it's my turn to halt as I look around. This isn't just any clearing. This is the clearing from my dreams. The pink, purple, and yellow wildflowers move and sway in the wind. Everything is exactly like my dream. The only thing missing is the woman I believe to be my mother with the flowers reaching up to meet her hands.

I sit on the grass, running my fingers through it, and close my eyes. I see it clearly, me as a small child running through this clearing with my mother. Why would I be dreaming about this place? Surely it can't be a memory. I would know if I had been here before. Wouldn't I?

My tears start falling faster now. Not just because of the hurt I experienced finding Sebastyn with his lips locked with that bitch, but out of confusion. I can't really blame Seb for wanting her. She's gorgeous, with long blonde hair, alabaster skin, pouty lips, with the body of a model. Of course he would want her rather than me. She's everything I'm not.

I feel someone sit beside me, and I open my eyes to see Skarlyt looking at me. "Are you okay?" she asks.

"I don't know," I tell her honestly. Because the more I rationalize it in my head, I realize that I have no claim to Sebastyn. As much as his words gave me hope for a better life and my body craves him, he's not mine, and I can't fathom why on earth he would want me when he could have someone like Barbie back there. On top of that, the feeling of serenity I felt when I first arrived on coven land has increased since walking into this clearing, and it's making me confused. I don't understand how I can be so utterly crushed yet feel more at peace than I ever have.

"You don't have to tell me unless you want to, but what just happened?" Skarlyt asks. Do I tell her that her brother and I shared some passionate moments last night, and he whispered everything I've ever wanted to hear to me, and then hours later I find him locking lips with a real-life Barbie?

At the thought of Seb and lips, a sob escapes my mouth. How can I be this upset over a relationship that never even really started, when my husband of ten years dying didn't phase me one bit? Skarlyt leans closer to me, wrapping her arm around my shoulder.

My tears start to slow, and Skarlyt scoots over on the grass so that we're facing each other. Instinctively, I reach up and begin playing with my crescent moon necklace, gathering up the courage to speak.

"What's that?" Skarlyt asks, her brows pinched in confusion, gesturing toward my necklace.

"This?" I ask, holding out my necklace. She confirms with a nod. "It's the only thing of my mother's that my dad let me have."

"What about this?" She reaches out and touches the small crystal pendant hanging off the moon.

"Oh, that is from my dad. He said the only way I could wear my mom's necklace was if he could add something of his to it," I tell her, growing even more confused by the direction this conversation is going.

"Can I see it?" she asks, and I bite my lip. I've never taken it off before. It may seem stupid, but wearing the necklace has always made me feel close to my mom.

I look between her and my necklace a few times before deciding she must have a good reason. Nodding, I release the clasp and hand it over to her. She moves it around in her hand, inspecting it before ripping off the crystal.

"Hey!" I say, snatching the necklace back out of her hand.

"There's a spell on this," she tells me, holding the crystal between her fingers.

"What?" I ask, utterly horrified at the thought of my father making me wear spelled jewelry, but I shouldn't be surprised after all. Joe spelled me to make me think I was in love with him.

"It feels like a binding spell or tether, or maybe even a combination of both. Either way, it's better for you if you're not wearing it," she says, putting it in her pocket.

"No, that can't be right. My tether connecting me to my father was a purity ring." I say, looking at her in confusion. "And my wedding rings replaced that when I got married connecting me to Joe."

"I don't know about those tethers, but I do know that this crystal," she says, patting her pocket, "feels very similar to the tethers that Phoebe and the boys were wearing when they first got here. But there's another spell in here, too. I will figure it out. I promise," she says, patting me on the knee. I bob my head with a small smile, looking down at my necklace. As I am fastening it back around my neck, she starts talking again. "So, did you want to talk about what happened back there?"

"Last night, Seb and I spent some time together. He told me that he thinks we're mates." Her face briefly shows shock, so I know that, unlike Samara, she didn't know. "I feel so stupid for believing him now. I opened myself up, shared my story with him, kissed him, and now I find him kissing another woman. I should have known I'm not good enough to compete with someone like that. I bet she's crazy powerful too, where I have barely any magic," I have never voiced out loud the fact that I don't have access to much magic. I convinced myself that it doesn't matter since I never used it, but the more time I spend around these insanely beautiful and powerful women, the more I think it does.

She places her hands on either side of my face. "First, you are more than enough. You are just as gorgeous on the outside as you are inside, which is pretty fucking beautiful. Second, that was Opal, and I know for a fact that Sebastyn wants absolutely nothing to do with her. And lastly, Sebastyn would never tell you that he thinks you're mates if he didn't mean it. That's just not who he is," her eyes dart over my shoulder and widen. "Just listen to what he has to say, okay?" She gives me one last squeeze before standing up and heading off in the direction we came.

Chapter Nine

Sebastyn

S amara and I walk in the direction of the clearing, following Sarah's path thanks to Samara's lion. If she wasn't with me, I'd be searching for hours.

We reach the break in the trees, and I see Skarlyt and Sarah sitting on the grass. Seeing Sarah's sunken shoulders, a sharp pain goes through my heart. I did that. I made her feel that pain again.

As we're walking, Skarlyt gives Sarah a hug, gets up and walks toward me. "Don't fuck this up," she says, as she passes me, links her arm with Samara's and heads back the way we came.

"Sarah?" I whisper as I get closer, and she looks up at me. I can still see the wetness in her eyes, and I mentally berate myself again for being the cause of her pain. "It wasn't what it looked like," I plead as I sit in front of her.

She takes a deep breath. "It looked like you were kissing that Opal chick hours after telling me that you think we're mates."

"No. Well, yes. That is what it was, but I wasn't kissing her; she kissed me," I fumble out my words. Man, I'm fucking this up.

"How is that different?" she asks, tears beginning to pool once more.

I reach out to wipe a falling tear off her cheek, and she jerks back. I place my hand on my lap. Obviously, she doesn't want me to touch her.

"Remember last night how I told you that I left because I was getting unwanted advances from some women in the coven?" At her nod, I continue. "Well, Opal is the worst. She's convinced herself that we're fated mates, even though I've told her a million times that we're not.

"This morning, when she came to my mom's, I was disappointed because she wasn't you. Then she cornered me up against the island and kissed me. I would never hurt a woman, so I didn't know what to do." Instinctively, I reach for her hands. Thankfully, she allows me to hold them. "I promise you, everything I said last night is the truth, and I don't want anything to do with Opal. I only want you," I fight the urge to kiss her, knowing that would be no better than what Opal did to me.

"But why? I just don't understand. She's gorgeous and perfect and.."

"Absolutely fucking insane," I interrupt her, coaxing a small chuckle from her lips.

"She may be crazy, but that still doesn't explain why you would want me instead." I gather my thoughts quickly, trying to figure out how to ease her self-doubts.

"I wish you could see yourself through my eyes. Not only are you beautiful with your olive skin, big green eyes, and long chestnut hair, but you have a heart of gold. I've watched you from afar when you thought no one was looking. I see the little things you do. Scooping up Aurora when she begins fussing so that Phoebe doesn't have to stop whatever she's doing. Picking up the boys' toys they leave strewn around the yard so that they don't get in trouble. The way you sit and listen to them when they're upset, not once telling them that they shouldn't be crying, especially when it's over something silly. The way your eyes shine with so much love when you look at Phoebe and Sophia that it makes my heart want to burst from being so full. You do so many things for everyone, not once expecting something in return. You may not think that anyone notices but I do." She's shocked at my words, her brows shooting up.

"Sebastyn," she begins, pulling her hands away, twisting them in her lap. "Even though you may see me that way, it doesn't change the fact that Opal is everything I'm not, and probably the better choice for you," I can see the pain on her face as she says the words.

I reach up to her face. "It wouldn't matter to me if Opal was the Queen of England. The fact is that I don't want her. I never have. I want you." She nuzzles my palms briefly before surprising me by pressing her lips to mine.

I kiss her back passionately, lifting her into my lap so she's straddling me. I push her hips down a little so she can feel just how much I want her. She sucks in a breath, pulling back and looking into my eyes.

"See how much I want you, sweetheart?" She nods, and I wrap my arms around her, pulling her close. I have a feeling she needs to be shown tenderness right now, and I shouldn't give in to my hormones, so I just hold her.

"Sebastyn?" She whispers after a little while.

"Hmm?"

She leans back a bit but doesn't move from my lap. "Can you tell me something no one else knows?"

I nod and think about what to tell her. What is something no one else knows about me? I'm a pretty open book but..."I like to read romance novels."

"What? Really?" She asks with a smile.

"Yup. I was on my way to Egypt and didn't bring anything to

read on the plane. The woman beside me offered me a Christine Feehan novel from her Dark Series to read, and it got me hooked. From there, I purchased every single one of her books. Have you read them?"

She shakes her head *no*. "I had to get my reading material approved by Joe and something like that definitely wouldn't have been on the list." I grind my teeth, again wanting nothing more than to bring him back from the dead and make him suffer. She wasn't even allowed to read the types of books she wanted? That's insane.

"Well, I have every single one on my Kindle if you want to borrow it."

Her smile gets even bigger as she bobs her head enthusiastically. "I'd like that."

We sit and talk for just under an hour about the different series by Christine Feehan. She seems to be most interested in the Dark Series about the Carpanthians, which is my favorite too, and I promise her that I will give her my Kindle as soon as we get back to the house.

"Alright, sweetheart. We should head back. My mom wanted to meet you," I say, brushing her hair off her face.

"What if she doesn't like me?" Her voice is so small, and it breaks my heart.

"She's going to love you," I tell her adamantly. Because it's the truth.

"But..."

"No but's. She is. Just be yourself and don't worry about anything else, okay?" I interrupt her.

She nods her head, but I still see the vulnerability in her eyes. She so badly wants to find a place to belong. But she already does; she just hasn't realized it yet.

We stand up, and I teleport us back to the front porch of my mom's house. "Ready?" I ask, reaching for the door handle.

"As I'll ever be," she responds. I link my fingers with hers and walk through the door.

"Mom?" I call out but I didn't need to; she's still standing in the kitchen where I left her, making a fresh batch of eggs like she knew we were coming.

"Oh good. You're back," she exclaims, instantly putting two plates piled high with food on the island next to Samara. Sarah shies away a little at my mom's boisterous tone, but I give her hand a small squeeze and pull her along with me.

"And you must be Sarah," she says, as she sets a plate in front of her with a smile which Sarah returns.

"It's so good to finally meet you. Both Skarlyt and my son have told me all about you." Sarah goes pale obviously thinking that we told her *everything*.

"Don't worry, I didn't tell her your story," I whisper while Samara nods in agreement. Sarah deflates after her confirmation sending a small pang of hurt through me that she doesn't trust my word, but I push it away quickly. I can't expect her to change her entire view on men or life overnight. I need to be patient and show her that she can trust me.

"No, of course not. Your story is yours to tell. When you're ready," my mom says with soft eyes.

Sarah inclines her head, looking between both Samara and I for something. Samara must pick up on whatever it is because she gives Sarah a subtle nod while I just look at her confused. She takes a deep breath and then speaks. She tells my mom her story, in even more detail than she did me. She tells her about her English teacher who desperately tried to help her, that Joe spelled her to make her believe she loved him, and everything in between. By the end, tears are flowing down my mom's face, and she doesn't waste a second, moving around the island and wrapping Sarah up in a hug. For a moment, Sarah stiffens, not returning the hug but gives in and melts into my mom's embrace, her face visibly relaxing with a look of peace on it. If I know my mom, and I do, she's putting a little magic into the hug, the kind only she can.

When they let go, Sarah's body language is vastly different than before. She begins shovelling food into her mouth, moaning with each bite just like a member of the family would. Goddess, she's perfect.

"Sebastyn?" My mom says, now standing behind the island once again, and I turn to face her.

"Yeah, Mom?"

"I was thinking about handing the reins over to your sister," she says, but she bites her lip in worry.

"That's a great idea. Have you talked to Skar about it yet?"

She bobs her head. "I have but she doesn't know it's going to be this soon. I wanted to make sure you were okay with it first."

My eyebrows furrow in confusion. "Why would it matter if I'm okay with it?"

My mom sighs. "Because her mate is not a witch, and there may be some who... Well, let's just say they may not be too happy. They may prefer to speak with you about certain things instead, so you would need to be your sister's right hand."

I walk over to my mom and wrap her in a hug. "That was always the plan, Mom. No matter who Skarlyt's mate turned out to be, her and I are a team, just like you taught us to be."

She visibly relaxes in my arms, breathing out all of her stress. "I'm so glad," she says, patting my cheek.

We all go back to sitting on the couch, talking about things going on in the coven. More like gossip in the coven, but I don't say that out loud. I just sit there, holding Sarah's hand, watching the way her eyes light up, hanging on every word my mom says.

"Oh good, you're here. We were just talking about how it would be best if we induct Sarah to the coven," my mom says.

"I had to run a quick errand, but I think that's a fantastic idea," Skarlyt responds, and we get up, walking outside to the backyard.

"Okay, Sarah, you stand here," my mom moves her so she's standing in front of the altar, as Skarlyt and I take our places beside her.

"Sarah, do you wish to join the Coven of the Moon?" she asks.

"Yes," Sarah responds.

"And do you pledge your allegiance to Skarlyt Moon as your coven leader?" I watch as my sister's eyes snap to our mother in surprise, and she winks at her.

"Yes, I do," Sarah replies, and Skarlyt takes her outstretched hands. Tears brim in Sarah's eyes, and I can only imagine the feelings she's experiencing. I silently thank the goddess for my family and for giving me the chance to meet my mate.

"In front of the Mother, I accept your allegiance and make a pledge of my own. I promise to stand by your side and do everything within my power to protect and guide you on your journey," Skarlyt says the words I've heard my mother say many times. Her magic reaches out, encircling them with a gust. Something seems to snap, and all of a sudden Sarah's magic flows out, joining Skarlyt's. Where her magic is an aqua blue, Sarah's is a deep purple, and I watch in amazement as shock and then excitement registers on her face. So much for her not having powerful magic.

"Well, I haven't seen that before," my mom says as their magic dies out.

"What do you mean?" It's Sarah who speaks.

"I mean that Skarlyt's magic reacted as it should, but yours seeping out to join wouldn't have normally happened," she explains.

"But I don't have very much magic." Sarah says confused.

"Now, I don't know who told you that, but you are probably almost evenly matched with Skarlyt. And are definitely stronger than most of the witches in the coven."

"No. That can't be. My dad always told me that because my

mom was such a weak mage, I would never have very much magic," a still confused Sarah tries to explain.

"Well, he obviously lied," my mom starts and Skarlyt interrupts.

"Wait. I forgot. I bet this has something to do with it," I watch as Skarlyt reaches into her pocket and pulls out a crystal. It's the same crystal that I remember seeing on Sarah's necklace. I glance at Sarah's neck and immediately see the crescent moon, but the crystal hanging from it is no longer there. Skarlyt hands it to my mom. As soon as she places it in her hand, she drops it and shoots a concerned look at me before looking back at Sarah.

"It definitely does. Sebastyn, why don't you and the girls head inside to get something ready for dinner," my mom says and we all start walking inside, noticing for the first time that it's gone dark.

"Skarlyt, can you help me clean this up first?" My mom says, and I look back toward them. My mom gives me a subtle nod, and I grip Sarah's hand, linking my fingers with hers, continuing into the house. I'm sure they'll tell me if what they're talking about is important.

We head inside and Samara stops right in front of us, spinning around. "What was that? I've never seen anything like that before."

I chuckle. "That was an induction ceremony for Sarah, making her a part of the coven."

She waves her hand in dismissal. "I know that. I meant the magic show."

"Oh. I've never seen that happen before," I tell her and feel Sarah sink down, her shoulders turning inward so I quickly add. "If I had to guess it's because Sarah's been tethered for so long that her magic wanted to come out and play after being locked away for so long. It's either that or..." I pause, not knowing if I want to voice my other thoughts.

"Or what?" Sarah asks, straightening up.

"Or because you are my mate, your induction was not only to the coven as a member but as one of the leaders." She sucks in a breath. "Skarlyt is the High Priestess or will be once Mom does their ceremony and the rest of the coven swears their allegiance to her, but because she and I are both of the Moon bloodline and our magic is almost perfectly matched, the coven could've went to either of us. Skarlyt and I made an oath to each other when we were young that we would share equal responsibilities, so it didn't fall solely on her shoulders. Now we know that her mate is a wolf, it makes more sense why we felt compelled to do that." Both women nod, and I gesture with my head to move to the living room.

"So your mom could've been wrong about me being powerful? And my magic just lashed out like that because I'm your mate?" Sarah whispers as we take our seats.

I shake my head. "No. Not at all. You're definitely powerful; otherwise, you wouldn't have had enough magic to push out to swirl with Skarlyt's." She inclines her head in agreement but doesn't look like she believes me. I want to reassure her, to tell her that I know it's true, but that's something she needs to figure out on her own. She needs to see it for herself.

"Alright, guys. What's on the agenda for tonight? I want to spend some time with Sarah," my mom says, walking in the room. Samara stands to leave and I remain in my spot. My mom gives me a pointed look. "Alone."

"Is that okay?" I ask Sarah, not caring in the slightest about what my mom just said. She looks up at me.

"Yes. Thank you for everything. I'll see you later. Okay?" She places a soft kiss on my cheek, a dismissal if I ever saw one, but one that I don't mind. If anyone can help Sarah see the woman that I do, it's my mom.

After both Samara and I say goodbye, we walk out the front door. "Want me to teleport you home?" I ask.

"That'd be great. Thanks, Sebastyn." I nod, taking her hand and popping back in right in front of her house.

"You know she's going to need you to be patient, right?" she says, turning after walking up the first couple of steps.

"Yup, and I'm more than willing to be. She's worth it."

"She is," Samara agrees as Trev comes out the front door to greet his mate. He pulls her in for a passionate kiss, both of them wrapping their arms around one another. Guess that's my cue to leave. I pop out with a chuckle, heading for Alaric's to talk to Skarlyt, knowing that after what happened she would want to tell Phoebe and needing to make sure I don't need to know what she and my mom talked about after we left.

"I thought you might show up here," The woman in question says sitting on the front porch.

I walk up and take a seat beside her. "Do I need to know what you and Mom were talking about?" I question, not bothering to beat around the bush.

She lets out a soft sigh, the first indication that I should, in fact, know, but she doesn't want to tell me. She looks into my eyes, searching for something. "You wouldn't be able to tell anyone. Not even Sarah."

Shit. "Is it bad?"

She shakes her head *no*. "Not at all. Just if she knows and I'm wrong, it could cause her more hurt, and I don't want to do that."

I sit back in the chair closing my eyes. Do I want to know? Is it something that I should know? Skarlyt's initial reaction makes me feel that I should probably know but then not being able to tell Sarah means I'd have to lie to her and that's not how I want to start a relationship. And I promised her last night that I wouldn't keep secrets from her.

I open my eyes and look at my sister. "No. Don't tell me. Unless she's in danger of being hurt, I don't want to have to keep anything from her."

Skarlyt deflates. "That's probably smart. But I promise it's not bad. In fact, if I'm right, it will make her very, very happy."

That makes me feel a whole lot better, though I wish I could know what it is. I know if I want to earn Sarah's trust, keeping things from her is not the way to go about it, no matter if it's good or bad.

Chapter Ten

Sarah

As soon as Sebastyn and Samara leave the house, my anxiety ramps up at being left alone with Sebastyn's mom. I know I practically pushed them out the door, but that was before, when I was still feeling the buzz of my magic under my skin. Or maybe it was because I was so comfortable having them both here. Now, with them gone, I can't help thinking that having them leave was a mistake. I'm sure that Seb's mom is a very nice lady.

"So, Sarah, Skarlyt tells me you are a master at creating personal care products," she says, bringing two teas for us and setting them on the coffee table before sitting down herself.

I incline my head, not enjoying talking about myself. I understand why she feels the need to get to know me and that hug from earlier did feel really nice, but I don't know how to turn off the anxiety I feel.

"No need to be modest. She says Phoebe loves the shampoo and conditioner you make."

"Yeah, she does. But I make a special one for her with coconut oil because of her unruly hair."

"Have you ever infused your magic into them?" She asks, and my mouth drops open in shock.

I shake my head. "No, I didn't realize I could do that."

"You can do a lot of things with magic. You probably already do without knowing it." She says with a large smile. "Want to see?"

Excitement flutters in my belly at the prospect of actually learning magic, and I vigorously nod my head yes. "Come on, then." She says, getting up and leading me down the hallway and into a large work room. Its setup isn't much different than Skarlyt's back at Alaric and Phoebe's house, though it's much bigger. Almost the size of an elementary school gymnasium.

"This is where the magic happens," she chuckles.

"Literally," I say joining in on her chuckle. She turns to me with wide eyes.

"I knew you had a spark in there somewhere," she says, and I blush. "No need to be shy with me. You are free to speak your mind at all times, even if you think it may upset me."

I bob my head in agreement though I don't think I'll ever feel confident enough to do that. That's the goal though. One day, I hope to be comfortable enough in my own skin to say whatever is on my mind.

I glance around the work room, taking a tentative step further inside. I look over at Constance to make sure it's okay and at her subtle nod, I begin to walk around. Books line the wall with the door, floor to ceiling. Every colour, age, and binding imaginable. I run my fingers across one of the rows, savoring the feeling. I've never seen this many books in my life, magical or not. One book catches my eye 'Storm Family Grimoire'. Without thinking, I reach out and pull it off the shelf, immediately flipping it open. On the first page, it has the family tree, at least a dozen generations deep with a single name at the bottom *Alexandra Storm*. I run my fingers over the name, a tingling sensation flowing through them. There's a connection being created between myself and the book.

Constance comes to stand behind me, looking over my shoulder. "Ah. That's my friend Rita's family grimoire. I keep most of the grimoires here for the members of the coven." She gestures to the wall holding the bookshelves.

"Why?" I ask, turning to her.

"Mainly because they're safest here with the wards I have set up. But most of the witches in this coven know their family spells by heart and are happy to share them with others. With the grimoires here, anyone can come and read them at any time through that door." She points to a door in the adjacent wall that I somehow missed. "It allows coven members, and only coven members, to enter and use the workshop when they need, but nothing can be removed without permission. When I get ready for bed, I put a ward up so that no one can enter my private residence, but I leave this room open. Some of the members are night owls and prefer to work at night."

"That's incredible. What's stopping someone from taking something, though?"

She gives me a sly smile. "If you were to try and walk out of here with that book, it would pop right back into its spot on the shelf the second you stepped beyond the threshold. My mother's ward was a little bit more cruel--it would give the person an electric shock, not big enough to really hurt--but after a few accidents where the members unknowingly carried something out with them, I changed it." I look at her, confused. How does someone unknowingly carry something? "Some of these books are finicky and feel attached to certain people. With that said, though, if someone were to come and take their own family's grimoire, they would be able to pass without issue. After all, it belongs to them."

"I didn't know magic could do that," I admit, turning my attention back to the book in my hand, flipping through the pages carefully.

"Magic can do almost anything, but caution is always to be

used. Respect goes both ways. You have to respect it for it to respect you."

My brows crease together in confusion again. It almost feels like it should just be a permanent look on my face. "You speak as if magic is a living being."

"It is alive and even though it is part of us, it's also separate. If you abuse it, it will warp and become twisted; that's how the dark witches begin. They push their magic to do things it doesn't want to do, using blood for their spells, and in turn, it corrupts not only their magic but their souls. Do it for too long and they turn into a mage: evil, vile creatures. But then you know that all too well, don't you?"

"Yes, I do. But I've never heard magic explained like that. As if it's a separate entity inside of you."

"The reason is probably because mages don't think like that. They believe that magic is a tool for them to use, bend to their will, but it's not," she reasons.

"They think like that about women, too," I add.

I slide the book back in its place, continuing onto the shelves of herbs lining the wall covered by windows. They smell so good. I close my eyes and take a deep inhale of the lavender and instantly my anxiety over the mages calms. When I open my eyes, the grimoire I just put back is sitting on the counter in front of me. "What the..." I begin but Constance just chuckles.

"Like I said, some books can get attached. This one seems to like you for some reason," she says, and I run my hand over the deep blue cover, feeling the gold indents of lightning.

"It's beautiful."

"It is. It's the symbol of the storm family. Remind me some-time to introduce you to Rita. I think you'd really like her. She stays home most of the time now after she lost her husband and daughter, but she doesn't mind company." She pauses a second. "Well, the right kind of company."

"Can I ask you a question?" I lift the book into my arms and turn to look at her.

"Anything."

"Why are you being so nice to me? I mean, I get that I'm now a member of this coven, and you're the high priestess, but you seem to be going the extra mile for me. Especially knowing how Sebastyn feels about me. Wouldn't you be happier if he was paired with a witch from your coven? Like Opal?" I ask, dropping my head in shame, surely she would want her son to be mates with someone more than me, someone who isn't broken.

She places a finger under my chin raising it up. "Now, you listen here. You are now part of our coven, our family. The way Sebastyn feels about you is a moot point. I feel a connection to you. I can tell you have a good heart. It's one of my gifts. But the fact that you could be my Seb's mate rather than that vile woman is a blessing." I nod, not knowing what to say.

Her eyes soften. "I don't know if you know this, but Opal wasn't always like this. Once she was a vibrant young witch, so carefree and loving, and I would've been happy to see her and Sebastyn mated. But something happened to her. Her mind twisted and warped reality. She's obsessed with Sebastyn to the point of insanity, not knowing how to take *no* for an answer, something a true mate would never do."

"I didn't know that," I say quietly, though I'm not sure if it changes anything of my perspective of her. I still don't agree with how she's treating Sebastyn, making him feel like an object rather than a person. Whether she was a good person or not when she was younger really doesn't matter.

She claps her hands together, breaking me out of my thoughts. "Okay. Enough with the serious stuff. Let's get to working on your magic."

With a smile on my face, I follow her over to her workstation and spend the next couple hours showing her how I make my products while she shows me how to infuse them with my magic. It's incredible. I didn't know that it was possible. I set to work on a new batch of shampoo and conditioner for Phoebe, infusing it with magic, sharing my intent to control her frizz with that pool of purple inside my chest, hoping to impress Phoebe with it. For the boys, I make another set of bath bombs but with magic to help calm them and lull them to sleep. For Aurora, I make some scented oil to dab under her ears to help with teething because she's bound to be starting to get teeth soon, and if she's anything like the boys, she's not going to be a happy camper for a while.

"You know we have a market each week where the locals come to buy all of our natural and homemade products. I think you'd make a killing, if you are interested." My ears perk up at the prospect of making money and being able to pay my way while I'm living here.

"When is it?" I ask, already calculating in my head the different products I'd want to make in order to sell.

"In two days. I can help you get a good stock made if you want. I make salves and package herbs for teas and sell them. You can share my booth." Excitement bleeds into her words, and it ramps up my own.

"I think I'd really like that," I tell her and set to work making a list of things I need for what I want to make.

"So, tell me, Sarah, what did you want to be when you grew up?"

I don't look up from my list. "I tried not to think about it often but when I did, I dreamt about being a teacher. I think I told you earlier that I was accepted into University as an English Major and would've gone on to Teacher's College but being a woman and a mage, that didn't happen."

"You could still do that. You could teach at the Westwood Academy. They'll be adding new classes soon and could always use more teachers."

I glance up at her to see a smile on her face. "Skarlyt, Sophia, and Phoebe have been trying to talk me into it. But I don't know how I would do with that many people around, especially men right now. I still need to close my eyes and breathe deep to keep the panic attacks at bay. If one of the older male students were to yell, it would scare me, and I'd be a cowering mess rather than a composed teacher that they would need me to be."

"You could teach the younger grades," she supplies, and I mull it over in my head.

"I don't even know how to use my own magic yet; I can't possibly teach anyone else."

"But they don't just learn magic there. They need to learn regular studies, too, just like everyone else. So, you could be their home room teacher, or teach math, English, geography," she suggests. "Sciences are usually separated for each supernatural faction so that they can learn the magic of their species, as well as history. They learn regular history, too, but it's important that they know the supernatural past just as much, if not more, so they don't make the same mistakes or unknowingly walk into danger."

A small smile slips onto my face. "I could probably do that. But right now, I need to heal my soul from the lifetime of damage caused by my father and Joe. I want to be able to walk with my head held high, to not flinch when a door slams or fly into a panic if someone is upset with me."

She nods. "And you will. The best way to do that is to practice your magic. If you have a way to defend yourself, it will go a long way to showing that you needn't be afraid. Connecting with your magic will also help settle your soul. It's a part of you that has been trapped and locked away for your entire life."

"That's the plan," I tell her, going back to my list.

"I'll grab us something to eat while you finish your list, and then I'll have Sebastyn run into town tomorrow morning to get any supplies we need," she says, and I freeze. I didn't think about that.

"But I don't have any money to pay for..."

She waves her hand. "We have more than enough to get you the supplies you need."

"But..."

"No but's. If you need to, you can call it a loan and pay us back after you sell everything. But we don't expect to be." With her believing the discussion is over, she walks through the door and back into the house.

Curiosity getting the better of me, I turn back to the Storm Family Grimoire and wonder why it's attached to me. All of a sudden, the pages flip on their own, landing on a passage close to the back.

The Storm Family is gifted with the ability to control the weather. It is our responsibility to keep a healthy balance between ourselves and our magic, lest the world suffer. With each new generation, the power will only grow until the one who will lead our family into the future is born with control of all four elements, as well. When that child is born, they must be protected, for unseen forces will try to control them.

I run my fingers over the scribbled words, feeling a deep connection to them for some reason. But this isn't my family grimoire, I'm not of the Storm bloodline, so I don't know why. All I know is that a feeling of rightness settled over me the moment I touched this book. It must feel the same since it came to me after I put it back.

But all that does is add more questions to my life as to why. Why did my father tell me my magic is weak when it's not? Why did he have a block and tether on my necklace when I was already tethered? Why do I dream about the clearing? Why have I been dreaming about my mother every night? Why do I feel so drawn to Sebastyn and his family? Is he right? Am I really his true mate? And if so, why would he want me? There's nothing special about me.

Constance comes back before I can really fall down the rabbit hole, holding two plates of sandwiches. "I hope you like turkey," she says, placing one in front of me.

"I sure do." I tell her before taking a large bite. It's made perfectly with mayo, cheese, turkey, and lettuce. I can tell that the lettuce is organic, being able to taste the difference. It's delicious.

A few bites later, the sandwich is finished, and I look up to see Constance staring at me with a smirk. "Was it good?" She asks and I sheepishly look down at my empty plate and then at her full one.

"Yes, it was delicious."

"Seemed like it," she chuckles, and I can feel my cheeks turning pink in embarrassment. "Nothing to be embarrassed about. I'm glad you enjoyed it. But I was wondering something."

"Okay." I respond, not knowing exactly what to say.

"Would you like to stay here for a few days so we can practice your magic each day? You can stay in Sebastyn's old room." Her face almost looks anxious, but I push the thought away. There is no way this amazing woman would be anxious for me to stay here.

"Sure," I agree. It makes sense. If I want to learn as much as I can about magic, staying here would be the quickest way.

We spend the next few hours using the limited supplies we have on hand to get some things ready for market while also working on my magic. Constance tests me for different elements but my magic doesn't want to cooperate. She explains that it could be due to me wearing my tether for so long that my magic needs a little time to recuperate, especially after the light show Skarlyt and I put on earlier. We decide to start with the theory of magic and different spells. I find that, when trying to infuse different things with my magic, I'm able to, but I can't make my magic appear outwardly.

As I begin to get extremely frustrated, Constance places her hand on my shoulder. "That's enough for today. We'll pick this up tomorrow."

I sigh but nod and follow her back into the house. "This is Seb's room. I changed the sheets earlier," she says, opening the door to a very masculine room. The walls are a dark blue, covered in posters of Blink 182, Simple Plan and Smashing Pumpkins. The cherry wood queen size bed has a light gray comforter with the matching desk placed underneath the window. On the top of it, there's a duffel bag that looks exactly like one of Phoebe's, and I walk over to it.

"Phoebe had Sebastyn bring you some clothes and your toiletries." Tears spring to my eyes at the thoughtfulness. No one has ever done anything like this for me before. I expected to have to walk back to the cabin and pack my own bag. The fact that they did this without me asking means everything to me.

"Can you thank them for me please," I say turning to look at her. She just smiles.

"Of course, though you can thank them yourself when you see them next. If you want a shower before bed, Seb has an ensuite bathroom right through that door, and if you need anything else, just grab it. I'm going to have a nice long soak in the tub before heading to bed myself."

She turns to walk away. "Constance?" I call out.

"Yes?"

"Thank you for everything."

She walks over to me and wraps me up in a hug much like the one she gave me earlier, and I melt into her. It feels just like the one hug I got from Mrs. Jones: maternal and everything I've been missing in my life. "You don't have to thank me, honey. I'm not doing anything any good person wouldn't."

I step back from our hug. "But that's the thing. I haven't been around a lot of good people, so everything that you're doing now is foreign to me. Amazing and incredible, but foreign."

She wipes a couple stray tears from my eyes. "Well, now you're here, and that's going to change."

I incline my head, and she walks out the door, closing it behind her and leaving me in the room. After having the best, most relaxing shower in my life, I crawl into the bed. Unfortunately, it doesn't smell like Sebastyn since Constance just changed the sheets, but knowing that he slept here, even if distantly, makes my entire body relax. Today was an incredible day. I have no idea how I'm going to top it, but I can't wait to try. I fall asleep quickly, eager to see what tomorrow holds for me.

Chapter Eleven

Sarah

The next two days pass in a blur, and before I know it, I'm helping Constance load up the truck with all her salves and herbs. I also load up the bath bombs, shampoo, and conditioner stock that I made up just for the market. Hopefully, I'll be able to make enough money to at least pay Sebastyn and Constance back for the supplies. Though it would be great if I can make a little more to buy myself some new clothes so I don't have to keep borrowing Phoebe's. But even if I don't, I added a minor spell of longevity to each product so that they won't spoil. I also have hair growth, frizz control, or relaxation spells in others. It's really exciting. Constance thinks that my stuff is going to go over so well I could possibly open up my own shop. In fact, she loved everything so much she kept a lot for herself. She insisted on paying me for it, saying that just because we're 'family' doesn't mean I shouldn't get paid for my hard work. I put the money in a drawer in Seb's room. I plan on giving back to her, subtly, of course.

Sebastyn has come to see me each day, and despite my aching

pussy's protests, nothing other than some stolen kisses has happened. Constance told me the first night after he left that I needed to make him work for it. At first, I thought it would be weird talking to his mom about us, but it's not at all. She said that he's never had to work for a woman before, and that mate or not, I need to show him who's boss now before he gets a different idea. I laughed out loud at that, thinking of sweet Sebastyn trying to be the boss of anything. He may be rugged with tattoos, looking like the baddest motherfucker on earth, but I've learned over the past few days, he's really a big sweetheart. She also told me not to be fooled. Just because he's sweet to me doesn't mean he's sweet to anyone else. I have yet to see that, but I could imagine it if he was protecting someone he loves.

"Are you ready?" I'm snapped out of my inner thoughts by Constance.

"Yup," I say cheerfully, rounding the truck and hopping in the passenger seat, feeling so much more comfortable with her than I did the first day. Turns out that spending two days straight with someone will do that to you. She's an incredible friend and mother; she's fiercely loyal and protective of those she cares about. She also isn't shy at all about showing that she cares. I've received more hugs, pats on the back, and soft smiles in the last two days than I have in my entire life, and I can't help wishing that I had a mom like her growing up.

"Let's go," she says as she starts the truck and pulls out. I watch out the window as the dense forest thins, and we hit the main high-way. I've been in the area for a couple of weeks now but have yet to really explore. I'm sure when the snow hits that I'm not going to want to do much driving, but maybe Seb will teleport us to sightsee a bit.

We pull into an extensive market area with dozens of covered booths. I know Constance said it was a big market, but I wasn't expecting it to be quite this size.

"We're going to be selling some of my friend Rita's herbs today too, so once we're set up, I'll head over and grab them from the storage shed. She had someone drop them off for me yesterday," she says, as we drop the tailgate and begin unloading.

It doesn't take us long to get everything set up, and she's off to grab the herbs. I busy myself, shuffling the display around, trying to make it more visually appealing.

I'm moving the hair products away from the cleaning products when I hear a throat clearing behind me. I slowly turn with a smile and am met face to face with Opal.

"You need to stay away from Sebastyn," she says with a sneer. Rather than respond, I turn back to my business, not wanting to engage in what I'm sure is going to be an argument.

"Did you hear me, bitch?" she asks. Once again, I turn. This time, though, I don't smile. I let my annoyance show on my face.

"Yes, I heard you. I just don't particularly care to listen to anything you have to say regarding Sebastyn," I respond.

"Well, you should. I'm his mate. We're meant to be together," she spits at me.

"The way I heard it you're an obsessed psycho who thinks she has a claim to a man who doesn't want her." Where the strength came from to talk to her like that, I don't know. Maybe being around confident women is rubbing off on me, or maybe it's just the fact that I fucking hate this bitch.

She's shocked for a second before she schools her features. "That's not true at all. You're just jealous because you know that you're just going to be another notch in his belt before he finally settles down with me."

This bitch is delusional and rather than playing into her game, I turn back around. Apparently, that isn't what she wants me to do because she grabs me by the hair and pulls me back. My magic flares up at her actions, lashing out and giving her a small electric shock. She jumps back, startled. Hell, I'm startled myself.

My magic hasn't made an appearance since my induction ceremony.

I rub my hand on the part of my head that was pulled with my hair. Holy fuck that hurt. I turn my furious gaze to her. She looks afraid, but it's too late. Like a switch flipped inside me, rage spreads through my body. I'm fucking pissed now. As if the weather is in tune with my mood, storm clouds roll in and thunder shakes the ground.

"Don't you ever fucking touch me again," I spit out through clenched teeth as the rain begins.

I advance on her, hands raised, surrounded by a purple glow. She backs up until she bumps into a booth.

"I'm sorry," she pleads, her voice shaking.

"It's too fucking late for sorry," I growl, not recognizing my own voice. I feel like I'm having an out of body experience, like I am hovering above my body, looking at myself. I can see the purple hue surrounding me, my hair is whipping around in the wind. Even my eyes look like there's a storm raging inside of me. Just when I think I'm going to do something I will regret, muscular arms envelop me. I know instantly that it's Sebastyn.

"It's okay, love," he whispers in my ear, and I feel my heartbeat return to normal and my magic fade.

"Go," he spits at Opal.

Her movement brings my awareness back to the present. "Wait," I call out and she turns back.

"Don't look at Sebastyn ever again. Don't even mention his name. And if you think about touching him, I'll make you wish you were never born," my voice comes out hoarse, like I've been yelling for hours, but does the trick, and she scurries away with her tail between her legs.

Sebastyn spins me around, and a pang of embarrassment flows through me. What did I just do? Does this mean I'm evil like my father? I don't know how far I would've gone if Sebastyn hadn't come.

As I hang my head in shame, Sebastyn places his hand under my chin, raising it back up. "That was the sexiest thing I've ever seen."

My eyes go wide at his words. I was expecting to be berated for hurting a member of his coven, not being called sexy. And although I'm getting more comfortable with him, getting praise from a man still makes me uncomfortable.

I try to step away, but he squeezes his arms around me tighter, securing me to him. I look up into his eyes, and my breath catches. The tenderness I see in them makes my heart begin to race.

His lips press to mine in a tender kiss. Again, as if the weather is in tune with my mood, the rain fades away and a ray of sun hits us. As we break apart, I look up to see a cloudless blue sky with a bright, shining sun.

It's not possible though, right? It's just a coincidence. The only family with the ability to control the weather is the Storm Family, and I'm not one of them.

"That was a quick storm," Constance says as she returns. Not knowing what to say or how to broach the subject, I simply nod. Sebastyn waves his arms, and a warm breeze surrounds me, drying my wet clothes. I give him a smile of thanks, and he returns it.

I move behind the table at the front of the booth to help Constance organize her friend's herbs. As I reach out and touch one of the packages, I get a flash of a vision: a woman with olive skin, sun-kissed blonde hair and bright green eyes. The same woman who I dream about most nights. My mother.

"Sarah?" I'm snapped out of the vision by both Constance and Seb calling out to me. Wait, when did Sebastyn come to this side of the booth?

"Hmm?" I say, shaking my head out to clear the fog from my brain.

"You were staring off into space. Is everything okay?" Constance asks, looking concerned.

"What? Oh, yeah. I'm fine. Sorry," I respond. Much like the weather, I'm not sure visions are a common gift, so I opt to keep my mouth shut.

The rest of the day goes off without a hitch. Constance was right. People love my creations. I sold out within the first hour and had to start taking orders for next week. Although I won't be here, Constance said that she will sell them for me. I have four days to get the inventory ready before I leave with Seb, Samara, and Trev to the Amazon.

I just finish helping Constance pack up when Seb teleports next to us. "I was wondering if you might want to go on a date with me?" The way he asks is almost as if he's expecting me to say *no*.

"Of course. Let me just help your mom unload at the house."

"Oh, no need. I've got it. You two go have fun," she says with a wink.

That's all the encouragement Seb needs because next thing I know, he's grabbing my waist and we're arriving in a beautiful covered gazebo with fairy lights hanging. As I turn in a circle, I see the candlelit dinner on a table for two in the center. There is soft romantic music playing from a Bluetooth speaker off to the side. Tears come to my eyes. No one has ever done anything like this for me before.

"This is beautiful, Sebastyn. Thank you," I say, ending with my gaze on him.

"You don't need to thank me, sweetheart; you deserve the world. This is just a small way I can show you how much you mean to me," he responds, coming and engulfing me in a hug.

My body melts into his, soaking up the warmth. I lift my head up to look into his eyes, and once again I'm awestruck by what I see: love. After watching Phoebe and Alaric together, I knew it was possible for two people to love each other passionately, though I never fathomed I would have anything close. Now, though, standing here under the fairy lights, swaying to romantic music in the arms of a man who is looking at me like I'm the sun and the moon, I think that maybe I can.

His lips press to mine passionately, snaking his tongue into my mouth. I kiss him back with the same passion. I've never wanted anything more in my life than to be able to call this man mine. But even with that thought, I know that I'm not ready. There are times still when, even though I know deep down that he would never do anything to hurt me or deprive me in any way, years of emotional–and sometimes physical–abuse from Joe has me questioning everything.

I know it's not fair to him to have to wait because of another man's actions, but it's not like it's a switch I can turn off. I know that I'm falling in love with him. There is no doubt about that, and for now, that's going to have to be enough.

He pulls back with heavy breathing. "We should eat before it gets cold."

I give a small chuckle and step out of his warm arms and take a seat. He sits across from me and lifts the covers. I'm floored by the sight: a beautifully cooked lasagna. Sebastyn stares at me as I take my first bite, and a moan escapes my mouth. This has to be the best lasagna I've ever had.

"Do you like it?" he asks.

"It is the most delicious thing I've ever eaten. Did you make it?"

He nods. "Yeah, my mom taught me to make it. I didn't know what your favorite food was, so I figured everyone loves lasagna."

"Well, it was a good choice because it just so happens that it is my favorite," I say, before taking another bite. As reluctant as I am to admit, I think this lasagna may even be better than mine, and I like to think that I make an amazing one. Not that I will ever admit that.

We eat in a comfortable silence, not because we have nothing to say, but because the food is just too good.

Once we finish up, he takes my hand and pulls me to my feet. "May I have this dance?" I let out a giggle at his theatrics but incline my head in agreement, placing my hand in his. As he pulls me into him and he guides me across our private dance floor, I visualize the life I could have with him: one where I would wake up feeling loved, where I could have children, where I could be myself with a partner who puts as much into our relationship as I do. All I have to do is say yes.

I come out of a spin and look into his eyes. Why am I holding off? As if my brain senses the fact that I could be happy, it chooses to plant doubts. Why would he want someone like me when he could have someone like Opal? What can I bring into any relationship? I have no job, no money. Sure, I made a little money today, but not nearly enough to contribute to a relationship. I don't even have a handle on my magic yet.

I slow our dance and walk toward the beach just outside the gazebo to sit and look at the stars.

"Where did you just go?" he asks, sitting next to me.

"Why would you want me over someone like Opal? I just don't understand. With Opal, you wouldn't have to wait for anything. I'm damaged goods who will always question everything. Why would a man as amazing as you want someone like me?" I ask.

"Now you listen here," he says forcefully, and I shrink back. He softens his tone, realizing his mistake. "Sorry, love. I just hate to hear you talk about yourself like that. You are amazing. You are beautiful, inside and out. You're generous, kind, and protective of those you care about. Any man would be lucky to have you, but none will appreciate you as much as me. I will wait forever for you to be ready and remind you every day for the rest of our lives just how amazing you are, if need be.

"Earlier today, when you stood up to Opal, I saw the fierce woman you are meant to be. The woman that you will be." As he finishes, I think back to my interaction with Opal, but I don't feel proud, like he seems to think I should. I feel ashamed.

"I almost hurt her, Seb. I wasn't in control. I think I might be evil like my father."

"You are not evil. You could never be evil. Opal crossed a line, and you defended yourself. No one would ever fault you for that," he says confidently.

"You don't know that. I didn't even know what I was doing. All I was thinking about is making sure she stays away from you forever. If you hadn't shown up, I honestly don't know what would've happened," A stray tear slips out of my eyes. Not for Opal, but for me. The last thing I want is to become like my father or, worse, Joe.

His face softens once more, and he brushes the tear from my cheek. "The fact that you are worried about that shows just how unlikely it is. Someone who is going to turn evil isn't worried about it. They let it happen. That will never be you," he moves his hands, cupping my face as he continues. "Besides, you will always have me here to remind you."

I search his eyes for any trace of a lie and find none. "I'm not ready to say *yes* yet, Seb. I really want to be. But I am a lot closer to *yes* than *no*," I really want to tell him that I'm falling in love with him, but I want to be able to give him the option to change his mind.

"I know, love. I already told you that I will wait as long as you need me to. All I wanted was a chance for us to get to know each other, and you've given me that. So, thank you. Even if you're never ready, as long as I can be close to you, I'll die happy," he leans in for a kiss before I can respond to his declaration.

I move my body so I'm straddling him and deepen the kiss. I rock my body back and forth against his very obvious erection, causing us both to begin to pant. I stop as I feel my release get closer and break our kiss. We are both breathing heavily, and I can tell that it's taking all of his control not to continue.

"We should stop," I whisper. Not wanting to, but knowing that if I let it go too much further, I won't be able to. He agrees but puts his lips back on mine.

"Let me make you feel good, love. Just that, nothing else," he whispers, and I nod my agreement, never wanting anything more. He carries me back up to the gazebo and lays me down on the ground where we were dancing. He kisses me again, but only for a moment before his lips begin a trail down my body.

As he reaches my pants, he unbuttons them and kisses a trail along the hem from left to right, pulling them down slowly. As soon as they are off, my body arches up to his mouth, wanting more than anything to feel his talented tongue on my clit. This causes him to chuckle and me to growl at him.

"Patience, love," he says as he moves his mouth to my pussy over the top of my underwear.

"Oh my goddess," I whisper, never having felt anything as exquisite as this before. Even with the fabric separating us, I've never felt anything this good.

"Please, Seb," I cry out as he swipes his tongue over the fabric before pulling it to the side.

Two soft flicks of his tongue on my clit has me moaning in pleasure, already feeling close to release. Joe never did this, always being in a rush to get his own release. The only orgasm I've ever had was by myself.

A quick suck and some tantalizing tongue flicks of my clit later, and I'm falling over the edge, seeing stars behind my closed eyes.

"Sebastyn!" I scream, my legs shaking.

He licks his lips, returning my panties to their original position and helping me back into my skinny jeans. "You taste divine love."

A wave of guilt crashes over me at the thought of him not finding his own release, so I reach for him. He softly grabs my hand and kisses it. "Not tonight, love. Tonight was all about you. There will be time for me in the future, but first we need for you to recognize your worth.

"Loathe as I am to admit it, I know there was a man before me. As much of an asshole as he was, not knowing or treasuring the gem that he had in you, he made you feel like a lesser being rather than the goddess you are. And I will enjoy every second of showing you exactly what you're worth without expecting anything in return," he moves back up and merges his mouth with mine once more, and I can taste myself on his tongue. I didn't think that it would ever be something I would enjoy. Having read a couple of romance novels in high school where the women would get turned on tasting themselves on their partners' tongues always seemed such a foreign concept to me. But now, as I am kissing Seb, I realize what they mean. And dear goddess, do I want this man.

He breaks our kiss and stands up, adjusting what must be a painful erection before reaching out a hand to help me up.

"Thank you," I say once standing.

"It should be me thanking you. This is the best moment of my life thus far. But we should really get you home. Are you going back to your cottage or my mom's?" he asks and for a split second I want to say neither and tell him to take me to his home, but I think better of it.

"To your mom's, I think. I have to make a good amount of stock before we leave next week," I tell him, straightening my clothes.

We teleport back into the bedroom I've been staying in with his mom, and he bids me goodnight, promising to see me tomorrow.

Tomorrow can't come soon enough. I fall asleep quickly with

dreams of my mother, but these dreams seem different, prophetic even. They're still of me and my mother, but instead of being young, I am my current age. We're sitting in the clearing, laughing and talking as if we have spent no time apart. I really need to figure out what these dreams mean. It can't be a coincidence that they are coming more frequently now that my magic has been released. Like they're trying to tell me something.

Chapter Twelve

Sebastyn

As much as it pains me to leave Sarah in my old bedroom, I know I must, or I won't be able to hold myself back from claiming her as my own. I adjust the bulge in my pants and teleport back to the gazebo to begin cleaning up. The second I pop in, I'm greeted by my sister. Good thing she came now and not half an hour before; things would've been a little awkward. I know I have felt pretty awkward when I've interrupted her and Lennox, which has happened a lot more than I'd like to admit. I blame them, though. They knew I was on my way over a few of those times, yet they still let me walk in on them.

"How did it go?" she asks. She had helped me set up and get everything ready for my date. I've been on plenty of dates in my lifetime but none as important as this, and I needed a woman's perspective to make it perfect. Luckily, my sister seems just as invested in everything between Sarah and I working out as I am.

"Better than I could've dreamed," I say with an enormous smile on my face.

"I'm glad," she responds. Wait, she's not being her bubbly, over-excited self. Something isn't right.

"What's wrong?" I ask, turning around to face her.

She sets down the tray she is holding with a sigh. "I'm just finding it really hard to keep this secret from you."

I walk over and put my hand on her shoulder. "I know. I don't like keeping things from you, either, but I won't be able to keep anything from Sarah, and if you're still insisting she doesn't know, then I can't know either."

She nods sullenly, so I change the subject, walking over to clean up the food. "Did you hear about what happened at the market today between Opal and Sarah?

"No. Why? What happened?" she questions.

"Well, I didn't see the entire thing, but Opal cornered Sarah at the market today," I watch as her fists clench and she gets a murderous look on her face. "It's okay, Sarah handled it, but some really weird things happened."

"Like what?" she moves to sit down, patting the seat next to her.

"Well, when I first got there, it was beautiful and sunny, then it was like a switch flipped, the clouds rolled in, and thunder started booming. I remember thinking that I needed to go check on Sarah because I didn't want her to get caught in the storm. But when I found her, magic was surrounding her like a mist. Her hands glowed purple as she was walking toward Opal, who was pissing her pants in fear." Skarlyt snorts out a laugh. "Not literally, but she was terrified. Anyway, I wrapped Sarah in a hug from behind and got her to calm down. As Opal was walking away, Sarah told her to stay away from me and that if she even thought about touching me, she'd make her wish she was never born. It was so fucking hot. You should've seen her," I get a goofy smile, having to adjust my pants to hide the raging boner I was sporting from remembering the scene.

"Did anything else happen?" she snaps at me impatiently.

"Well, yeah. After that, it seemed like, as soon as the storm rolled in, it rolled back out again. Sarah said she's worried about being evil like her dad. She said she didn't feel in control when she was going after Opal and that, if I hadn't intervened, she didn't know what would've happened." Skarlyt looks at me skeptically.

"Don't get me wrong, I know she would never turn evil, but I think her powers are a lot stronger than any of us realize, and without proper training and because they were locked up for so long, they're trying to take over. We need to help her, Skarlyt. I just don't know how," I let my shoulders slump, and she wraps her arm around my shoulders.

"She is insanely powerful, and I don't care what mom says, I think if given the chance she could even give me a run for my money. But also, like us, her powers are linked to her emotions. Where we had years of training since birth to learn to harness and control our emotions and magic, she's had to repress both. She doesn't need us worrying about her; what she needs is for to let her free, to allow her to feel what she wants to feel, what she needs to feel, become the woman she was meant to be. Then, and only then, will she gain the control she wants. As backwards as it sounds, because she's had to control everything for her entire life— she's never been able to act as herself, to cry or laugh freely— instead of practicing control, she needs to let it go," she finishes, and I'm staring at her with wide eyes. It goes against everything they ever taught us, but it also sorta makes sense.

"How do we do that?" I ask.

"I have a few ideas, but you're not going to be able to be present. She is already beginning to recognize you as safe. If you're around, she won't let go like she needs to."

"Or, she will let go more with me there because she trusts I won't let her go too far," I argue.

She sighs again. "It's possible. But honestly, Seb, she's less likely to want you around when she loses control. She won't want you to see her like that."

Damn it. I know she's right. I don't like it, but she is. It's been hard enough getting her to open up and be herself when magic's not involved.

"We just need to figure out who she trusts enough to let go with," she places her hand on her chin in thought.

"Samara," I say and her eyes snap to mine in question. "She trusts Samara enough to let go. She trusts Phoebe and Sophia, too. But Phoebe has children, so she would be worried about hurting her, and Sophia is in the Amazon. She probably trusts you enough, too, but you also have Kayne, so you're out; she'd be too worried about something happening to you. It has to be Samara."

She nods at that and before saying anything, pops out and returns with a very pissed-off looking Samara.

"What the fuck?" Samara growls at Skarlyt, and I burst out laughing. Leave it to my sister to piss off the most powerful feline shifter in our area.

She turns her scowl on me, and I raise my hands in defense.

"It's about Sarah," Skarlyt speaks up.

"What about her? Is she okay?" I can see the panic beginning to form on Samara's face, and I know I was right. She's the right choice for this.

"She's fine. Better than fine, I hope. We just wanted to talk to you about how to help her with her magic," I watch as she visually relaxes at my words.

"But I don't know anything about magic," she looks between us both in confusion.

"No, but she trusts you. She needs to let go of her control. She's never been able to be herself and feel. Feel the anger, sadness, joy and whatever other emotions those mage assholes didn't let her. She needs someone she feels safe with to let everything out, or she risks her magic lashing out and taking over," Skarlyt explains.

"Wait. I thought magic was like shifting: you need control over your magic just like we need to control our animals?" Samara asks.

"But you don't control your lion, do you? You've come to a mutual agreement with her, right?" I ask, and she nods.

"It's the same with magic. Although our magic can't speak to us the same way your animals do, in a way it's the same. And normally, a witch is taught from birth to have a healthy respect for our magic and how to let out our emotions without losing control. Sarah was not. She was taught to suppress everything about herself, magic included. Before she and her magic can form an alliance or agreement, she needs to give up that control," Skarlyt explains.

Samara inclines her head. "'That makes sense. But I still don't understand what it has to do with me."

"We need you to let her lose control with you. Just be her safe space. We are going to talk with her about it tomorrow. I'm sure she will agree, but before we do that, we wanted to make sure you would be okay with it," Skarlyt says.

"Of course. Anything for Sarah," Samara agrees, and I let out a breath of relief.

"I'm going to make you a protection totem just in case her magic takes control, but I know deep down she will never hurt you. It will just put her at ease knowing she won't be able to harm you, no matter what," I tell her, and Skar's eyes snap to mine. Shit, I forgot. That's another thing that I haven't taught her yet. "You can help Skar," she seems appeased by the prospect of being able to watch—or more likely take over the entire thing once she knows how. Thank the Mother. My sister is amazing and I love her, but she also terrifies me.

"So, what am I supposed to do?" Samara asks, walking over and sitting down on the stairs to the gazebo.

I share a look with Skarlyt and shrug my shoulders. Luckily, she seems to know. "You need her to express as many emotions as strongly as possible. Everything she's held in needs to come out. I would start with anger since that one will be the easiest. Hopefully, she will just think about her father and Joe and her magic will rise up, but if that fails, just mention Opal. After what happened today, I'm sure that will do the trick," Skarlyt says with a snicker.

Samara looks between us both. "Why? What happened with Opal?"

I shoot my sister a pointed look before explaining, stopping a couple times to keep Samara from going to find Opal.

"She really did that?"

I nod. "Yup. She was a badass. I can't wait for you to see her in action."

"I can't wait," Samara says with a smile, rubbing her hands together.

We finish cleaning up, which goes a lot quicker with Samara's help. A third set of hands makes it one trip instead of two, which is great because I'm ready to go to bed. Not because I'm particularly tired, but more because it means I can see Sarah sooner.

After dropping Samara back off at home, Skarlyt and I teleport over to my house to create the totem. To say she's excited is an understatement. Of course, she knew about jewelry being able to hold protection spells, but the one that I have is so much stronger and doesn't just protect from outward attacks. It protects the wearer from all magic. It also means that if Samara is wearing it, we might not be able to teleport with her. I've never tested it out before.

I pull out the thick, ancient book gifted to me by the High Priestess of the Egyptian coven and flip to the page. Luckily whoever wrote this book spoke English so there's no need to translate anything.

"So how is this different from our regular protection spells? You called it a totem," Skar says, breaking my concentration.

"First, it is a whole lot stronger. It can only be tied to a red jasper stone, hung with hemp twine, and nothing man made can be included in the set up. Once it's done, the person wearing it– Samara in this case–will be immune to magic in all forms. I'm thinking even teleporting with her will be out, at least while she's wearing it."

"Really?" Her eyes sparkle with excitement, and I smile. I pass her the book while grabbing the red jasper and hemp twine and set it in front of her.

"The instructions are all there," I tell her, tapping on the page. I had intended to do it myself and just show her but that's not how she learns. She picks things up a lot quicker when she is physically doing something, and right now, we only need one.

As with anything she does, it's perfect when she's done. I can feel the hum of magic as she settles it into my hand. "This should do the trick," I tell her with a wink, handing it back. "Bring this to Samara and drape it around her neck. Don't let it go around anyone else's. It needs to bond with Samara."

"Bond?"

"Yes. It will only work for the first person who ties it around their neck. Once it's been secured there, it can not be transferred to another person."

"Can she put it on and off?"

"Of course, but it won't work for anyone else and, in extreme cases, if the stone bonds strongly with Samara, it could lash out magically at anyone else who puts it on, so please warn her."

Skarlyt nods, placing the stone and twine in her pocket. "I will. Sweet dreams little brother." She doesn't say anything more, just pops back out of my house leaving me to my bed.

∞∞∞

. . .

After having one of the best sleeps of my life, I wake up completely refreshed and more than ready to go see Sarah. I get dressed quickly before teleporting to my mom's. Normally, I would have just popped myself inside, but with Sarah staying here, I don't want to invade her privacy.

I raise my hand and place a soft knock on the door before turning the handle and stepping inside. My mom greets me, already making her way to the door. "Why'd you bother knocking if you were just going to walk in anyway?" She chuckles.

"I didn't want to invade Sarah's privacy," I say with a shrug.

"Knocking before just walking in is the exact same thing as just walking in," she challenges.

"No, it's not. The knock is an obvious warning to the fact that I'm coming inside."

"Whatever you say," she laughs, shaking her head. "Sarah's in the back room making some of her products for me to sell while you guys are gone."

I place a soft kiss on her cheek and make my way to the back room. I hear soft humming coming from beyond the open door, and I lean against the door frame taking in the scene. Sarah has a pair of earbuds hanging out of her ears, her body swaying to whatever music is playing. It's insanely sexy. I stand and watch her for a few minutes, enjoying seeing the smile on her face. She looks very relaxed, the most relaxed I've ever seen her before, and it warms my heart. It starts to feel a little creepy, and I knock loudly on the wall. Her eyes dart upward and widen in surprise, quickly pulling the ear buds out of her ears.

"Oh, hey, Seb!" She exclaims with a smile.

"Good morning, sweetheart." I walk around the worktable to her side and place a soft kiss on her head while wrapping my arms around her. She melts into me, letting out a sigh, her body seeming to lose all tension in my embrace. "What are you working on?"

116

She steps back, turning back toward the workstation. "I've been trying to make some extra stock so that your mom can sell it for me next week, and I had this idea that since I've been using magic to enhance everything else, perhaps I could go a step further and make a nail polish that magically changes color to match any outfit. But so far, it's a bust."

"Maybe I can help. Show me what spell you're using." She pulls out a couple of different grimoires and shows me the spells she's been using. I immediately see why they're not working. "These are all for specific items."

She sighs. "I know. I thought maybe I could substitute a word in there."

I rub her back. "Sometimes that works, and other times it doesn't. Here, try this." I say, rushing over to the bookshelf and grabbing one of the older grimoires. It's written in Latin so that's probably why she didn't check it, but I remember seeing something in here to change fingernails colors.

"Ah. Here it is. Let's try this."

"What does that say?"

"*Digiti reflexionis vestis.* It means fingernails reflect the color of your clothes. I think it's meant to be used directly on your nails but maybe it will work if we infuse it into the polish." I place my hand on the bottle of nail polish and whisper the spell. "Only one way to know for sure."

Sarah smiles, picking up the white bottle of nail polish and swiping a stripe on her nails. It instantly changes to a pale blue color that matches her shirt perfectly.

"Oh my goddess! It worked!" She exclaims, wrapping her arms around me and jumping up and down.

"I'm glad I could help," I chuckle.

We spend the next couple hours making her stock, spending the day together. By the time my mom comes in with dinner, we've got boxes and boxes of different products. The smile on her face is incredible; in fact, her entire body seems to have a glow around her. She's radiating happiness. I'm going to do anything in my power to make sure it stays that way.

Chapter Thirteen

Sarah

The last two days flew by. Between Sebastyn, Constance, and I, we made more than enough stock so that if I sell everything, I will get a nice chunk of change. Definitely enough to pay them back for the supplies, get myself some new clothes and set some aside to hopefully pay rent on the cabin that I've been staying in on pack land. I looked up the rental prices for the resorts that the pack owns and while I definitely can't afford the four thousand a month that it would cost to stay in one of those, I at least want to pay something. Although being here, with the coven, feels right, too. I'm considering asking Constance if she knows of any apartments, rooms, or houses for rent. There's something about this land that feels like home. It may only be a hop, skip, and a jump from the pack, but being here settles something in my soul. I haven't brought it up yet because I know Constance will offer for me to stay here or Sebastyn will insist that I stay with him. As much as I care for them both, I feel like maybe I need to be on my own for a little bit. Take care of myself for once. Stand on my own two feet.

It's a surreal feeling, this belonging. It's something I never felt before, never even dared to hope for in my life. I thought I was resigned to a fate of constant fear. Now, I wake up in the morning with a smile on my face. Instead of needing to hop to it and get chores done, I can lounge around the house in my pajamas if I want and no one would say anything. Heck, Constance would probably join me.

I chuckle to myself as I hop in the shower, washing away the sleep fog from my brain. Today is special. Samara and I will be going to the clearing to let my magic loose. I'll admit, when Skarlyt and Seb explained their theory to me, I was skeptical, but the more I thought about it, the more it made sense. Both the losing control and that Samara would be the one with me while doing it. I need to get a handle on my magic so that something doesn't happen like it did with Opal. The last thing I want is to lose control at the wrong time and hurt someone. Even her. Knowing that Skarlyt and Sebastyn made Samara a protection totem, making it impossible for my magic to hurt her will go a long way in helping me relax enough to let my magic out the way it needs to.

Skarlyt explained that, in order to accomplish my task, I need to talk about my past, and that's another reason I'm glad they asked Samara to help instead of either of them. As much as I'm falling for Seb and feel a connection to Skarlyt, there are parts of my past I would rather they not know. So far, I've told them most, but other than Sophia, no one could know what I'm not saying, and there's no good way to tell them about the punishments.

I get dressed quickly and walk out in the kitchen, finding Samara sitting there, already stuffing her face full of food at the island. "Good morning."

"Morning." She says with a mouth full of food, and I chuckle.

"Hungry?"

"Always," she responds, immediately going back to her plate. The way she's shovelling it in there, you would think that she hasn't eaten in a year.

"Are you even chewing?" I ask, as I sit down in front of my own plate. She just nods.

"She's a shifter, that's how they all eat." Constance says, sitting down with her own breakfast.

"Phoebe doesn't eat like that," I say, wrinkling my nose.

"That's because she was raised as a human," Samara says, pointing her fork at me between bites.

Not wanting to accidentally see the chewed food in Samara's mouth, I keep the rest of my thoughts to myself: like how Alaric doesn't seem to eat with his mouth open or how I've seen Lennox actually chew his food.

By the time I'm done eating, she's had seconds, and I stare at her stomach for a moment wondering where the heck she puts it all.

"Shifter metabolism. Couldn't gain weight if I tried. Besides, I train regularly."

"Must be nice," I grumble under my breath. I'm not over-weight, but I'm not a twig either. I've got nice curves; although, I do wish my ass were a little smaller and firmer. But if I were to eat like Samara, I'm sure I would blow up like a balloon. I've gained at least ten pounds since arriving here. Joe always watched what I ate to make sure I didn't gain any weight. And my father was the same before him. Whenever I asked for an extra slice of cake or chocolate syrup on my ice cream, he used to tell me no man wants a pig for a wife and that I needed to 'stay fit' for my future husband.

"Ready to go?" Samara asks, breaking my mental musings.

"Yup," I tell her and the two of us walk out of the house toward the clearing.

"Are you ready for this?" she asks, and I think about it for a second.

"I think so. I mean I don't know exactly what's going to happen, or if my magic is even going to make an appearance, but I can't allow myself to lose control like I did with Opal. Someone could've gotten hurt."

"What happened with Opal was justified. You have nothing to feel bad for. She deserved much more than the scare you gave her. Much more," Samara growls.

"I know." I sigh but still I've always tried to forgive and forget, holding grudges only hurts the grudge holder. Most often the other person doesn't even care.

"Okay, let's sit," Samara says, gesturing to the grass. "Skarlyt says that you don't even need to say anything out loud, that simply envisioning it in your head will do the trick. So, close your eyes and think about your father first," she tells me. I sit down and close my eyes. Nothing seems to be happening, and I scrunch my eyes together in determination.

"Okay. That's not working. You look like you're trying to take a shit," she says with a chuckle. I open my eyes and glare at her. "Let's try this. Close your eyes again." When I do, she continues, "What's the first word that comes to your mind when you think of him?"

"Oppression," I answer without hesitation.

"Okay, let that feeling out," she tells me. "Replay every moment he made you feel oppressed, like a movie, and let it out." I do as she asks and allow every time he told me not to express my feelings to play on a reel in my mind. I remember the time, as a little girl, I fell down and scraped my knee, and instead of telling me it would be okay, he barked at me to clean myself up and not to cry. Then, I allow every time he demanded I not speak or remember my role to come forward, too.

I feel the rage at him and the sadness for myself come out, and my magic rises up in response. I raise my hands to the sky and scream out my frustrations, watching as the purple flows up to meet a quickly darkening sky. I listen as the thunder crashes down, mixing in with my screams, fueling them, giving me permission to keep going.

I don't direct my magic on what to do; I just let it go. As it crashes back down to the earth and the first droplets of rain fall, I see small flowers spring up. I know that they will die soon because winter is coming, but watching something beautiful come from a place of pain for me is awakening. Maybe my magic isn't bad; maybe I won't turn out like my father. If these horrid feelings are creating something so beautiful, how can I?

"That was incredible, Sarah. I've never seen anything like that before." Samara says, completely awestruck, looking around at the small flowers now growing in a circle around us.

"Me neither." I admit, awestruck myself.

"Okay, next, think about Joe. What's the first word that comes to mind when you think about him?" Samara asks.

Again, there is no hesitation. "Monster."

Without her direction, I close my eyes once more and play my ten years with Joe on the reel: the beatings, the belittling, my 'wifely duties'. I scream louder this time as I release my magic, and the rain pelts down on us. I think about stopping, but it feels like something inside of me is releasing, like a lock opening, and for the first time, I'm becoming who I'm meant to be.

The magic again seeps into the ground where it falls, growing small vines that weave together into beautiful benches. I didn't know magic could do that. But it's magic and I guess anything is possible.

"Now your mom," she says, and my eyes shoot to hers in surprise. "We need to express as many emotions as possible. We got the hardest two out of the way first."

I nod, closing my eyes and thinking of my mom. "Loss," I say sadly, as tears fall down my face. All my life, my father told me I killed her coming into this world. That it was my fault. I believed him for a long time, longer than I care to admit. Too long. Even when I should've known that it was not my fault. A child is never at fault for complications in a birth. They are innocent. As my tears fall faster, I once again let my magic flow upward. This time, though, it floats slower. Instead of raging outward, it floats up leisurely like it's dancing to a sad song.

As it falls, each bench gets thicker and sprouts little flowers over them. Samara doesn't say anything. She places her hand on my knee, giving it a small squeeze of support. I bob my head in thanks, wiping the tears off my face.

"Last one. What's the first word you think of when I say Sebastyn," she says, and I know the word.

"Home," for he is my home. She nods and smiles at my answer.

I allow the love I feel for him to pour out, but instead of shooting to the sky, I place my hands on the ground. I pull up Seb's reel and realize I am not just falling in love with him; I've fallen completely. There is no going back for me now. He has quickly become a permanent fixture in my heart. I open my eyes and watch as everything in the clearing that was changing colors and withering with the change of season has now perked back up and grown thicker. But more than that, where the storm clouds were, the sun is now shining brightly, directly on the spot where Samara and I sit.

"That's amazing!" she exclaims, wrapping me in a hug. "But I think you need to talk to someone about your ability to influence the weather. I'm pretty sure that's something that isn't very common."

"That wasn't me." But as the words come out, I know they're not true. Just like at the market, the weather seemed to react to my mood. "It's not possible. Right?" I ask.

"It was you, hun. There's no way that a storm rolled in and out that quickly, perfectly in sync with your moods." As she answers, anxiety begins to roll through me. This isn't possible. I was coming to terms with the fact that I have magic after years of my father telling me I didn't have any. I am working on learning to control said magic, and it's starting to get easier, especially after today. But now she's saying I can influence the weather? Only the Storm family can do that right? What if someone pisses me off, and I let a tornado loose on their house—or worse—I strike someone down by lightning?

As if sensing where my thought process is going, Samara snaps me out of it. "Don't stress until we talk to Constance, Skar, and Seb. I'm sure one of them will be able to help you figure it out."

We hurry back to Constance's house, and all the while I'm lost in thought at the repercussions of having this gift. Wondering how, if I'm not of the Storm family line, that I even have it. When we finally arrive, I'm so distracted by my inner turmoil that I vaguely register Samara telling them what happened.

Seb, realizing that I'm not present, engulfs me in a hug. "This is a very special gift. One that the Mother does not bestow on many. I've only ever met one other witch who can influence the weather, and she's part of our coven. I'm sure she can help you learn to harness it."

"Can I meet her?" I ask excitedly, looking at all three. Constance and Skarlyt share a look that I will need to unpack another time. I'm not sure what it was about, but I have a feeling it involves me.

"When you get back from the Amazon, we will set up some lessons with Rita," Constance answers, and Skarlyt shoots her a look that I can only decipher as 'what the fuck'. Okay, now I really need to know.

"Why don't you want me to meet her Skar?" I ask.

She sighs, probably kicking herself mentally for getting caught. "It's not that I don't want you to meet her. It's just Rita has been through a lot and generally keeps to herself. I want to ask her permission before getting your hopes up and offering you a lesson with her."

Oh, that makes sense, so I nod in agreement. Wait. Rita, that's Constance's friend who has shut herself in after losing her mate and daughter. I hear them all whispering as I numbly walk toward the shower. I'm already wet from the torrential downpour I seem to have caused, but I'm freezing. The weather isn't warm anymore, so the wind that helped dry my clothes was cold and didn't do much.

As I step out of my clothes and step under the hot spray, I think about my magic. I close my eyes and reach inside, finding that pool of purple in my chest. I mentally caress it, pushing my gratitude and love into it. It seems like it reaches back, stroking my heart, trying to ease some of my pain. I can't help feeling like it has an awareness and is more present in my life than I thought. "Thank you," I whisper to it, and I go about my business in the shower.

Stepping out and into my towel, I almost feel like a new woman. Where there used to be fear, there is now confidence; where there was rage, there is now the prospect of happiness; where there was loneliness, there is now love. I don't think I've gotten rid of all my insecurities. I still don't think I'm good enough for Sebastyn, but now I find I don't care about that as much because I want him and he wants me. For now, that's enough.

I find him waiting for me when I step out of the bathroom. "Everything okay, love?" he asks.

"More than. But I'm tired and could use a nap. Will you hold me?" I ask. He immediately grabs my hand, leading us to the bed. He helps me into a nightgown over my towel which I drop as soon as the nightgown is covering me and slide on a pair of underwear. We crawl under the covers, where he pulls me close and wraps his arms around me, and I drift off to sleep. What an emotional rollercoaster of a day. Not only did I use some of my magic, but something inside me feels different. Better. Settled. Like something inside of me was broken but has now been put back together.

Chapter Fourteen

Sebastyn

I'm stronger than I thought I was because seeing Sarah's barely covered body in that towel was almost my undoing. It took everything I had not to rip it off her body, push her down on the bed and show her just what she means to me. But that's not what she needed right then. She looked exhausted and, from what Samara told me of their time in the clearing, combined with witnessing the storm with my own eyes, she used a lot of magic and needs rest.

I run back through what Samara told us and then replay the events from the market the other day. I don't know how I didn't see before that she could influence the weather. Probably because only those of the Storm bloodline have that ability and after Rita's daughter died along with her husband, Rita is all that's left.

I look down at a sleeping Sarah and pull up the image of Rita in my mind and gasp. Shit. Is this what Skarlyt believes?

I slide my phone out of my pocket, careful not to disturb the sleeping beauty next to me and pull up Skar's contact.

> Me: You think Rita is Sarah's mother don't you?

I type and watch the three dots flutter and disappear before returning again.

> The Best Sister in the World: Yes but I need to be sure before I say anything.

She responds and I chuckle to myself. I wonder when she got a hold of my phone long enough to change her contact name?

> Me: What are you doing to find out?

I type, looking back down at a sleeping Sarah, gently rolling her over. Once her breathing evens out once more, I quickly teleport to the porch where I know Skarlyt and my mom are still.

"Okay spill," I tell them both, seeing the guilty looks on their faces.

My mom sighs, patting the chair in front of her. "There's a lot to catch you up on. We wanted to keep you out of it because you said that you didn't want to keep things from Sarah."

"That was before I figured it out on my own. Now I understand why you don't want to tell her until you're sure."

My sister smiles. "I'll start at the beginning." I nod.

"That usually works best." I snark, and she taps me on the leg.

"I first suspected it when she walked in on you and Opal in mom's kitchen..." She begins and I growl.

"There's no me and Opal."

"I know. Okay, I'll rephrase. I first suspected it after we walked in on Opal kissing you." She says, and I incline my head, agreeing with her choice of words. "After I followed Sarah back to the clearing, she began playing with her necklace, and I thought it looked familiar. Remember that necklace Rita always wears, the moon with a sliver cut out?" I scrunch my eyebrows together and try to remember but come up blank. I shake my head *no*. She waves her hand. "No matter. Anyway, she does have a necklace, it's like one of those friendship necklaces where, when you put two necklaces together, they make one. Only it's in the shape of a full moon with a sliver cut out of one side. She had given the crescent moon to her daughter and kept the other half herself."

"And you think Sarah's necklace is the other half? But Rita's daughter and mate died, right?" I look over at my mom for confirmation.

She sighs sullenly. "We believe that Robert–that's Rita's mate's name–may have faked their deaths and hidden Alexandra away from Rita, though we don't know why."

"Wait. Alexandra? Don't you mean Sarah?"

"No. Rita's daughter was called Alexandra. You were very young when she died, or went missing or was stolen, that you wouldn't remember."

"Okay, but there are probably hundreds of those necklaces out in circulation."

"Exactly." My sister says. "But combine that with the looks: if you replace Sarah's brown hair with blonde and add a couple inches more height, you'd be looking at a younger version of Rita."

I nod. "That's what gave it away to me too. Along with the weather stuff."

"The fact that the Storm Family grimoire calls to her and is so attached that it will magically appear in her hands each time she enters the workshop should be proof enough without even the weather. But if there's even the slightest chance we're wrong, it will destroy both of them," my mom says. She's right. Even with all the signs pointing to us being right, if, on the off chance we're wrong, we won't only send Rita back into another depression, but Sarah will probably not be much better.

"So how are you going to prove it?"

129

My mom and Skarlyt share a look, and I have a feeling I'm not going to particularly like what they're going to say. "Sarah cut her hand the other day when she was cleaning up a vial in the work room. I saved a few drops of her blood. We just need to get a couple drops of Rita's–though I don't know how–and put them together to see what happens."

"What do you mean 'see what happens'?"

"I mean that, if they are in fact mother and daughter, the blood from both will merge, the slight amount of magic residue within it calling out to each other. If they're not, the blood will stay separate like oil and water."

"Well that should only take a few minutes; why haven't you done it yet?" I demand a little forcefully, looking between my mother and sister.

"Because it doesn't only take a few minutes, Sebastyn." My sister scolds. "Sometimes the blood can take up to forty-eight hours to blend. We will need to allow it to sit. I'm heading over to Rita's now. Hopefully I'll figure out a way to get a couple drops of blood, and we'll have our answer within the next two days," she says, popping away.

"You know she's just as frustrated as you," my mom says, and I snort.

"Doubtful."

"Sebastyn," My mother scolds, and I turn to look at her. "You were too young to remember but Skarlyt, Alexandra and Opal were the best of friends since they were in diapers; they were 'the three amigos.' When Alexandra died, it was extremely hard for your sister. She was too young to truly know what happened. She just knew that one day her best friend was here and the next she was gone. She cried for Alexandra for months until she woke up one day and just stopped asking for her."

"I didn't know that," I whisper, now feeling a little bad for snapping at my sister.

"Of course you didn't; why would you? But with the possibility that Sarah is Alexandra, it's opened up an old wound in your sister, and if we're wrong, she's going to need us."

"How do you think Rita will react if it is true?"

My mom sighs. "I honestly don't know how we're even going to get them in the same place. They both have extremely strong Storm magic. If the two of them lose control at the same time, it could be disastrous."

"Shit," I whisper and she nods. I wasn't even thinking of that. Depending on the emotions they are feeling when they find out, we could get a bright sunny day or a hurricane level storm.

"That's part of the problem. Say we find out tomorrow that we're right, and I go tell Rita her daughter is alive; she'll never believe me. If you tell Sarah her mother's not dead, it will be the same. They need to see each other. Their magic will tell them."

"So why not just introduce them now and see?" I ask, confused as to why we're going through all this if the answer is that simple.

"Because if they are mother and daughter, and their magic reacts in a volatile way, then we need to be prepared."

"But couldn't we do that even without the blood confirmation?" I ask, genuinely still confused. This seems like a way better and way easier answer.

"No. Even with their magic reaching out and recognizing one another, there is still the chance that they, or others in the coven, would try to deny it. With the blood, there is no room for it to be disputed."

I agree, though I still think we should put a protection barrier around the two of them and throw them in a room together. We'll know one way or another extremely quickly whether they are related or not. No matter what happens, it feels like the truth; I could feel it the moment the thought popped into my head when I was snuggling with Sarah.

"I'm going to go snuggle with my mate," I tell my mom, placing a soft kiss on her head.

"I'm so happy for you, my boy. She's a good one."

"Better than even you know, Mom," I tell her and pop myself back onto the bed, rolling Sarah back over toward me. She instantly wraps her arms around my middle and hooks her legs over mine with a sigh, as if I'm a body pillow. I caress her hair softly, listen to her breathing, and relax. I'm not tired enough to sleep, but I have no problem sitting here and staring at my sleeping mate for however long she needs.

Chapter Fifteen

Sarah

I wake to the smell of bacon frying, and my stomach rumbles loudly. As I start to roll out of bed, something heavily draped over my waist stops me. I panic, immediately thinking the past few weeks have been a dream, and that Joe is laying beside me. My entire body freezes in terror.

I close my eyes and will away the panic that is rising within me. But just as my breathing starts to slow, the arm around my middle pulls me closer, and I feel someone nuzzle into my neck. Wait. Joe would never do that, sleeping or not. I open my eyes as I turn to face the person next to me, and I am greeted by Sebastyn's sapphire blue eyes.

"Good morning, gorgeous," he says with a smile.

"Hi," I say back, letting the tension slip from my body, and I relax in his hold. Just as I'm starting to get comfortable again, my stomach rumbles louder. Peeking over Seb to look out the window, I notice the morning sky. Holy crap! I must've slept for at least sixteen hours. No wonder I'm so hungry; I've skipped lunch and dinner!

"Someone's hungry," Seb says with a chuckle as he places a

kiss on my forehead and hops out of bed. After another whiff of delicious bacon fills the room, I reluctantly follow. "I'll meet you out there. Mom made a huge breakfast, and you must be hungry after yesterday."

After visiting the bathroom to do my business and brush my teeth, I round the corner in the kitchen and stop in awe, my mouth watering at the sight. The entire island is covered: pancakes, bacon, hash browns, sausages, toast, and an enormous plate of scrambled eggs.

I let out a giggle. "Are we feeding the entire coven?" I joke.

Constance laughs along with me. "Nope. Just Skarlyt and Lennox. But Lennox eats as much as ten witches combined, so I always make extra. Although he does have better manners than Samara," she chuckles.

I nod, agreeing with her. I didn't realize the difference in metabolisms between shifters and everyone else until I came to stay with Phoebe. To say that shifters eat a lot is an understatement. I've seen Alaric finish off an entire pot of spaghetti to himself in one sitting. Though I think, after watching Samara yesterday morning, I feel like she may be able to give him a run for his money.

"Is there anything I can help with?" I ask, even though I already know the answer.

Constance shakes her head, "Just grab a plate of food and sit at the table. Skarlyt and Lennox should be here any minute with Kayne." I do as she asks and am just sitting down when they arrive.

"How are you feeling today, Sarah?" Skarlyt asks, sitting down at the table next to me.

"Pretty good, actually. But then that much sleep would make anyone feel good," I chuckle.

"That's true," she says, looking at me differently this morning than she has before. I can't put my finger quite on what it is. It's almost as if she's seeing a different person when she looks at me.

I'm not even sure why that thought pops into my head. Maybe it has something to do with my magic. I shake my head to clear the thoughts and go back to my plate.

We eat with light-hearted conversation between bites. It's refreshing. Growing up just me and my dad, and then with Joe, I never had this. I was not to speak during meals, and if we had company, I was not entitled to even sit at the table, being forced to sit and eat in my room.

Once we are all finished with our food and beginning to clean up, Skarlyt pulls me out to the porch, "Let the men clean up." I go to protest, but she gives me a look that tells me the argument won't end in my favor, so I follow her.

Once we are seated, she turns to me. "Sarah, tell me about your mother." A pang of sadness rolls through me, remembering my time in the clearing yesterday, but I give Skarlyt a soft smile. My magic spreads through my body, not trying to come out, but soothing me in a way, letting me know that I'm not alone. At least, that's what I think it's trying to say.

"My dad always told me that she died giving birth to me, so there's nothing really to tell." She gives me another look that makes me think someone has told her about my dreams, so I continue. "But sometimes I have these dreams. Well, really, they seem more like memories. I'm a little girl, spinning in circles and running around a clearing very similar to the one here, with a woman who looks exactly like my mother in the only picture of her I was allowed to keep. But if what my dad said was true, it would be impossible for them to be memories. Right?"

"What does she look like," she asks, quickly adding on, "in your dreams, I mean."

"Here," I pull out the picture I carry with me at all times. Her face is slightly hidden in the picture, as she is turning away. But from what you can see, she has beautiful olive skin and bright green eyes with sandy blonde hair.

I watch as her eyes go wide, taking in the picture.

"What are we looking at?" Constance says, making me jump. I didn't hear her join us.

"It's a picture of Sarah's mother," Skarlyt says, handing the picture to Constance. I watch as her eyes go wide, as well, sharing a look with Skar before handing it back to me. I run my fingers over her face in the picture, caressing her.

"I know you can't really see her because she's looking away, but that's all I have," I whisper.

"She's beautiful," Constance comes and sits beside me, wrapping her arms around my shoulders much like I always envisioned my mother would.

I'm about to ask what the looks were about when Seb rushes to the porch. "Sarah, are you packed? We need to go. Darren called. He needs us to come earlier than expected. Like a lot earlier," he spits out the words so fast they almost blend together.

"I'll finish packing now. Go get Samara and Trev and grab me after," I say, rushing into the house and throwing things in my bag. I could tell from the anxiety pouring off Sebastyn that he's worried, and we need to get there now. I don't know what happened, but I'm sure I'll find out when I get there.

I'm just throwing my toothbrush and toothpaste in the bag when he teleports into my room.

"Ready?" he asks. I nod, and next thing I know we're landing in the middle of the jungle next to a concerned, and naked Darren, a shifted Samara, a shifted Sophia, and a very confused Trevan. That's when I hear it. The very distinctive screech of a phoenix. But having been around Phoebe and Sophia enough when they are shifted, I can tell that this one is young and not fully shifted as it doesn't hurt my ears.

As Sophia takes off in the sound's direction, Darren shifts, starting to pace as soon as all four paws hit the ground, impatiently waiting for something.

"What kind of magic do you have?" Trevan asks both Seb and I.

"I can access all four elements like Skarlyt, but my water is the strongest, and Sarah can influence the weather and probably has an element in there, but we haven't had too much time to figure that out."

Trevan inclines his head, coming to grip my shoulders. I would love to say that it isn't bothering me, that I am completely okay with this man touching me, but that would be a lie. My entire body freezes up, my back snaps straight, and a slight tremble flows through me. I am able to stop myself from having a full-blown panic attack with the knowledge that this is Samara's mate, that she and Sebastyn would never let anyone hurt me, that I am safe.

Seeing my discomfort, he releases me, and Samara comes over and rubs up against me. I reach out and stroke her, my heart calming a little with the feel of her soft fur under my fingers. I close my eyes and control my breathing, feeling my heartbeat return to its normal cadence.

"Sorry," he says, looking ashamed. I give him a small smile to show him that I don't have any hard feelings. "Okay, Sarah, close your eyes." I look at him skeptically for a moment but eventually do as he asks. "Now, reach out to your magic. Tell it that you need help and think of the wind. Pull it to you. Imagine it caressing you like an old friend, lifting you higher off the ground, until you're suspended in midair." I do as he asks, closing my eyes and calling on my magic. It comes to my call quickly, but other than a slight breeze flowing through my hair, I don't feel anything.

"I don't know what I'm supposed to be doing," I say, getting frustrated. But as I open my eyes and look around, instead of looking at my friends on the forest floor, I'm looking straight at the treetops. As soon as I look at the ground and realize that I'm at least fifty feet off the ground, that brief moment of panic causes me to fall as the wind released me. I close my eyes once more, calling on my magic.

Please don't let me fall, I whisper. As if understanding, I stop, suspended in mid-air, with the wind circling me, almost like my own personal tornado, ten feet above the ground.

"Amazing control, Sarah. You should be able to direct the wind like this," Trevan says as he launches himself into the air, as well. Instead of trying to fly, Sebastyn climbs on the back of Darren's wolf, and we take off.

As I raise myself up with the cyclone of air, I catch sight of Sophia's flames and push the wind to spin faster, hurdling me in that direction. It's amazing. This feeling is like nothing I've ever experienced before. And it's me who is doing it. No one else. I'm the one controlling the wind lifting me higher; I'm the one controlling the speed and setting the pace for myself, no one else.

I leave Trevan behind me, spreading my arms out wide and spinning through the sky toward Sophia. I seem to be making up the distance but feel a sense of urgency, and I push myself even faster. Something is happening over there, and I need to figure out what it is. I may not have gut instincts as good as Phoebe, but there's a heaviness to the air surrounding me, almost as if it's telling me something is wrong. I really need to figure out why I have this power and what it all means.

I am extremely surprised at my control, though. Never in a million years would I have thought I would be able to control a cyclone like this. Although 'control' isn't the right word. I'm not controlling it or forcing it to do anything. It's more like we're a team, and my magic is anticipating what I need, reaching out and supplying it. I wonder if that's what Constance, Skarlyt, and Sebastyn meant about my magic having an awareness and needing to respect your magic. I know the mages definitely don't feel like this when they use their magic; otherwise, they would be using it all the time rather than only when they need to. And they sure as hell wouldn't need to tether anyone to get more power.

Or maybe my dad was just wrong, and my magic isn't weak and not all people feel like this. If he was, I'll never know why because I don't think I ever want to see him again. Not after the last message he left for me. "Marry a widower." Hah. Not in his lifetime. Not if I'd have to give this up.

Sophia's phoenix takes a nosedive into the clearing below as a third screech sounds. I'm sucked out of my own head and back into the present. That can't be good.

Chapter Sixteen

Sarah

As I come upon the clearing that Sophia just flew into, another screech sounds. I look down and take in the scene. A small village is settled within the clearing, with a large crowd of people standing in the center, looking toward the forest. Just at the edge, I see a woman with small flames licking up her arms, attempting to get free of a man who is holding her back and a small child clinging to her leg. What draws my attention is the young woman being pulled into the trees by a group of men.

She screams, and it comes out in a phoenix screech. I seethe, directing the air to bring me closer, and hover above the ground out of sight. I wait and watch as Sophia flies down with a loud screech of her own, causing the man to release the girl and step back. As she lands between them, Sophia's flames fly from her hands and create a barrier between the men in the forest and the rest of the people. I look closer into the forest and see several pairs of glowing yellow eyes. I squint to try and see the rest that I know must be in there, but I can't; the jungle seems to conceal them. I remain in my hidden spot to stop anyone from being able to sneak up on Sophia.

I turn my attention back to the young girl who's sobbing behind Sophia's back, and I do everything within my power to control my rage. I don't know what is happening here, but I do know that I don't agree with whatever it is. This girl is far too young to be this scared.

"This is no concern of yours, bitch," spits the man who was forced to release the girl. Sophia lets loose a wave of flames with the intent to push the men back, rather than burn them. If she wanted to, I'm sure they would all be extra crispy right now. As the heat forces them further into the trees, the man who had the hold on the girl digs his feet in and hisses at her.

"She is my mate. *My* property. She will come with me, and you will not stop me from taking her." Property? I clench my fists tighter as the cyclone encircling me gets stronger, fueled by my rage. They sound just like the mages. I don't care if she is his mate, she's not going with them.

I turn back toward Sophia and the girl, who's watching in awe as Sophia smoothly transitions back to human. "Is this true? Is he your mate?" Sophia questions. Rather than speak, the young girl looks up at her with wide eyes, shaking her head *no*.

"She will not be leaving with you," Sophia says, turning back to face the dark-skinned man with a murderous look on his face. I want so badly to rush in there and help, but this girl is a phoenix, and Sophia's phoenix seems to be doing a fine job as it is.

"Who are you to deny me?" he asks and begins stepping toward her. A blink later, a large black wolf is in front of her, baring his teeth at the man.

The man in question shifts into a large black jaguar, growling and hissing. So that's why I couldn't see them in the trees. The jungle is too dense and dark, their black coats camouflage. Just as I watch his back legs sink down, ready to pounce, a large mountain lion roars and skids to a stop in front of Sophia as well.

I smile at the scene, enjoying watching my friends. The jaguar looks wary now, realizing that he may be outmatched. But as Trev and Seb appear on either side of Sophia, he shifts back.

"She's mine. You can't keep her from me. You hear me? I'll be back for her by the end of the week. I suggest you have her ready, or you will suffer the consequences," he spits, straining his neck to try to get one last look at the terrified girl behind Sophia's back.

That's it! I can't stand around anymore. I know they can handle themselves, and I was really enjoying watching, but no more. I move myself into the clearing, putting myself completely in between the asshole of a man and my friends, my purple magic and small bolts of lightning showing in the cyclone . He thinks better of challenging me, turning and walking back into the jungle. That's right. I'll be here all week. Just try and come get her. See what you get. Of course, I don't say that out loud, but I think it. Loudly.

As soon as he is past the tree line, I join my friends in front of the girl. "Are you okay?" Sophia asks. She looks up at us with striking green eyes and nods. I take in her features properly for the first time. She has deep cherry red hair and sun-kissed skin. She is wearing a simple fabric dress.

"Thank you," an older woman with the same looks says, running up and wrapping her arms around the girl. A younger girl follows with a dress for both Samara and Sophia, as Sebastyn hands Darren a pair of pants out of his pack.

"You're a phoenix like me," the younger girl, who must be around eight, says to Sophia. She looks like the other two with a slightly lighter red tinge to her hair and the same green eyes.

"I am," Sophia responds with a chuckle. Sophia turns her focus on the older woman. "I don't understand; you're obviously a phoenix. Why didn't you shift to protect who I'm assuming is your daughter?"

She looks down at the ground briefly before meeting Sophia's gaze. "A pride of jaguar shifters captured me as a teenager. They had teamed up with a group of hunters. Together, they performed awful experiments on me. Finally, one day I'd had enough, escaped and flung myself off a building, hoping to die. Instead, I lived, but something is damaged inside me, and I've never been able to fully shift. The most I can get is a small flicker when I'm extremely upset. Once they realized I was 'damaged goods', they tossed me aside. I thank the Mother every day for that. Otherwise, I'd probably still be there.

"I owe you a great debt that I'm afraid I'll never be able to repay. I refuse to watch my daughter suffer that fate-or worse-if that pride gets their hands on her. So, thank you, all of you." She has tears brimming in her eyes, and I get a pang in my chest. I know what it's like being forced to do something or be somewhere you don't want to. I refuse to allow that to happen to anyone else.

"You owe me nothing. I'm Sophia," Sophia says, introducing herself, sticking out her hand.

She clasps it. "I'm..."

"*Cinder!*" yells a male walking up from the large group gathered. We all turn to face him. "Do you know what you have done?" he screams.

"Hey! You don't talk to her like that," Sophia says, stepping in front of the woman who I guess is Cinder.

He rounds on Sophia, reaching his hand out to poke her in the chest. "You." Bad move, buddy. I call my magic back up, ready to jump in and defend my friend. But I don't need to.

Just before his finger hits her in the chest, a large hand grabs it and forces it backwards. "You don't speak to my mate that way," Darren growls out, releasing the finger and pushing it toward the male.

"You don't understand. The jaguars will be back for her and if they don't get her, we will all suffer," he says, trying and failing miserably at keeping the shake from his voice. And as soon as those words are out of his mouth, my body begins to vibrate with rage.

How dare he? The storm clouds begin to roll in and thunder booms so loudly that it shakes the ground.

"As far as I'm concerned, you all should be ashamed of yourselves. Can't you see that she doesn't want to go with them? How dare you force this young girl to do anything?" I yell.

He postures as if he's going to do something, his pale blue magic flaring to life in his hands, and I look to Sophia, who nods, forcing the phoenix family behind her.

I will never intentionally attack anyone, not even this idiot of a man, but I'm just learning control. If a stray lightning bolt were to hit someone, I would be upset. Sophia shifts into her phoenix, and I return my gaze back to the man in front of me, knowing that I can't hurt her while shifted.

Sebastyn teleports to my side, his glowing green hand reaching through the cyclone, which parts easily for him and closes to encircle us both. He clasps my glowing purple hand, creating a beautiful show of purple and green. "Try it," he dares the man, who steps back, seeing that he's outnumbered.

"I'm sorry," he bows his head. "It's just that the alpha of the jaguars is a cruel man who will use any excuse to wipe us from the earth. We are a small coven and nowhere near powerful enough to take on their pride." I don't want to, but I can't help but feel a little sorry for the man. It's one of those 'rock and a hard place' situations. If he doesn't give the girl over, they could wipe his entire coven out. But on the other hand, that is no reason to force anyone to do anything. Especially someone as young and innocent as a child

I share a look with Sophia and can tell she wants to try and talk to the man. I nod, but keep my magic level up, just in case. I will let her try talking, but I will be ready if it doesn't work.

"Listen," she says with a sigh. "I don't like it, but I do understand the position you're in. I will tell you right now, though, that girl is not going with them," she turns to point at the young girl.

"Not today, not tomorrow. Not unless she tells me while looking in my eyes that it is her choice.

"That being said: we will stay and help you. Sebastyn has knowledge of lost magic, and obviously Sarah is an extremely powerful witch, as well. Trevan is from a highborn family of Fae and, of course, the two alpha shifters we have in our party, as well as me. We will stay for the week. Help set up your defenses. Train who we can; hide who we can't." His eyes aren't the only ones wide as she finishes. The entire coven is staring at me wide-eyed, murmurs beginning to sound.

Although I let Sophia handle the diplomatic solution, I can't hold my tongue. "We are not here to help you," I say, pointing at everyone except the girl and her family. "We are here to help them. I don't give a fuck what happens to you. For you to stand by and watch a young girl be dragged away and her mother screaming in agony after her, I'm disgusted.

"What if she were your daughter? Your sister? Would you be so quick to trade her?" I watch as people in the crowd shake their heads. "No, you wouldn't. And she, the same as any one of you, deserves a choice in what will affect the rest of her life. Notice I say *her* life. That is because it doesn't mean anything to you if she's forced into a mating with a cruel man who is not her mate. It doesn't hurt *you* if he raises his hand to her or forces her to perform sexual acts. It only affects *her*.

"Before you try to push this young girl into a situation most decent people would find horrendous, ask yourself: would you force a woman in your family in that situation? If the answer is no, then you don't fucking do it," I'm still seething, my power over-taking my body as the thunder sounds louder and more frequent. I feel just as out of control as the day at the market. Luckily Sebastyn turns to face me from where he stands beside me, turning my face so our eyes meet.

"It's okay, love. No one is going to force her to do anything," he whispers and some of my rage settles.

"We didn't..." the assface speaks again. I turn to face him, my rage igniting more and more.

"Will you shut the fuck up?" Seb snarls at him. He uses his hands to guide my face back to his. "Shh, love. It's okay. Come back to me," he says as Sophia and Samara step up, placing a hand on each of my shoulders.

I close my eyes and focus on the feeling of their hands on my body. I take deep breaths, allowing my racing heartbeat to slow.

As my eyes slowly open, I glance around, realizing that instead of the large group gathered, it is just our small group and the family of phoenixes. My eyes find Seb's once more, and he gives me a small smile. "There you are," and he places a soft kiss on my lips.

"I'm sorry," I say, melting into Seb's embrace and burying my head in his chest.

"Don't be sorry," the father of the young girl says. "You're not the first to lose control, and you won't be the last. But it normally only happens when a block is removed."

Seb nods. "Her block was removed a few days ago."

The man nods in understanding. "I can give you some techniques if you like. I'm Calder, by the way," he sticks his hand out to me first. I glance down at his hand and keep my left firmly planted in Sebastyn's as I reach out and clasp it with my right. For the first time since I got to Parry Sound, I'm able to touch a man other than Sebastyn without having a panic attack. Maybe I'm getting better or perhaps having Sebastyn touching me helps. He shakes hands with the rest of our group.

"My wife, Cinder, you've already met. These are my daughters: Blaze who is seventeen and Fyre who just turned eight," Calder gestures to his family. I smile and give each girl a small wave.

Sebastyn introduces our group to the family, each of us smiling and shaking hands. "So, what do we do now?" Samara asks.

"You can stay with us. We don't have much room, but you're more than welcome," Cinder offers.

"I can use my magic to make an extension and enlarge the space so that we aren't on top of one another," Sebastyn states.

Calder's mouth hangs open in shock. "That magic was lost centuries ago."

Now, it's Sebastyn's turn to be shocked. "Really? It's one of the first spells we teach our children when they come into their magic. I can show you if you like." Calder's eyes go wide, and I swear if he nods his head any harder, it's going to fall off. Chuckling, our group follows the family to their home.

It's a small cabin on the outskirts of what I'm assuming is their coven. It is completely made of unrefined wood, looking like each beam or plank was hand crafted, and topped with a thatched roof.

I walk up the two steps onto the covered porch and follow as Cinder pushes a heavy wooden door inward. The inside is dark; Cinder lights lanterns as we walk through the room. It's smaller than I expected but cozy. I see two doors that must lead to smaller bedrooms off the side of the kitchen and another door off the small dining room, or what I think is the dining room since there's a table with chairs.

"Like I said, we don't have much room," Calder says, almost sounding like he's ashamed. I'm about to tell him how perfect it is for their small family, but Sebastyn beats me to it.

"It's exactly right for your family," he says clasping him on the shoulder. "But if you would prefer it to be bigger, I can show you how to create a permanent extension and between your coven and those with magic here, we will have more than enough strength."

Calder's eyes water and he nods. "Thank you."

I watch as Sophia walks over to Cinder, Blaze, and Fyre to

have a discussion about phoenix powers, and I snag Sebastyn's hand, pulling him outside with me.

"Can we go for a walk around the coven?" I ask him. He smiles down at me.

"Of course, my love. Too many people?" He questions, and I smile knowingly, needing to get out of the cramped space inside their home. It's quaint and perfect for them, but when you add another six people, it gets a little stuffy.

As I step onto the green grass, I pull each of my shoes off, enjoying the feeling of the grass under my feet. There's something about this place, being here surrounded by all this green, and my magic is humming peacefully just below the surface, happy to be outside as well.

Sebastyn and I walk around the coven. All the homes are similar to Calder's and Cinder's, except closer together. I wonder why Calder and Cinder chose to build further out, almost like they're not connected to the coven at all. I file that away in the 'questions to ask later' folder in my brain and continue taking in the scenery. The jungle is thick and the sounds of monkeys swinging through the trees are loud. It's like one of those jungle documentaries, and it's incredible.

Chapter Seventeen

Sarah

"Phoebe!" I exclaim, seeing her on the porch with Alaric and Skarlyt. I rush over and wrap my arms around her. I feel like I haven't seen her in forever, even though it's only been just over a week. She hugs me back tightly.

She pushes me back but keeps her hands on my shoulders. "So why did I have to hear about you having magic from my sister and not you?" Her tone is light, but I can see the lingering hurt there in her eyes.

I look down at the floor, then back up at her. I'm a little ashamed. She's right. We've been friends the longest, and I haven't told her anything about what's happened in the past week. "I was so caught up in the rush of learning to control it that I didn't think to tell you. I'm sorry, Pheebs," I say using her nickname for the first time ever. She stares at me in shock, nodding her head with a smile on her face.

"It's okay. I am just so happy for you! We need to celebrate when we get home." I bob my head in agreement. I think that's a wonderful idea.

A round of introductions go around as I introduce her to Cinder, Calder, Fyre, and Blaze. I can see the connection between them, her flames coming up and dancing happily on the tips of her fingers as she touches each of them.

"How long have you lived here? Are there more phoenix shifters nearby?" She blurts out, and I chuckle, waiting for the explosive verbal diarrhea that would normally follow. She turns and glares at all of us. "What? That wasn't nearly as many questions as I usually ask," she says, pinning us with a glare.

Cinder answers, "We thought we were the last. A group of jaguar shifters kidnapped and brought me here as a teenager."

"Didn't you want to return to the place where you were born? You know, find your family?" She asks, and I turn toward Cinder, wondering myself.

She shakes her head *no*, tears pooling in her eyes. "When they were taking me, my parents fought with everything they had, but it wasn't enough. At the end, after seeing my father die, my mother sacrificed herself to allow me a chance to get away. She went nuclear, taking out as many shifters and mages as she could, but instead of running at my opportunity, I froze. They captured me anyway." Her mate tucks her into his side, and she wipes her tears. "Besides, I met my mate here," she gives him a soft smile, which he returns, kissing her on the forehead.

"Okay," Alaric asks, going into alpha mode, "what allies do you have in the area?" Darren had obviously given him and Lennox the extremely abbreviated version of what happened while I was talking with Phoebe.

"Not many," Calder explains, leading us toward a room full of maps in the house. He spreads a map of the jungle out onto the table with a bunch of x's placed sporadically. He points to an X on the left of the map. "Here is where the jaguar pride you just met lives: 'Jungle King,' as he so named himself, and his pride. Over here," pointing to an X below the first one, "is where a small coven of Amazon witches live. I wouldn't say they are an ally, but they're not an enemy either. They find us weak, so they don't associate with us at all.

"This," pointing to an X in the upper corner of the map, "is where a flock of harpy shifters live. Again, they find us weak and tend not to associate with us but aren't overly hostile either. There are anaconda shifters here and caiman shifters over here.

"But our biggest ally will be the jaguar pride over here on the other side of the jungle." He points to an X in the bottom right-hand corner of the map. "Their alpha, Kenji, is actually the brother of the Jungle King's Pride alpha, Koto, and hates them almost as much as we do. He left a few years ago because he didn't agree with their practices. Kenji believes in the Mother and true mates, where Koto is only interested in power. He rejected his mate because she wasn't dominant enough for him, which is why he now wants Blaze. She is the strongest shifter in this jungle aside from the two of you." He nods to Phoebe and Sophia.

"If we are going to start gathering allies, I suggest we start with Kenji and his pride." We all glance at each other as Calder finishes. I know we're all thinking the same thing. What the fuck did we just sign up for?

Since I don't have much to input, I leave the room while everyone is looking over the maps of the jungle, pointing out the different allies. Blaze gestures for me to follow her outside. Once we are out on the porch, she takes a deep breath and turns toward me. "I want to thank you."

"You don't need to thank me; we all stood up to protect you," I respond, feeling uncomfortable under her praise. "I mean, Sophia is the one you should be thanking. Without her, we wouldn't be here at all."

She nods, turning to look out at the forest. "Yes, and I am

extremely grateful to her. But I don't think anyone in our coven ever looked at it as if we were people rather than things to be traded. When the jaguar alpha came, I was around eight, and Fyre was just born. He beat my father almost to death until the coven agreed to hand each of us over at eighteen. We were to be mated with the strongest of their pride, true mate or not," she wipes away the moisture in her eyes as she takes a steadying breath.

"My father would have died happily that day. I know that he would've. He has never wanted this, but without my mom able to shift and us being too young to shift, it would be us against a coven of witches, a pride of jaguars and whoever else was on their side. So, I thank you. You made them see what they are doing is wrong. It may not mean much to you, but for another witch to stand up to them, especially one as powerful as you, telling them what they were doing was wrong means everything to us."

I walk up and wrap my arms around her, letting her tears soak my shirt. "You know, my father was not a nice man, not like yours," I begin, and we return to sitting on the porch. "He was a very evil man who thought it was the woman's place to sit still, stay quiet, and do all the housework. At eighteen, I knew that he was going to pair me with a man who was not my mate, but I was too young to do anything about it. They paired me with a man more evil than my father could ever have been," I turn to look at her.

"But, one day my friend Phoebe, the phoenix who showed up a little while ago, came into my life and things changed. Not only did she make my bleak existence brighter by being my friend, she ended up saving me. Now I live with them, away from all the people who would want to hurt me. It's taking me a while, but I'm slowly becoming the woman I was meant to be. And I have to thank you for helping me with that.

"When I saw you earlier and heard those people talking about your life as if you didn't get a choice in the matter, something inside me flipped. I couldn't stand by and let them take you. And I promise you this: if we don't find a solution to this, I will take you and your sister away from here, where they will never find you again. I will not let them take you," I'm gripping her arms at the end, attempting to show her just how much I mean that.

"You would do that?" A feminine voice comes from the doorway. I turn to see Cinder standing there.

"Of course, I would. No one deserves to be stripped of choice in their own life. And I'm sure if you ask any of my family inside, they will tell you the same. Most of us, especially the women, have lived through more than you can imagine, and will not stand by and watch as another is put through what we were, or worse."

"Damn Right!" Phoebe says walking out the door. "Not one of us will leave these girls, or you, here defenseless." Cinder is clutching her chest, tears streaming down her face, as if she has never had anyone stand up for them before.

I share a look with Phoebe. She obviously notices and gives a small nod. We need to help this family no matter what. I understand if the rest need to return home; they have kids and families to protect. But I will not be leaving them. And, after the look I just shared with Phoebe, I have a hard time believing she will either. She will need to because of the kids; though I have every faith that she will find a way to come back.

Sebastyn walks straight toward me with Calder. "Hey, love. Calder told me of this place in the jungle called Tepuis where we can go to let your magic free. He gave me some tips on how to help you gain control after being blocked for so long. We can see what you're truly capable of without fear of hurting anyone." My eyes snap to Calder in surprise. I know he spoke earlier of knowing others who lost control, but I didn't expect him to have the knowledge to actually help. Or be so quick to share it.

"That would be amazing. Thank you," I respond.

"There is a legend in the jungle that those who go to the top of the ridge at Tepuis and pray to the Mother will gain her favor. In return, she helps them gain control over their magic. In rare cases, she gives them access to magic buried deep within themselves. We have sent our children there on the night of their eighteenth birthday for generations. I truly believe it can help you, as you already seem to have ancient magic deep within you," he looks from me to Seb. "Both of you." It's Sebastyn's turn to look surprised.

"Thank you, Calder," Seb says, clasping his hands and then reaching for mine. He pulls me in close and the next thing I know, we are standing atop a beautiful ridge overlooking the forest. The mist from the waterfall peppers my face, and I giggle.

"This is the most gorgeous thing I've ever seen," I say, looking around.

"Not me," Sebastyn responds. I turn and quirk an eyebrow. "You are." Oh, my Mother, this man is going to be the death of me.

"I thought you couldn't teleport somewhere you've never been before?" I question.

"After Skarlyt was able to teleport here with only a picture, I figured I could probably do the same. Calder showed me a picture of this place and here we are." He smiles at me, and I can't help but smile back.

"Okay. What do we do first?" I ask.

He gestures for me to sit beside him on the edge of the ridge. I take a quick look down and gulp at the distance to the ground. "It will be okay. I won't let you fall, love." With his words, I sit next to him, so close our legs are touching. "First, we need to see what elements you have. I want you to close your eyes. Feel the spray from the waterfall as it crosses your face. It feels wet and warm." I dip my chin to let him know that I do. "Good. Now, I want you to gather all those droplets into a ball, creating a water balloon of sorts." I strain but picture each droplet merging with one another until I see a large ball of water in my mind. As I open my eyes, I see exactly that right in front of my face. I get so excited that it pops gushing water over both me and Sebastyn.

Instead of being upset, Sebastyn laughs. "I guess we can say water is one of your elements." I join in his laughter, only quieting when he presses his lips to mine. "You're amazing," he whispers.

I bat him away playfully. "What's next?"

"Let's see about air. This one will be tricky because you already have a lot of control over the weather. Close your eyes again. This time, I want you to focus on the air and the way it feels. I want you to try and bring the surrounding air in a bubble, protecting us from the spray of the water. Not in the same as the wind, where it creates a cyclone around you. I want you to picture a solid bubble of air surrounding us." I do as he says, trying to separate the air from the water. I imagine the water within the air separating and focus on bringing a big gust of wind toward us, encasing us in a bubble. I try to take it one step further and get the air to dry our clothes. To my utter surprise, I can feel the air taking the place of the water in my clothing, forcing the droplets outward.

"Amazing," Seb says breathily, causing me to open my eyes. I look around and can see the shimmer of where the bubble of air begins and ends. I never thought I would have this much control over anything. It makes me feel powerful, like I'm indestructible and anything in my past doesn't matter anymore.

"Let's try earth. This one should be easy. I want you to close your eyes and envision vines growing and twisting together to create a ledge directly under our feet." As the last of his words are out, I'm already picturing it. I can feel each vine grow and slither toward each other like a snake, twirling and braiding together until I open my eyes and see a sturdy platform of vines beneath our dangling feet.

"Last one. Fire," Seb says, taking out a lighter from his pocket. He flicks it open and sets it alight. "You don't have to close your eyes for this one. This time I want you to look at the flames and make them grow bigger or smaller at your will. Mold them into whatever you want. Make them dance or fly, even." I know exactly what I'm going to make. I will the flames to grow and, to my astonishment, they do. I perfectly imagine the scene I want them to play out and push that picture toward the flame. All at once, the flame spins and turns into an image of Sebastyn and I dancing under the gazebo.

Sebastyn stares at the image in awe before raising his eyes to meet mine. I was going to wait for the perfect time to tell him that I want him forever, but I've come to the realization that even if we aren't true mates, I choose him. My choice is my own. For the first time in my life, no one and nothing is forcing me into anything. I am also not naïve and know that time is precious. We've already each spent so much time without each other. Why am I waiting when I've known since that first glance that he is the man of my dreams?

I let the flame fall back to normal. "Sebastyn." His name comes out a lot breathier than I mean it to, but it doesn't matter because if the lust in his eyes is anything to go by, he's feeling the same as I do. I walk back away from the ledge a bit, taking off my shirt and dropping it to the ground as I go. Next is my bra. As I unhook the clasp, I hear his short inhale of breath and him scurrying to stand up. I sneak a peek behind me and see his jaw dropped in shock as his eyes roam my body.

I have never felt this in control of anything in my entire life. Even my magic. I feel like I hold all the power and with that thought, I unbutton my pants and slide them down my legs, bending over and showing him my hunter green thong. I slip off each shoe as I pull my legs out and turn to face him.

A small giggle escapes me as I look at his face; there's heat mixed with love, and a small amount of drool slipping out of his mouth. His eyes snap up to mine and he races toward me. "Are you sure?" he asks, and I nod. That's all he needs before he reaches for me. "I love you, Sarah," he whispers, moving his mouth up my neck to my lips.

"I love you too, Sebastyn Moon," I whisper back just as our lips meet. I run my tongue along the seam of his lips, asking for entry. His own tongue thrusts out to meet mine in a passionate kiss. He grabs me under my ass, lifting me up so my legs wrap around his waist, before he sits on a smooth boulder so I'm straddling him without breaking our kiss.

I lean back and grasp the bottom of his shirt, pulling it over his head. My breath catches as I take in his upper body. He has tattoos covering his arms and chest. I'm sure that his back is much the same with some poking up his neck. His well-defined muscles still show through, making me the one to drool now. I lift my hips up and begin to unbuckle his pants. He shimmies them down his legs, freeing his massive erection. I lick my lips in anticipation and follow the path of his pants to kneel between his legs.

I dart my tongue out to taste the small amount of pre-cum glistening at the top, moaning in delight at the taste. I engulf him in my mouth, taking him as deep as I can. I use his moans to guide me on what he likes. And just as I am getting into a grove, he lifts me up to stand, trading our positions, sliding my panties down my legs and guiding me to sit. As he kneels between my legs, I am forced to remember that night under the gazebo.

He swipes his tongue over my clit, once, twice, before sucking it into his mouth and flicking it with his tongue. A few seconds later and I scream out my release. "Sebastyn!" I expected him to line himself up with me and thrust inside. Instead, he trades spots with me again, lifting me so I'm straddling him once more.

At my surprised look, he explains, "You will always be the one with the power when you're with me." I melt with his words and merge my lips with his, tasting both of us on our tongues. I pour all the love I feel for this man into this one kiss as I reach down and guide him inside me. I give a sharp inhale of breath at first. It's been so long since I've been with a man. After Phoebe escaped and Tanner died, Joe became obsessed with finding her, leaving his focus elsewhere and away from me. Thankfully.

I drift my body downwards, taking more of him inside, pausing briefly to accommodate his size. When I'm fully seated, we break our kiss and his mouth moves down my neck to my breasts, taking a nipple in his mouth and sucking on it. I moan loudly.

I slowly move my body up and down the length of him, moaning with each thrust. As I begin to feel my release, he switches nipples, clutching me around the waist, lifting me up and slamming me down harder and faster than before.

I close my eyes and throw my head back, clinging to Sebastyn's shoulders as my orgasm takes over. I feel the wind and water whipping around us as rain begins to shower down. I open my eyes and see a cyclone of green and purple magic circling, lifting us from the ground.

My magic reaches out and I place my hand above his heart and feel it pulse out, leaving a full moon with a lightning bolt striking across it blended into his tattoos. His arm wraps around the back of my neck and as he merges his mouth with mine, I feel his magic branding me on the back of my neck.

We slowly float to the ground, our magic still flaring brightly. As we land, wave after wave of magic pulses out from both of us, sending vibrations out over the forest floor. "I knew it," Sebastyn says, pulling back from our kiss. "I knew you were my mate." I giggle and nod. I guess we are.

Our magic slowly releases, and the ground begins to shake. "Is that still us?" I whisper to Sebastyn.

"I don't think so, love," he says quickly, setting me down and tossing me my clothes before putting his own on.

I'm about to ask what it could be when the rumbling finally stops, and a gigantic dragon with mossy gray scales takes flight into the sky with a roar. Awestruck, I watch the mythological creature circle a few times before landing in front of us and shifting into the biggest man I've ever seen. He opens his mouth to speak, but I don't understand the words. I look at Seb and see that he is just as confused. The large olive-skinned man tilts his head to the side and tries to speak again.

"Was the power I felt from your mating?" he asks.

I'm too frozen in place to speak, but luckily Sebastyn isn't. "Yes. I suppose it was."

"I haven't felt power like that in centuries. It has awoken me from my slumber. I am called Andres." He bows as he finishes.

"I am Sebastyn, and this is my mate, Sarah." Seb puts his hand out to clasp Andres', who simply looks at him in question. Seb chuckles and guides their hands together, demonstrating how to shake hands.

"This is a new custom?" Andres asks.

"Yes. This is how we greet one another," Seb responds.

"I must leave to attempt to locate my family. But I will come and find you again. I owe you a debt. The time of the prophecy is coming near. You both will need my help in the coming days. Gather your allies," Andres says cryptically before shifting and taking to the sky.

"How will he know where we are?" I ask Seb, who just shrugs.

"I don't know. Maybe he has some kind of magic to help him locate us. I didn't think dragon shifters were actually real. I thought it was all just a myth. And what was that about a prophecy? I hope he doesn't think we have something to do with it," Sebastyn says quizzically, still staring at the sky.

"We just met a dragon," I whisper, excitement overtaking the paralysis that was trapping my body in place. "I can't wait to tell the girls!" I squeal.

Sebastyn chuckles, but I can still see the worry in his eyes as he turns to me. I raise my hand to caress his face. "Let's not stress over what we don't know. He may take years to come back, or it could be days. We don't know. But what we do know is that we are mates, and our friends are going to need our help soon. Let's head back," I try to keep my voice strong. He places a kiss on my lips, and we head back to the village.

Chapter Eighteen

Sarah

S ebastyn and I teleport back to the front porch of Calder and Cinder's house, expecting to find everyone still inside or more likely hanging around outside. "Blaze? Fyre? Cinder? Are you in there?" I call out as I walk into their home, finding it empty.

"Maybe they went with the others to gather allies?" I ask Sebastyn.

He shakes his head. "There is no way Alaric would've allowed them to go." At my sharp inhale of breath, he knows he used the wrong word. I detest the word *allow*. It is something that my father or Joe would've said. "Sorry, love. Poor choice of words. I simply meant that he would've been more concerned about their safety and would have suggested they stay here."

"I know. That word just brings up bad memories for me," I say, and he wraps his arms around me in a brief hug. "We should go check outside."

He nods, and together, we do just that. It almost seems like a ghost town walking outside. Where I assume there will be people walking around, soaking in the late afternoon sun, we find no one.

F. D. Fair

But voices coming from the far end of the village have my heart racing, and I rush toward them.

The scene that is playing out in front of me gets my blood boiling. Cinder and Fyre are being held tightly against two large men, while Blaze is kicking an equally large male in the shins, desperately trying to get away. "Stop it. This is what's best for the coven. We have no choice. We will not allow you to bring their wrath upon us."

"And you all agree with that?" I say loudly, causing everyone to turn toward me. Some, being ashamed, look downward at the ground, but the few at the front stare at me with pure evil shown on their faces.

My magic flares, recognizing the taint on them immediately. I don't know how I didn't see it before. They may not be mages yet, but they are well on their way and have obviously been dealing with dark magic. Cinder and Fyre are the first ones to be released.

"You were not supposed to be here," the man holding Blaze sneers.

"Well, we are, and you will let her go or suffer *my* wrath, which I promise is far worse than any jaguar pride could ever bring upon you," I grind out. He doesn't budge.

"You don't understand. They will be here soon. If we don't hand her over, I don't know what they will do with us," he once again tries to convince me.

"So, what you're saying is that, even after our conversation earlier, you reached out to the pride, offering her up on a silver platter." He has the intelligence to look slightly ashamed by his actions, but I don't give a shit if he's ashamed or not. "I can promise you that if you do turn her over, you will not live to see tomorrow." My magic is now covering my entire body, lifting me up from the ground. Storm clouds are rolling in with loud rumbles of thunder shaking the ground.

A flicker of fear passes over his face before rustling from the bushes reveal two large jaguars. I'm sure there are more, but I can't spend the time looking right now. If I split my focus, Blaze could be long gone before I get the chance to do anything about it.

The man, seeing the jaguars as well, breathes a sigh of relief. It's short-lived though, because Sebastyn teleports next to him, punching him in the throat. He releases Blaze to clutch his throat, allowing Seb to grab Blaze and pops back next to me, bringing her with him.

The two jaguars I saw in the underbrush quickly multiply until we are surrounded. Sebastyn's green magic hovers over his hands and Cinder's small flames lick up her arms as we force Calder and the two girls together and surround them in a protective circle. I'm sure Calder could hold his own, but he's needed as a last line of defense.

Sebastyn throws up a barrier around the six of us. The jaguars take no time before they start pouncing at it, slashing it with their claws. Cinder goes to push a jaguar back with her flames, and they hit the shield, creating a small hole. Sebastyn is quick to fill it, but not before a particularly fast swipe from one of their claws rakes down a momentarily distracted Cinder and she screams in agony.

I close my eyes and focus on the storm raging above, willing the lighting to strike. At my fifth attempt, it finally hits its mark, striking one of the jaguars. It seems to only further piss them off, rather than doing the damage that I was hoping, as they renew their efforts to get at us.

I look around, realizing just how dire our situation is. We are completely surrounded, and no help seems to be in sight. Calder's entire coven is gone. Cowards. I reach for Sebastyn beside me, but he's too far. I turn to look and notice the sweat on his brow from keeping the shield up and sending blasts out at the same time. I wish I was better trained to help. Instead of stressing, I focus on what I can do and continue to call the lighting, pleading with my magic. *Please send Sebastyn strength and let my lightning hit its mark.*

A minute or fifteen later, I'm not sure, I sigh in relief as a phoenix screeches from the sky. Thank the Mother. I didn't think they would be back this soon, but I also know we wouldn't have been able to wait them out forever. The first wave of flames goes out, singeing the fur of the jaguars. They are rolling on the ground to get them out when the wolves show up. I'm still not able to tell Darren and Alaric apart, so I'm not sure which one attacks first, but it's a welcoming sight.

Samara and Lennox join next, allowing the stragglers to tuck tail and run. Like Darren, Alaric, and Sophia, they aim for the ones closest to us, attempting to join our protective circle.

We seem to be making a dent, but we are still greatly outnumbered when the second phoenix screech goes out. I watch in awe as Phoebe and Sophia join each other above us, grasping each other and forcing out wave after wave of heat. Like me, they aren't aiming to kill. None of us wants blood on our hands, especially when most of our opponents are just following orders, but I have a feeling we are going to regret that when it's all over.

Once Phoebe joins, the jaguars disperse quickly, turning and running into the safety of the forest. At the first sign of safety, Sebastyn falls to the ground, clutching his head.

"What's wrong?" I rush to him, squatting in front of him, roaming my hands over his body, trying to find a source of pain.

"It hurts so much," he cries out.

"What hurts?" I plead with him.

"Everything. I can feel everything," he says, confusing me further.

"What's wrong with him?" Skarlyt asks, rushing to my side.

"I don't know. He said it hurts, and he can feel everything. I don't understand," I say.

She looks at me in confusion before saying, "I'll be right back for you," and teleports away with Sebastyn, leaving me crouching there alone with tears brimming in my eyes. I don't understand at all.

Within seconds, Skarlyt is back, and we teleport into her mom's living room, where I find Constance hovering over Sebastyn, who is laying in the fetal position.

"What exactly happened?" she asks.

"I don't know. One minute he was holding up a barrier to keep the jaguars away, and the next he dropped it and was clutching his head in pain," I tell her, moving to Sebastyn's side.

"Did he get hit by a spell?" she asks, and I shake my head *no*. There were no witches or mages fighting us. "What about poison? Did he eat or drink anything?" Again, I shake my head no.

"The last thing we ate was here," I respond. My tears come in faster, my worry for Sebastyn becoming worse by the second.

"What about before the fight? What happened?" my cheeks redden at her question, remembering our activities.

"Um," I start and twist my hands together.

"You mated?" she asks, and being unable to speak, I nod my head yes. "Did anything unusual happen?"

"Well... uh. We kind of floated and were surrounded by a mixture of our magic." Both she and Skarlyt stop what they are doing and stare at me. "What? That's not normal?" I ask.

"No. Definitely not normal. Where did you two cement the bond?" Constance asks.

"Uhh... we were practicing my magic on a ridge called Tepuis in the Amazon. Calder told us that it is where they go to reconnect with the mother," I explain.

"And that's where you finalized your mating?" she asks. I dip my chin in agreement.

"Sebastyn, can you feel this?" she reaches over and starts tickling Skarlyt as she asks, causing her to laugh hysterically. Sebastyn starts laughing, still clutching his head.

Constance stops tickling Skarlyt and rushes to her back room, leaving us sitting there. I rub my hands over Sebastyn, trying to stay as calm as possible but not understanding why Sebastyn would laugh at the same time as Skarlyt was. "I'm going to go let the others know where we are before they get too worried," Skarlyt says to me, and I nod in agreement. Knowing Lennox, he's probably flipping the fuck out.

I hear Kayne fussing in the other room and get up to go check on him. I find him lying in his playpen, crying and reaching for me. I scoop him up and he quickly quiets down. I bounce him for a few minutes before we head back to the living room. To my surprise, Sebastyn is now sitting up, looking a lot better than before.

"I'm sorry for worrying you, love. I don't know what that was," he says, and Kayne and I rush to his side.

"Are you feeling better?" I ask.

"A bit, although I still feel weird. I can't explain it," he says.

"I can," Constance says, coming back into the room. "It seems the Mother has granted you a new gift."

"What?" we ask in unison.

She agrees, "Yes. It seems that the Mother has blessed you with empathic abilities. But rather than having years to learn to cope with it as the power grew, it hit you all at once. You will need to learn to quiet the feelings of others. In the meantime, drink this. It will help dull your abilities."

She hands Sebastyn a drink, which he quickly gulps down. I sigh in relief as his gorgeous blue eyes meet mine.

He lifts up his soaked shirt over his head and Constance sucks in a breath. I quickly look over his chest, trying to find the cause. Was he hurt, and we didn't know? But all I find are his tattoos, mate mark and his well-defined muscles.

"What? What is it?" he asks.

"When did you get that tattoo?" she asks, pointing right at my mate mark.

"It was the mark that my magic left when we mated. Why? Is there something wrong with it?" I knew I was no good for him. I probably cursed him or something. I should have believed my father and Joe that I would never be good enough.

"No, of course not," Constance tries to reassure me, but it's too late. The spiral has already begun. My breaths come in quick, and my chest begins to tighten.

"Love. There's nothing wrong with your mate mark. It's perfect and exactly where it's supposed to be," Seb leans over, grasping my face. He tilts my head up until my eyes meet his. I watch his chest rise and fall and try to regulate my breathing. Kayne squirms in my arms a bit, bringing my attention back to the present.

I look down at Kayne while readjusting him before bringing my eyes back up to Seb's eyes. "It's okay, love," he comforts, "I don't want anyone other than you. Only you. There is nothing wrong with your mate mark. It's right here on my chest where it's meant to be. Just like you are right here in my arms where you are meant to be." He kisses my forehead.

"I don't understand, Constance. Why the urgency for me to come to your house?" A voice draws my attention to the front door. As the owner of the voice turns, I begin to shake. It can't be. The woman from my dreams. From my picture. My mother. "And why the..." she stops mid-sentence as she makes eye contact with me. "Alexandra?" she says, looking at me as she drops to her knees.

My brows crinkle in confusion. "Alexandra? Why does that seem familiar?" I whisper to myself.

"I don't understand, Constance. Is this a trick?" she asks.

"No, Rita. I had my suspicions, but Sebastyn's mate mark just confirmed it. Sarah is your daughter, Alexandra." At Constance's words, my heart wedges in my throat. My mother is alive. I didn't kill her. My dad kept her from me my entire life. Feeling rage bubble up inside me, I pass Kayne to Sebastyn, standing up and walking out the door. I let the rage bubble up; bubble isn't the right word, more like a burst from me like a volcano erupting.

I raise my hands to the sky and let my magic loose. Thunder rolls in, the wind whips around me, the rain pelts down, and the lightning strikes all around me.

"Sarah, love?" I hear Seb calling to me, but I can't stop. The storm rages on. I let my pain and feelings of betrayal out in my screams as I am raised from the ground.

"Alexandra!" I hear the woman said to be my mother yell, and my head snaps to her. She walks toward me despite Constance trying to hold her back. She walks straight into the surrounding cyclone I have created, like it was nothing. With a simple wave of her hand, the wind separates, obeying her command.

She rises into the air in front of me. "Calm the storm, Sarah," she states calmly, reaching a hand out to brush my cheek.

"He kept you from me for my entire life. Aren't you angry?" I sob.

"Of course, I am, my sweet girl. But you can't let it consume you. It won't do anything but corrupt your soul," she whispers, pulling me into her arms. I sob harder.

"Shh," she coos in my ear while rubbing my back. My tears continue to fall as I struggle to match my breathing to hers. "It's okay, my sweet. It will all be okay." I feel us lower to the ground until we are both kneeling on the ground.

The wind dies down and the lighting stops, but the rain continues to pour. I feel sobs wrack my mother's body as her hands clutch me, so tight it's as if she were stopping me from disappearing again. "I've dreamed of this so many times that I'm afraid I'm going to wake up in my bed, and you'll have been nothing but a figment of my imagination," she cries out.

"Me, too," I whisper back.

We sit there for I don't know how long, clinging to one another. "What did I miss?" I hear Skarlyt ask. Leave it to Skar to break a beautiful moment with her mouth. A fit of giggles overtakes the both of us as we turn to her.

"A lot," Constance says, causing my mother and I to laugh harder.

I look over at Skarlyt and see tears brimming in her eyes as she looks at me, as if seeing me for the first time, happiness overflowing from her before she clears her throat and shakes her head. "Well, so have you. Blaze is about to have her coming of age ceremony with Phoebe and Sophia, and she really wants you there," I hop up right away.

"What ceremony?" I ask walking toward her.

"Apparently there's this ceremony that, if performed by two fully shifting phoenixes, can coax out Blaze's flames. According to Cinder, it was done at the age of twelve in the past, but it's been a few centuries since there were two phoenixes together to perform it, and their shifts were delayed as a defense mechanism," Skarlyt explains.

"That is so cool," I exclaim and walk toward her.

I just about reach her when my mother's voice rings out. "Can I come?"

I turn to Skarlyt and Sebastyn, with Skar shrugging and Seb nodding. I walk to Seb, wrapping my arms around him while my mom heads over to Skarlyt, and seconds later we arrive in the middle of the village amongst a small crowd.

Chapter Nineteen

Sarah

As I am looking around to find our group, I'm tackled by Blaze. "You came!"

"Of course, I did. I wouldn't miss it for anything!" I say, hugging her back tightly. As I release her, I notice her eyes get wide, looking behind me. Following her line of sight, I see Skarlyt and my mom walking our way.

"Blaze, this is my mom, Rita," I introduce them. At my use of the word 'mom', Rita's eyes get misty, and she looks at me in surprise. I'm not sure why, though. Did she expect me to call her Rita? Or maybe it's just because she hasn't heard it in a very long time. But that's a puzzle for another time. I can only imagine what she must be feeling. I assume it's similar to what I feel but multiplied by a thousand. A child expects to one day lose their parents, but a parent should never outlive their children. But then to find out that you grieved the loss of a child who wasn't even really dead? She must be really confused by how to act or what to feel.

"It's very nice to meet you," my mom says, reaching out a hand. Blaze bats her hand away and immediately engulfs her in a hug, which she returns.

"Blaze," Cinder calls out, walking up to us. "It's time."

"Mom, look. Sarah made it," she exclaims.

"So, I see. I'm glad you could make it back in time," Cinder says. "And Sebastyn. I'm so glad you're okay. We were worried."

"Yeah, I'm feeling much better now. Thank you," he replies.

Almost as if we were one, our small group follows Cinder through the crowd. We reach the front, where we find the rest of our friends. Sophia and Phoebe are facing us.

"Sebastyn!" Darren exclaims, walking up beside him and clasping him on the shoulder.

"Hey," he replies as Darren pulls him in for a hug.

"Are you okay? We've been so worried about you," Sophia says, rushing over as well.

"Yeah. Mom fixed me up. I'll explain more later when we aren't in the middle of a crowd," Sebastyn tells them quietly. They seem momentarily satisfied, but I know they will want an explanation sooner rather than later.

"Ready, Blaze?" Phoebe asks.

"Yup. I've been ready for this my entire life," she replies.

Phoebe, Sophia, and Blaze walk to the front of the group. Sophia and Phoebe face the crowd and shift while Blaze faces them, taking hold of each of their hands. Their flames immediately begin licking up her arms, trailing a path from each of them and creating a circle.

As one, the three of them take to the sky, flames surrounding them: Phoebe's crimson red, Sophia's burnt orange, and Blaze's amber coloring all blending together perfectly. I stare in awe as the flames begin to move faster and faster. I can't even tell where one begins and the others end. It's beautiful, and I am so grateful that I was able to see it. They slowly move back to the ground. Once their feet land, they release their hands and, to my shock, the flames don't leave Blaze. She remains ignited.

Cinder rushes to her daughter, wrapping her arms around her.

Blaze's flames don't burn Cinder but caress her as if greeting her, the same as Phoebe's and Sophia's do with their family. Alaric and Darren move forward at the same time, with robes in hand to wrap around their mates as they shift back.

As Blaze's flames begin to die out, Calder steps forward with a robe for his daughter. Once she's covered up, she begins jumping up and down in excitement. "It worked!"

"It sure did. And we will start training you tomorrow. But now, I need to get home to my kids. I'll see you first thing in the morning," Phoebe says, giving her a hug before walking toward Alaric and Skarlyt.

"We have to get home to Kayne, too. We will be back in the morning to train some of the coven," Skarlyt adds.

With that, Skarlyt takes Lennox, Alaric, and Phoebe back home, leaving us for the night. The rest of our group walk back to the house, allowing Blaze and her family to celebrate in peace.

"Trevan and I are going to take the first watch," Samara states.

"Darren and I will take the second watch so Sebastyn can get some rest. After the scare today, I think he needs it," Sophia adds.

"What was that anyway?" Darren asks.

"Apparently when Sarah and I mated, the Mother granted me or unlocked–I'm not sure which–an additional power. I am now an empath. Mom explained that most empaths are born with the empathic ability and have years to learn how to quiet the feelings; however, because it seemed to come on all at once, my brain was overloaded," Sebastyn explains.

"Wait. What do you mean the Mother granted or unlocked a new power?" Trevan steps forward. "I've never heard of that happening."

"Calder explained that there is a ridge here called Tepuis, and it has been used for centuries at the age of maturity for witches to get closer to the Mother. He told us that sometimes the Mother grants these witches favor in the form of new or stronger abilities," Seb says.

"Well, that is some cool shit," Darren says. "But you're okay now?"

"Yeah. Mom made me a potion that dulls the empathic abilities. I'm okay for now, but I will eventually have to learn how to control it," Sebastyn admits.

"That's all that you two got out of that explanation?" Sophia says with her jaw almost hitting the floor. Trev and Darren look at each other then back at her in confusion.

"Why? What were we supposed to get?" Darren asks.

"Uh. The fact that Sarah and Sebastyn mated," Samara says, rolling her eyes before turning to me with a huge smile.

"Let's see them!" Sophia demands, and I look at her in question.

"See what?"

"The mate marks, silly," she says. I spin around and lift my hair with my hand and show her my crescent moon mark on the back of my neck.

"It's beautiful." Samara says before turning to Sebastyn. "Alright. Let's see yours."

He raises his shirt and proudly shows off his chest. "That has to be the coolest one I've ever seen." Sophia says, reaching out and touching it. Normally, I probably wouldn't like another woman touching my mate's bare chest, but I know both she and Samara are happily mated.

"It's the mark of our family. Just like the Moon family has a very distinct mating mark, so does the Storm family. Both being the direct descendants of one of the original five families," my mom adds.

I turn to her in surprise. "Original families?"

"When the goddess first came to Earth and decided to create supernaturals, she created five families of each species to rule.

Four of those families were the Moon, Storm, Fleur, and Soleil families. The fifth was said to become the first mages and thus their name has been stricken from every book. No one knows what it was," she explains. Both Sophia and Samara look as shocked and intrigued as I am. I'm glad that I'm not the only one who didn't know this information.

"Are you saying there should be at least five phoenix blood-lines?" Sophia asks.

My mom nods. "In theory. Though like with any species, some died out while others thrived. It's hard to know how many are left now."

"That's something we should definitely look into. Maybe we can find more." Sophia announces hopefully, and I bob my head enthusiastically.

My mouth opens wide, a yawn bubbling up without my permission.

"Let's go to bed," Seb takes my hand and I dip my chin, whispering a quick goodnight to each before heading inside with him and my mom.

Sebastyn does his thing and creates an expansion bubble, extending the house, creating rooms for each couple, as well as my mom. "I'll show Calder how to do that tomorrow." He says, leading the way.

"I'll see you in the morning?" My mom asks.

I nod, "Absolutely." She gives me a hug, lingering as if she is afraid that I won't be here in the morning. If I'm honest, I hug her back with the same fear running through my brain. For so long she's been a figment of my imagination, only real in my dreams, and I would be lying if I didn't worry about waking up tomorrow to find this day to be another dream. Not only did I cement my mate bond with Sebastyn and gain better control over all four elements and the weather, but I found out my mom is alive. Pair that with the scare I got with Sebastyn and trying to protect Blaze from being taken again, and it is almost too much to be real.

Reluctantly, I release her, and we both turn to our separate rooms for the night, Sebastyn following behind me. Inside the room, I sit on the bed, allowing my body to release the tension of the day. "I'm afraid that I'm going to wake up tomorrow and this will just be a dream," I whisper.

"It's not a dream. I promise you. But it has been a crazy day, hasn't it?" he responds, wrapping his arm around me and pulling me close.

"It has. It has been the most wonderful, scary, emotionally draining day of my life. But if this is still my life when I wake up, I will be forever grateful," I say, turning to look up into his eyes.

"It is real. Let me show you just how real it is," he whispers, his mouth inches away from mine. His lips meet mine softly, with small, tender kisses until I can't stand it anymore and place my arms around his neck, pulling him closer to me.

He lays me back on the bed, inching his kisses down my neck. I reach down and grab the bottom of my shirt, breaking our contact for a brief moment to remove it. His mouth returns to my neck, traveling softly down my body, pulling the cup of my bra to the side and taking a nipple into his mouth. I moan when he gives it a soft tug between his teeth, and he continues his path to the other breast, repeating his motions. He uses his hands to unclasp my bra at the back and pulls each strap down before removing it completely to give him better access. I want to do nothing more than rush his movements and feel him inside me, but after the emotional day we had, I think we both need this.

I reach down and pull his head back to my face, kissing him passionately. I thrust my tongue into his mouth to dance seductively with his, all the while reaching for the bottom of his shirt and pulling it over his head. Breaking contact for another brief moment is almost torture, but his body once more lies atop mine with nothing in between us, and I relax. As he grinds his prominent erection into me, the friction causes a delicious feeling to spread; I moan loudly and freeze, worried that the sound will travel and be heard by the others.

"Don't worry. I made sure each room was soundproof. They won't hear us, just as we won't hear them. You can be as loud as you want. In fact, I encourage it." With his statement, he trails his hand down to the waistband of my pants, unbuttoning them before slinking his hand between the fabric, gaining access to my most vulnerable parts. He moans out, finding how wet and ready I am for him before sinking a finger inside of me. Then it's my turn to moan again.

I start to thrust myself onto his finger, chasing my release when he stops abruptly, pulling his hand out and sliding down my body. I was going to protest, but this is so much better. He slowly slides my pants and underwear down my legs at the same time, leaving me bare before him.

He trails up my legs, placing kisses and gentle sucks along his way. Finally, after what seems like an eternity, he arrives at my core. He flicks out his tongue over my clit, and I cry out, "Sebastyn!"

Rather than continuing, he raises his head to look at me. "Yes?" he asks before darting his tongue out once more and stopping again, making me squirm in place. "Did you want me to do something?" he asks. I try to give him a look promising payback, but I must not have succeeded because instead of continuing, he speaks again. "I can't hear you, love. You have to tell me if you want me to do something."

"I want you to..." I try, but I can't force the words out, as he lowers his mouth to me once more. This time he lingers, bringing me extremely close to release before stopping. I groan in frustration.

"What was it you wanted?" he asks, never breaking eye

contact and resuming his assault on my clit. I'm so close, I try to thrust my hips upward to chase the path of his mouth. Once again, when he's out of reach, he speaks. "Love. You have to tell me what you want."

"I want to cum," I rush out, utterly frustrated at his actions. Once again, I'm quickly brought to the brink with the flicks, sucks, and lashes of his tongue before he stops.

"Where would you like to cum, love?" This dirty talk would really be a turn on if he didn't keep denying me.

I groan in frustration again, and he resumes repeating the pattern. "I asked where you would like to cum, love. You're in charge," he repeats.

"On your tongue," I finally breathe out. This must've been the answer that he was waiting for because seconds later I'm crying out his name, my legs shaking and core pulsing with the largest orgasm I've ever had.

"I hate you," I whisper with a smile on my face.

"Now, love. That's not a nice thing to say," he responds, moving his body back up against mine, giving him access to my lips.

"Yeah, but that wasn't very nice either," I tell him and instead of responding, he merges his mouth with mine. I try to roll over to pay him back for his little game he just played with me, but my body is spent, and I can't find the strength.

He recognizes what I'm doing, but instead of helping, he simply says, "I need to be inside you tonight. You can pay me back anytime, love. But right now, I need to feel you."

I nod permission, and he removes his pants and pushes himself inside of me. "Oh goddess," I cry out as he sets a vigorous pace. With every single thrust, it seems that he hits that delicious spot inside me, and I quickly hit my peak again, tumbling over the edge. My inner walls grip him tightly, pulsing with my orgasm, causing him to follow me soon after.

He removes himself and picks me up bridal style, carrying me into a bathroom that I'm pretty sure wasn't there before. Once inside, he sets me in a tub, filling it quickly with his magic and heating it to a perfect temperature before sliding in behind me.

"I love you, Sarah Storm," he whispers in my ear, playing with my hair as I relax in the water.

"I love you too, Sebastyn Moon. Thank you," I whisper back.

"What are you thanking me for?" he asks, leaning over so we can see each other's faces.

"For loving me, for choosing me. Just for being you," I tell him.

He places a soft kiss on my forehead before returning to his position. "You never have to thank me for that. Besides, it's me who should be thanking you. You could've told me to beat it the first day we met or on the dock, and I would've listened. I wouldn't have liked it, but I would have respected it. The fact that you put your trust in me means everything, and I promise I will never take that for granted." I smile at his words and swear my heart just grew ten sizes, filling more with love for this man.

I must have fallen asleep in the bath because next thing I know, I'm being lifted from the water and carried to the bed. He softly towels off the water before pulling up the covers and sliding in behind me. When he pulls me close, wrapping his arms around me, I allow myself to go over the events of the day. I got a hold on my magic; I cemented my mate bond; I found my mother; I saved Blaze; I witnessed her access her flames for the first time; and oh, yeah, I met a dragon. "When do you think Andres is going to find us?" I say groggily, already half asleep.

"I don't know, love," he whispers back, just as tired.

The last thing that flits through my brain is a vision: Sebastyn and I are holding a beautiful baby girl while sitting on Constance's couch. If this is a vision of the future, sign me up.

Chapter Twenty

Sebastyn

I wake up early the next morning well-rested and ready to start the day. I roll over and place a soft kiss on Sarah's head. "Good morning, beautiful." I whisper.

Rather than the 'good morning' I expected, I get "Five more minutes" grumbling from a sleepy Sarah who pulls the covers up over her head. I let out a chuckle and make my way over to the bathroom. When I first made the extension with all the separate rooms, I didn't think about the bathroom situation, not realizing that there wasn't a single bathroom in the house to begin with. Instead, there was an out-house, which just wasn't going to do. I quickly added a bathroom to each room, going as far as extending both the original rooms to add bathrooms to them, as well. I hope they don't mind but I know I can't start the day without having at least a nice hot shower.

After doing just that, I dress and silently head out the door, letting Sarah sleep.

"Good morning, Sebastyn," Rita says, greeting me from the now large kitchen area. She's standing with the rest of our group minus Darren and Sophia, who had taken the last watch and are probably still sleeping.

"Good morning. Do some magic this morning?" I question, gesturing at the kitchen.

Rita waves her hand much the same way my mom does. "Cinder deserves to cook in a kitchen worthy of her skills."

I eye the espresso machine sitting on the counter. "And she needs an espresso machine too?"

She glances back at it. "Oh no. That's for me. And Sarah, if she likes coffee. Crap. Does she like coffee?" She gets a panicked look on her face, spewing the questions and I set my hand on hers.

"She prefers tea but will drink coffee. Now, Darren and Sophia? They love coffee and will be your best friends for life. Especially if you mix a little French vanilla coffee in it. Oh, I brought some of Sarah's favorite tea. You can have it."

She smiles and nods. "Thank you, Sebastyn. Or I guess I should call you 'son'?" She giggles.

"Rita, you can call me whatever you want as long as you know that I'm in love with your daughter and not going anywhere."

"Of course, I know that. Don't be silly," she says, shooing me out of the kitchen. I run back to the bedroom and grab Sarah's tea out of the side pocket of my bag, being quiet so I don't disturb her.

"Here you go." I pass Rita the bag of herbs that Sarah likes in her tea and take a seat at the table with Samara and Trevan.

"Morning, Sebastyn." Trev says with a smile. Samara looks up from her coffee cup and gives me a dip of her head in greeting.

"Not a morning person, Samara?" I chuckle, and Trev shakes his head *no* with a smile.

"Oh, good, Sebastyn. I wanted to thank you. It's been years since I had a hot shower," Calder says, as he and his girls sit down.

"Yes! That was amazing. I've never had a shower. We normally bathe in the river. Or dad will use his water magic to spray us down," Fyre says.

"Well, if your parents are okay with it, Rita, Sarah, your dad, me, and my sister—when she gets here—could probably make this extension permanent." I look to Rita for confirmation, knowing that I just volunteered her magic. She doesn't look upset but just gives me a nod in response.

"Really?" Blaze says, with wide eyes before turning to her father. "Can we, Daddy? Please?"

Calder smirks while making a show of thinking about it, but I already know his answer. If he could say no to the puppy dog eyes on those girls, I would have to question if he was human or not.

"I suppose," he groans, and both girls cheer, rushing out the front door and onto the porch to tell their mom the good news.

"Thank you for that," Calder says. "I haven't seen them that happy in what seems like forever."

"It's not a problem. Why don't you and Cinder think of some things you would like for the inside, and the rest of us will brainstorm, as well. The outside will remain the same, so the rest of your coven need not know about the changes we make unless you want them to know. However, in order for it to be permanent, we will need to set the spell into the house itself, which means you will be able to feel a slight pulse of magic coming from it, just so you know," I tell him.

"Unless you want to come to Canada with us," Trevan supplies.

"Really?" Calder asks, turning to him with wide eyes.

"Of course," I say, "my sister Skarlyt is our coven's high priestess, and Alaric is the alpha of the pack. We currently have two phoenixes living with us and a school for supernatural children. There is more than enough room for you."

"Thank you for the offer. Cinder and I will think about it. The Amazon has been my home since birth, though, so I'm not sure if I would be able to leave it."

I nod, completely understanding. As much as I love it here-it's beautiful and warm all year round-I'm not sure if I could leave Parry Sound. It's my home.

We eat breakfast, and soon my sister, Lennox, Alaric, and Phoebe are walking through the door.

Skarlyt lets off a whistle as she takes in the changes inside. "This place looks amazing."

"Are you feeling up to making it permanent?" I ask her.

"Of course! Between just the witches in our group, we should have more than enough power," she says, clapping her hands.

"That was my thought, too. I should see if Sarah's ready to get up now." The new group makes their way to the kitchen table while I head into our room. I slowly sit down on the edge of the bed and brush the hair out of her eyes.

"Good morning, my love. Are you ready to get up?"

"Good morning." She says with a smile, stretching her arms above her head. "Is everyone else up already?"

I chuckle. "Everyone except Darren and Sophia."

Her eyes widen. "Really? What time is it?"

"It's just before noon."

"Oh my gosh," she exclaims, throwing the covers off and rushing over to the bathroom. "Just give me five minutes, and I'll be ready," she calls out.

"No worries, love. Take your time."

As I turn to walk out of the door, she calls out once more, "Sebastyn?"

"Yes, sweetheart?"

"You didn't by chance pack any of my tea, did you?" She asks.

"Of course, I did. Your mom is already getting you a cup ready."

"Thank you. I won't be long," she says as I hear the shower turning on. I hear her sigh as the warm water hits her, and I smile. I love the noises she makes when she's happy.

"Oh. By the way, we're going to do the spell to make the extension permanent for Cinder and Calder. We're going to need your help."

"That sounds amazing. I can't wait."

With that, I head back out the door, allowing her to get ready in peace. I close the door and spot Darren and Sophia doing the same, rubbing the sleep out of their eyes.

"Rita brought an espresso machine," I whisper to them. Their sleepy demeanor quickly fades and is replaced by them racing each other to the kitchen. I laugh at their antics.

"Is she getting up?" Rita asks once I enter the kitchen. Both Darren and Sophia are bouncing excitedly in front of the gurgling espresso machine.

"Yup. She's just in the shower." She pours the hot water over the bowl of loose-leaf tea into a mug. "She likes a little honey in it, too." I whisper with a wink.

"Does mom have Kayne?" I ask my sister, sitting down at the table next to her.

"Yup, and Charleigh has Aurora and the boys," she says.

"Where are Phoebe and Alaric?" I ask, looking around. "They were here before I went and got Sarah, right? Or am I going crazy."

Skarlyt chuckles. "You are crazy, but they were here. They're outside with Cinder, Blaze, and Fyre, working on all their phoenix powers. Alaric is doing some kind of perimeter search or something or other before he and the other's head off to talk to the allies."

"Who's all going to talk to the different factions?" I ask.

"Lennox, Samara, Alaric and two of the guards from Kenji's Pride."

"Kenji's Pride?" I ask, not remembering anyone telling me that they had agreed to be involved.

"I forgot we didn't get a chance to tell you. Yesterday, Alaric and Phoebe were able to convince the Jaguar pride's alpha Kenji to help us with the other jaguar pride. They agreed, but we still need more help than just what they can give. According to Phoebe, he was skeptical at first but came around to the idea when she shifted. Oh, and I also forgot to tell you, a hunter showed up in Parry Sound the other day, looking for Phoebe."

"What?" I exclaim, instantly anxious about knowing that hunter is hanging around our home, where my nephew currently is, unprotected.

"Yupp. Her name is Rayne, and I think she and I are going to be good friends." She says adamantly and I am suddenly confused.

"Friends? What do you mean friends? She's a hunter."

"Well she is, but she isn't. It's hard to explain. All I know is that she loves giving Drake a hard time, and I'm absolutely loving it. Ohh, and also by the way, Drusilla came over, too."

"You mean she left the coven?" My mouth drops open in shock.

Skarlyt nods with a smile on her face. "Remember when Dru was captured and escaped? And she said that a hunter helped her escape?" She asks and I bob my head knowing exactly what she's talking about.

"You don't mean that hunter was this Rayne person?"

"The one in the same."

"This is insane. I feel like I missed so much, and we've only been here for a day."

"You have. But to be fair, you've had a lot going on in your life, too."

"Good morning, everyone." Sarah says. She walks straight to Rita, who is holding out a steaming mug of tea for her.

I get out of my chair, wrap my arms around her waist, and nuzzle into the side of her neck as she takes her first sip.

"Okay. Let's do this!" She says excitedly.

"Do what?" Skarlyt asks.

"The extension thingy," Sarah says, looking a little confused.

"You can wake up a little if you want before we get started," I tell her, and she shakes her head.

"No. I'm ready." She rubs her hands together.

"Okay, then. Everyone except for the witches out of the house," Skarlyt calls out, and everyone vacates the house except for Calder, Skarlyt, Rita, Sarah, and I.

"Did you think of anything else you want to add?" I ask, turning to Calder.

"Just one minor alteration to our room." Calder says, leading me through his bedroom door. "We want a small reading nook and a window on that wall, if we can."

I look where he's pointing. "Okay. You're going to envision it and take my hands. I'll guide you through how to do it yourself."

Excitement shows on his face before he schools his features once more. I chuckle, taking his hands in mine. "Close your eyes and picture exactly what you want it to look like, down to the very last detail. Imagine how the cushions are going to feel underneath you, how the window will look with the sun shining through, how the soft pillows will feel underneath you." I wait for him to nod before continuing. "Now reach down to your magic, ask it for help to create this space. It always helps to give it a reason why. If it's for Cinder, make sure you show that; our magic is always eager to help when it comes to pleasing our mates." I turn and look at the wall, watching the shimmering of his magic reaching out, morphing what was once a solid wall into a large bay window with a cushioned bench. Built into the wall at the bottom are two book-shelves, filling quickly with multiple books. The cushions change from a light gray to a deep purple before I feel his magic flow back inside him.

He opens his eyes. "Oh my goddess. That's exactly what I saw. I've never used magic like that before. We have been taught that the words are more important than anything."

"A lot of covens believe that but it's not true. Your magic is the only ingredient you need. And no matter what you're trying to do, it will help."

"Thank you," he says.

I clasp him on the shoulder. "Now let's go make this permanent," I tell him, leading him back into the main area of the house.

"Okay, then. We need to find the middle of the house." I do some mental measurements in an attempt to find the exact center of the house.

"I think it's here, Seb," Skarlyt says. She's standing in the space between what would be the new living room and kitchen.

I compare them with my mental measurements and quickly agree. "Okay, everyone needs to place their left hand on the person to the left of them and their right hand on the floor in front. Creating a circle. The most important thing is the intent, not the words. We could say gibberish and it would still work, though the words will help keep us focused." I wait until everyone is in position before continuing. "Now, close your eyes and repeat after me:

"We call upon our magic in our hour of need,"

"We ask that you bind this extension to the boards in the floor."

"So that temporary it is no more. As we will. So mote it be."

As they say the last words, power flows from the central spot where we stood, and a ripple goes through the frame of the house, up the walls and along the roof, locking this extension in so that it will not fade in a couple of days or continue to drain our magic. Instead, it will sink into the grains of the wooden boards of the floor.

I open my eyes and see a wide-eyed Calder. "This is incredible. I can feel the power radiating from the walls."

I nod, "You should put up a barrier to prevent others from being able to sense it."

He turns, closes his eyes and waves his hands while whispering his spell under his breath.

"That was incredible," Sarah says, wrapping her arms around me.

"You're incredible," I whisper, placing a soft kiss on her lips.

She deepens the kiss instantly, tightening her arms around me, and I meet her back with just as much passion. I lift her up, her legs wrapping around my waist just like her arms around my neck, and I forget everyone else in the room, walking her toward the bedroom.

A throat clearing has us breaking apart and turning toward the rest of our group. "As much as I'm sure you two would enjoy spending some time together, it's going to have to wait. My daughter needs to train and learn what she's capable of."

"Damn it, she's right," I whisper, lowering Sarah to the ground with a pout.

"We have the rest of our lives, Seb," she says, stepping back away from me with a pout on her own face. I groan and reach down, adjusting my painful erection before turning around.

"And I would very much like to have you train some of my coven, if you would, Sebastyn," Calder adds.

Internally, I groan, but outwardly, I plaster a smile on my face and head outside to train Calder's disrespectful cover. I'd much prefer to be in the bedroom with my mate, but Sarah's right: we do have the rest of our lives to be together and only a short period of time before those jaguars come back.

Outside, I pass Phoebe, Sophia, and the other phoenixes in training. Three of them have shifted and the other two have small flames licking up their arms. It looks like Sophia and Phoebe are trying to teach Blaze the Tidal Flame.

Next, we pass by Alaric, Darren, Trev, Lennox, Skarlyt, and Samara standing with two men I don't know. These must be the members of Kenji's pride sent to be our guides.

Skarlyt and Trevan see us and break apart from the group to walk with us. "Are we going to train the coven?" She asks.

I nod. "The ones that are willing."

When we reach the biggest hut at the edge of the village, we find a large group of people waiting.

I call out loud enough that they can all hear me. "Listen up! I'm only going to say this once. We are willing to help and train you but know this: it's going to be hard work. I refuse to train anyone that would be willing to give Blaze or Fyre to those monsters." All stop and stare while others squirm in place. "This is your chance. If you don't want to be here, leave now."

They all share looks with one another and, unsurprisingly, some actually walk away, leaving a group of around thirty people. I make mental notes of those that walk away. We will need to deal with them sooner rather than later. "Now that the unwilling have been weeded out, there is one more thing. You will all have to swear a magical oath to protect every member of your coven, including the young phoenixes. If broken, you will surrender your magic." Another round of murmurs goes around the crowd, but no one else leaves.

One by one, they come up to either Skarlyt or I, swearing to protect all members of the Amazon coven lest their magic leave them forever.

With that done, we get to work, breaking into three groups: Trevan helps those with elemental magic unlock their potential; Skarlyt teaches her group how to produce barriers; I work with my group on teleportation and extension.

We spend the rest of the day working with our groups until they get a handle on each skill, then call it a day. They're nowhere near where they need to be for the impending fight, but we're on our way. We will switch groups in the morning, repeating the same lessons, until all three groups are masters of them all. Hopefully, they can teach us some things that maybe we don't know.

Chapter Twenty-One

Sarah

The next two days go by with nonstop motion: my mom has been training me on how to use my powers, Sophia and Phoebe have been training Blaze, and Sebastyn, Trevan, and Skarlyt have been training the coven. Or well, what is left of the coven after we weeded out the corrupted witches. It was so potent that you could almost smell the taint on their magic. A lot of the coven found it unbelievable that they had been living alongside these corrupted witches, but the proof came when we called them out. They tried to fight dirty, spewing everything they could come up with, like 'It was us who were corrupted' and 'the Mother turned their backs on them', but at the end of the day, it didn't work and after realizing this, they tucked tail and ran away.

While we were all busy doing that, the alpha of the jaguar pride, Kenji, had sent us two guides to lead Samara, Darren, Lennox, and Alaric through the jungle to attempt to locate some more allies. They are supposed to all return tonight, including Kenji's entire pride, to get ready for the impending battle. Although if I'm being honest, I'm hoping we can find another solution. As bad as that Koto guy seems, any loss of life on either side will be devastating, and I really hope it doesn't come to that.

Spending time with my mom has been surreal, though. We decided to take a much-needed break and spend a day catching up on each other's lives. Twenty-five years of time is hard to catch up on when you're focused on training, so we have had little time to really talk.

Today is the day that I have been waiting for: I get to find out what happened to separate us. It's hard to believe that my father was always evil, especially since my mom seems so amazing. But then, just like the corrupted witches in the coven, or how Tanner hid his true self from Phoebe, it's easy to overlook the little slips when it's someone you care about.

"Are you ready to go, love?" Sebastyn asks, breaking me out of my thoughts.

"Yes, I am," I respond. I wrap my arms around his waist. "I feel like I've been waiting forever for this day."

"I know, sweetheart, and I'm glad that you two decided to spend the day in the clearing, rather than here. Especially since you've been dreaming of the two of you being there," he says as he places a loving kiss on my head. "Skarlyt is meeting us there with your mom because she wanted to get some stuff ready for your day."

At first, we had talked about waiting until everything calmed down here before taking this break, but after thinking about it, what if the worst were to happen before we got the chance? When I brought this up to my mom, she instantly teared up, promising that nothing was going to happen, but she also agreed that we should carve this time out for ourselves while we could.

"Is it weird that I'm a little nervous?" I ask, leaning back to look up into his eyes.

"Not at all, love. I think whatever you're feeling is completely normal." He lifts my hand and kisses it. "But I'm under strict instructions to make sure you get there on time, or it's my head."

I nod with a chuckle. "I'm ready." I may not know my mom well, but I know Skarlyt, and she is most definitely someone I do not want to cross.

With that, we arrive back in the clearing, and I look around, seeing the changes that have been made. After my little experiment with my magic creating the benches, someone used that as inspiration and placed little huts made of vines overtop each bench. I walk up to the closest one to inspect it, noticing the detail. Each vine is woven together perfectly, creating a seamless shelter. It's beautiful, and I bet in the summer they will be even better covered in flowers.

"Do you like them?" my mom's voice calls out from behind me.

I look at her in shock. "You did this?"

She inclines her head shyly. "I got the idea from the benches, which I recently found out was you. So, thank you. They are spread out enough that we can still hold gatherings within the clearing but now each family can adopt one or make their own."

"That's such an amazing idea," I tell her with an enormous smile on my face.

"I'm going to leave now, love. I'll be back at sundown, waiting right here for you," Sebastyn says, walking up and placing a kiss on my lips. I kiss him back, wrapping my arms around his neck. He pulls away far too soon and is on his way back to the jungle. A small weight feels like it has just been placed on my chest at his absence, and I begin to rub it.

"That's just the mate bond. It will get easier with time, but because you only cemented the bond a few days ago, it will feel like a small pressure on your chest the farther he is from you. I wouldn't be surprised if he ends up back here sooner than nightfall," my mom says, leading me over to one of the huts.

"So, you and my dad were, or are, mates? Is that how you

know?" I ask. I was planning on easing into this conversation, but since she brought it up...

She nods sadly, tears brimming in her eyes. "Robert and I met as children. He was a witch from a neighboring coven. Our mothers had grown up together and regularly kept in touch. By the time we were teenagers, we had begun dating. I knew from the first time he kissed me that he was my mate. I told him, but he laughed and said it was impossible to know for sure. But I knew.

"At eighteen, we took the last step and low and behold, I was right. We were, in fact, true mates. He was everything I had always dreamed of in a mate: kind, caring, passionate," at her last word, I make a face. I know I'm a grown ass woman, but I still don't want any details on how 'passionate' my father was with my mother.

"What happened? I don't understand?" Her definition of him does not fit at all with the father I grew up with.

"Well, I'm not quite sure. I've gone over it a lot over the past few days since finding out you're alive. He was acting strange in those last few months, spending more time with his old coven, meeting with new friends. But I never truly suspected anything out of the ordinary.

"When the two of you left to go shopping that day, I rushed around making your birthday cake and cooking your favorite dinner, lasagna. I had just finished setting the table and was getting ready to pull the lasagna out of the oven when the knock came on the door. It was a police officer telling me that there was an accident. He said that the two of you were driving on the highway when a tractor trailer hauling gasoline struck our car, causing an explosion. He said there was nothing left to identify or even bodies to bury.

"I remember standing there, denying it. There was no way that happened. I would've felt it. I was sure that it was some kind of mistake and that the two of you were going to walk through the door any minute. I dismissed the officer and went back to getting everything ready for your birthday dinner. You were so excited before you left. I just wanted everything to be perfect.

"An hour went by, and you didn't come home. I searched inside myself for my mate bond and felt nothing. Not pain as if your father had died, but instead, I felt hollow. Where I should've had a strand connecting me to your father and you, there was nothing. That's when I truly began to believe it." She pauses and wipes the tears from her eyes, obviously remembering the pain vividly.

"The storms that raged that month were excessive, I admit, but in my grief, I was unable to control them. I brought down tornados, caused a forest fire with my lighting and eventually an extensive flood before Constance finally convinced me to let it go," she places her hands on my shoulders, giving a slight squeeze. "If I thought for even a second that you were out there somewhere, nothing would have stopped me from finding you. Not a day goes by that you have not been consuming my thoughts."

"I thought of you all the time, too. I've always had these dreams of you and I running and spinning in circles while laughing through a clearing much like this one. I guess it probably was this clearing. They always felt like they were memories rather than dreams, but whenever I asked dad about them, he would fly off the handle and remind me that I killed you when you were bringing me into the world, blaming me for your death, which I now know isn't true. I just don't understand: the man you described to me does not fit the man who raised me," I tell her, tears brimming in my own eyes.

"I'm so sorry, sweetheart. I wish I could go back in time and make it so that never happened, but I can't. Those dreams, though. You were right: they were memories. Since you started walking, you and I would come to this clearing, roll in the flowers, spin until we were dizzy, fall down on the ground, and play tag. This was your absolute favorite spot.

"I'm sure it will be hard for me to hear, but can you please tell me about your life? Was there anything good?" she asks.

"Are you sure? There are a lot of things that happened in my past that are going to be painful to hear," I need to make sure she truly wants to know, because once she hears some of it, she can't go back. I'll try and keep the worst details to myself but I'm sure she'll fill in the blanks.

"I'm sure," she responds with a nod, visibly steeling herself for my tale.

I begin, "Well, dad wasn't the worst father I've met, but he also wasn't sunshine and rainbows. He was cold, distant. He loved to make sure I knew my place, my *role* in life: to be seen and not heard, to be responsible for the housework, and to one day bring him great honor by marrying a mage. Oh, and he loved to remind me how I killed you. He made sure whenever I would get a sliver of a backbone and stand up for myself that he brought me down a few pegs. He was just cruel enough to keep me in line, but not so cruel that I ever actively thought about running away.

"Even now, after I left, rather than calling or emailing me to see if I'm okay or even alive, he sent me a message demanding that I return to wed a widowed mage, or he would disown me. As if the man he originally chose for me wasn't bad enough." A shudder flows through me at the thought of Joe or marrying another like him.

"And you didn't have any children?" she asks. I'm sure she wants to ask more about Joe, but I'm glad she doesn't.

"No. But that was entirely on purpose. I had this amazing teacher in high school, Mrs. Jones. She knew of the expectations placed on me and didn't agree with them. First, she tried to get me out. She even got me accepted to university and offered for me to move in with her. When that didn't work, she helped me get birth control so I wouldn't have to bring a child into that life. I took it religiously for the first couple months, before Joe placed a spell on me to think I was in love with him and then again for the last four years, after I broke his spell.

Even without the birth control, though, I didn't get pregnant, and though it infuriated Joe, I'm so happy I didn't. I couldn't imagine having a child with that man. He was evil. No, evil is not quite a strong enough word. He was more than evil, and his father was even worse." Rather than cry like I thought I would be telling her about my old life, I feel grateful to not be living it anymore. But my mom, on the other hand, doesn't seem to feel the same. Her fists are clenched, and her eyes are closed tightly with the rumble of thunder sounding off in the distance.

I place my hands on hers. "It's okay. Everything that I went through with Joe or his father is in the past. I have some lingering anxiety, but after mating with Sebastyn, a feeling of peace has settled in. I don't think I'll ever truly be over everything that happened in my life, but I'm moving forward. I found Sebastyn. And you. That's all that matters. Dad will pay one day for the time he stole from us."

"Yes, he will," she grinds out through clenched teeth, but the storm starts fading. "At first, I was angry that you had been kept from me, but my happiness at finding you again had overridden it. Now, hearing more of your story, which I'm sure you have kept the worst parts from me," she gives me a pointed look as I nod to confirm, "the anger is bubbling up. I want him to pay for what he's done to you."

"To us. And he will, I promise. But for now, I want to get to know my mom on a deeper level, not just about how our magic is the same. I have dreamed of you for so long. Having you here within touching distance doesn't seem real," I whisper as I pull her into a hug.

"I know exactly what you mean," she whispers back.

We sit there and talk for another hour about our likes and dislikes, hobbies and such. Turns out I get my knack for my homemade concoctions from her. She uses her herbs to create healing balms and teas. The more we talk, the more it feels like the missing piece of my soul has reattached, and I notice where I would normally be second guessing myself, I feel confident and sure. Maybe I'm not as broken as I thought. Maybe I was just missing a part of me and didn't realize it.

We decide to go visit Constance for some lunch and are laughing and joking as she shares some of my finer moments as a child. But as we approach the house, I can hear yelling.

"What do you mean, he's not here? Where is he?" I can already tell exactly who that is: Opal. I quickly throw my hair into a high messy bun, proudly displaying my mate mark. I know she's going to see it, and I already know what her reaction will be.

I walk in the door without knocking, earning a sideways look from my mom. Guess she doesn't know the drama with Opal. I shrug my shoulders and give her a wink. This is going to be so much fun.

"Constance?" I call out.

"Sarah, sweetheart. Right on time," she says, coming to give me a hug whispering in my ear. "She's in a mood. Be careful."

"I've got this," I whisper back. I purposely turn to look at my mother, who is still standing in the doorway, waiting to come in.

"What the fuck is that?" Opal screams.

I spin back toward her. "What is what?" I put as much sweet- ness into my voice as I can muster.

"On your neck. What is that?" she says, pointing at me.

"Oh, you mean my mate mark. It's beautiful, isn't it?" I ask, still feigning innocence.

"Only the Moon's have that mark," she spits at me.

"Really? I didn't know. It's hard to see the back of my neck. Sebastyn held up a mirror for me, but it was still difficult to see. I suppose it makes sense though because it is very similar to Lennox's," I say with a shrug, walking toward the kitchen. I look back at the door again and see both Constance and my mom standing there, staring at me. My mom's mouth is hanging open while Constance has a smirk knowing exactly what I'm doing. I shoot them a wink and grins show on their faces, my mom finally catching onto what I'm doing.

"But that's impossible. There are no other members of the Moon family, just Skarlyt and..." she seems to get stuck, so I help her out.

"And Sebastyn. My mate," I don't keep the venom out of my words this time. Tears brim in her eyes, and if she were any other person, I would feel bad. But she isn't. She is a spiteful bitch who doesn't know how to take no for an answer.

"That's not possible," she whispers again, backing away from me.

"You know it is Opal. In fact, you probably already knew that you weren't his mate. You just wanted to try and force him into a relationship he didn't want. What you really need to be doing is going and finding your own mate. And leave mine alone," I walk toward her to show that I'm serious.

But instead of being her usual bitchy self, she surprises me. "I can't," she whispers, looking directly into my eyes. "He rejected me."

She knew the whole time Sebastyn wasn't her mate? She just wanted a replacement for the one who rejected her? I stand there in shock, trying and failing to stay angry with this obviously hurting woman.

"Then why did you continue to try and convince Sebastyn that you were mates?" I ask.

"Because it wasn't supposed to be like this. I was supposed to live happily ever after with my mate," she shrinks down to the floor, hugging her knees to herself, "but it turns out my mate is a bear shifter who was passing through and wanted nothing to do with a witch."

Constance is the first to soften and rushes over, wrapping her arms around Opal. My mom and I do the same. "Oh, Opal, when did this happen?" my mom asks.

Opal seems surprised at the turn of events but leans into our embrace, closing her eyes as she answers. "Two days after my eighteenth birthday."

We all suck in breath. "You've been living with this pain by yourself for ten years?" I ask. Damn it. I really wanted to hate this woman, but oddly, I'm finding myself admiring her strength. From what has been explained to me, it takes a special person to be able to survive a rejection. And for her to have done it alone for this long... Wow.

"Sarah?" I hear Sebastyn call from the door. I look up, meeting his eyes, and he smiles before noticing Opal in the middle of our hug. "Okay, what's going on?"

We all giggle at his question. "No," Opal says, standing up and walking toward him. I go to take a step, wanting to keep distance between them, but my mom and Constance each place a hand on my shoulder.

"Just wait," my mom whispers.

"Sebastyn, I owe you an apology. I should never have acted the way I have toward you. I have no excuse. It's a long story, but will you forgive me?" she asks him.

He looks shocked, sharing a quick look with me. I'm not sure, but it feels like he is asking my opinion, so I give a slight nod.

"I'm not going to pretend to understand what happened here while I was gone, or why you changed years ago." He pauses, taking a deep breath. "But, yes, Opal, I forgive you," he says, sticking his hand out for her to shake.

"You have a wonderful mate. I wish you both the best from the bottom of my heart," she says, turning to give me a soft smile before turning back to walk out the door.

"Opal. Wait," I rush after her, seeing the pain on her face, hearing it in her sobs and feeling it in the tremble of her petite body, changed something inside me. Where there used to be hate and fury toward Opal, I have understanding. Sure, her pain isn't the same as mine, but pain is pain, no matter the cause. If I can help someone like others helped me... Well, that's what I'm going to do. "Listen, I think we got off on the wrong foot. I would like to start over and maybe in the future we can be friends." She seems surprised by my statement, but the smile on her face says it all.

"I would like that very much." I wrap her in a hug. We promise to sit down and talk one day soon. For some reason, it feels right. I just can't explain why.

As I re-enter the kitchen, my mom pulls me to the side. "You know, you, Opal, and Skarlyt were best friends when you were little. There wasn't a day that went by where the three of you weren't at one of the other's houses or in the clearing. I'm not sure if she realizes who you are yet. But she will." So that's probably why Skarlyt's been looking at me like I'm someone else. She's been waiting to see if I'm her long-lost friend who she thought had died. Maybe a girls' night is in order. I know I have some things to talk to Sophia about too.

With that, we head inside for a late lunch, catching up with Constance. When the day is over, my mom decides to stay at home, providing that we promised to come get her for the show-down. Only a few more days and Sebastyn and I can come home and start our life together, even better now that it's going to be without the Opal cloud hanging over us.

Chapter Twenty-Two

Sarah

Arriving back in the Amazon still takes my breath away. Not just because of the beauty, but because it's so sweltering hot that it is literally hard to breathe. There's still a flurry of activity around the coven with some witches training and Sophia and Phoebe working with Blaze on their flames. Based on what I can see, everything is going very well.

"Sebastyn, everyone had an idea to do a barbeque, so you and I are going to teleport back home and get the food," Skarlyt says, walking up to us. I look at her in shock. There has got to be a couple hundred people here, not including the shifters that will be coming. How are we going to feed them all? It's going to take them forever to go back and forth.

"I just got back," he says to her.

"Yeah, I know. But we figured that it would be a nice way to greet our allies, and it was either this, or we sent out hunting parties to go catch some game. This seems like the easier option," she reasons.

"I think it's a great idea!" I tell them both.

Skarlyt beams at me while Seb gives me a look that says he

doesn't want to be away from me any longer than he already has been today. But seeing the looks on both of our faces, he gives me a soft smile and a kiss on my forehead before he and his sister are off to gather all the supplies.

I spend the next couple hours moving between each coven member, trying to help in any way I can. Although I'm not the most well-trained witch, I do know how to help them access their raw power. There are no witches here able to use all four elements, like me or the Moon siblings. Most are earth witches, which has helped them survive this long by allowing them to speed the growth of crops.

I am standing with a large group at the edge of the forest when I get a fantastic idea. "Hey, Calder!" I call out, and gesture for him to come stand by me.

"Hi, Sarah. Glad you're back," he replies warmly.

"Thanks. I was thinking, how many earth witches do you have that can help plants grow?" I ask.

He looks confused. "Um, a few, I think. Why?"

"Well, back home, when I was trying to get a handle on my magic, I did something. My magic seeped into vines, causing them to braid and twist together to create these benches. Then my mom and some of her earth witch friends went back and created huts on top of them, all using vines. I'm wondering if we could do something similar, but instead of benches or huts, we could create a wall of vines towering around the coven, forcing the battle to take place in one general area." He looks skeptically at me, but I can see the moment the idea takes hold when his eyes light up.

"If we could do that, it would not only protect us from this attack but could potentially work in the future. Okay. Let's try it."

He rushes over from group to group, gathering up about a dozen witches before returning to me. "These are the most talented earth witches we have. I told them your plan."

"I'm not even sure how exactly we start, but if we go to the tree line and coax the vines together, we should be able to get a lot done today," I say, walking them over. Once I'm there, I think about what Sebastyn said when we were building the ledge. I close my eyes and envision the vines shooting up and twisting and turning together. I throw in my intent that I want it to be thick enough to protect the people within. I feel the way the vines move, slithering like snakes, weaving in and out of each other, securing themselves between the trees.

I open my eyes when I hear gasps behind me and turn to see all the witches staring at me in shock. "What?" I ask.

Calder points to the treeline where I was just working, and I turn. Now it's my turn to be shocked. Where there was a large opening in the trees, there is now a fifteen-foot wall that is at least five feet wide, and as I walk around it, I realize it's about two feet thick. I run my hands over the vines, feeling how smooth they feel, but when I push on them, they start to grow thicker, reinforcing the section that is being attacked. Perfect.

"How did you do that?" One of the witches asks.

"I just envisioned what I wanted the vines to do and rein-forced it with the intent that I want to protect those inside. I'm sure you all are already aware, but if you share your intent with your magic, and it agrees, you can do amazing things. You try," I gesture for her to step up.

Reluctantly, she steps up, and her face scrunches up in deter-mination. Other than a few small vines sprouting, nothing happens.

"Okay, stop." I stand behind her with my hands on her shoul-ders. "Close your eyes. Now think of your family inside this coven. Think of the love you have for them and the desire to protect them. Think of your friends and their family." She nods, and I can feel that some of the tension in her shoulders has dissipated. "Good. Now I want you to see the vines growing and weaving together between the trees to help keep out those who would wish to harm. You need to feel them slither across each other like snakes. Show them in your mind what you need them to do and why. They need to know that you're not misusing them. Ask them for their help," I watch as the vines start to twist and turn together, creating a wall in front of us. It's not as big or as thick as mine, but it's still amazing to watch.

"Open your eyes," I say, and she does.

"I did that?" she asks, turning to look at me.

"Yes, you did. Now, watch," I say, taking her hand and standing beside her. I reach inside for my magic and begin to push it out into the vines. I feel the second that she catches on as her magic merges with mine, and it spreads out, growing the vines.

Another witch comes and takes my hand, adding to our magic, and the vines respond in kind. They grow faster and thicker than before, spreading out so that a large portion of this side of the clearing now has a large vine wall separating it from the jungle.

The line of witches gets longer as more people step up to clasp their neighbor's hand. I feel each individual person's magic flowing together, weaving along one another just like the vines in the wall. When I open up my eyes, just over half of the coven is surrounded by another fifteen-foot-high wall with large trumpet vines growing along the surface. It's absolutely gorgeous. "Alright, everyone," I say, stepping back and removing my magic from the line. They do the same. "That food smells delicious, so let's go grab something to eat."

A round of cheers go out from the group, and we all walk over to the barbecue. I quickly find Sebastyn and wrap my arms around him. "I want to show you something," I whisper.

He looks down at me and nods. "Oh, you, too, Skarlyt," I call out as I begin leading them over to the wall. I hear them both suck in a breath when they see it.

"You did this?" Skarlyt asks, walking up and pushing on the wall. Just like when I did it, the wall starts to slither and grows thicker in the spot. "That's incredible. Where did you learn to do this?"

"Well, it was Sebastyn who taught me, but the idea came from my mom when she made those huts in the clearing. I wondered why we wouldn't be able to do the same here with a wall around the coven. This way we can force them to attack in one area rather than be surrounded. It works like a natural protection barrier, one that doesn't drain our magic," I reply.

"This is amazing, love," Sebastyn says, lifting me up from the ground and spinning me around. I giggle.

"We have about half of the coven surrounded now. The other earth witches helped a lot. I'm hopeful that after dinner we will be able to finish," I say.

"Then let's go eat. I want to help with the rest," Skarlyt says excitedly, rushing over to give me a hug quickly before skipping back to the barbeque.

"You truly are amazing," Sebastyn says, sweeping me up against him and merging his mouth to mine. I wrap my arms around his neck as he places his hands under my ass, lifting me up so I can wrap my legs around his waist as well. Our heated kiss turns frantic as I begin to grind myself on him. Even though it's only been a day, it feels like it's been forever since we've been together, and I can't wait any longer.

As he pushes me up against the wall, I silently show the vines my thoughts. I swear they chuckle but comply as they create a small ledge for me to sit on and encase us. I open my eyes and look around with a gasp. Where the vines on the wall are just a mixture of brown and green covered in orange trumpet flowers, the vines surrounding us now are covered in little blue and purple flowers.

"Did you do this?" Sebastyn asks.

"Kind of. I just asked the vines to help me hide us from prying eyes so that I could show you how much I love you. The rest, the flowers, that's all them," I tell him.

His eyes heat with lust and his mouth is back on mine as he places me on the ledge. I reach down, unbuckling his pants and shoving them to the ground, before shimmying out of mine as well. "I can't wait," he whispers.

"I don't want you to. I just want you inside me," I whisper back. He uses his fingers to make sure I'm ready, which I am. I'm always ready for him. He thrusts in slowly, causing my back to arch, and I cry out. "Oh my goddess!"

Together, we move as one, like dance partners who have been dancing together their entire lives, rather than just the last week. Our mouths are fused together in hot and needy kisses, our tongues tangoing while the rest of our bodies move in sync. He pulls me forward so that my ass is on the edge of the ledge, adjusting the angle so that with every stroke he hits that delicious spot inside of me quickly, bringing me to climax.

Just as I'm thinking that I'm too hot and covered in sweat, a small hole appears in the top of the vines, and a cool wind seeps down as Sebastyn releases his seed inside me. We are both breathing heavily and coated in a sheen of sweat as he removes himself, reaching into his pocket and pulling out a small piece of fabric. He uses it to clean me up before helping me off the ledge the vines created, and we both get dressed.

"I love you, Sarah," he whispers, placing a soft kiss on my lips. I suck his bottom lip into my mouth, giving it a small tug with my teeth.

"And I love you, Sebastyn," I whisper back as I release his lip.

After putting our pants back on, I place my hands on the vines, sending them my thanks, and they open back up, merging in with the wall.

We are almost back to the barbeque when the first growl sounds out. "What the?" I say, coming to a stop and sharing a look with Sebastyn.

"They're here," he says, grabbing my hand and together we run. So much for eating dinner.

Arriving at the group, everyone is panicking. People are rushing around, unsure of what to do. We haven't even gone over battle strategies yet. No one is sure of their roles.

"Okay, everyone, calm down," Alaric starts, but I can see how unsure even he is.

"I need all the witches from earlier with me and anyone else who has access to earth magic. We need to finish this wall," I call out. Alaric looks at me in shock, probably because I've never spoken that confidently in front of him, but nods. With that, I rush to the edge of the wall we had created.

"I'm going to take half to the other side. We'll meet in the middle," Sebastyn says, giving me a kiss and rushing to the other side of the wall.

"Okay, same as before. We need to show the vines it is only our intent to protect those inside," I call out and once again, we all join in a line with our hands clasped together and raised. I feel a hand reach out, joining my outstretched one and open my eyes to see Skarlyt beside me. I give her a dip of my chin in encouragement and clasp her hand, holding it out toward the wall. The vines must sense the urgency because they grow faster and stronger than before.

By the time the wall is about to close, I can see the glowing eyes of the jaguar shifters in the trees. We double our efforts and before long, Sebastyn's group and my own are in one line, pushing our magic into the vines.

"Good job, everyone. Now, head back and see what Alaric needs," I say to the coven members, while turning toward Skarlyt and Sebastyn. "We need to allow our allies in. We have to show the vines who they would be." They both step up to the vines with me, and we place our hands on them. "We have aid coming. Please allow them passage through your wall," as I finish, the vine seems to pulse a response. "Thank you," I whisper as we all step back.

"I've never seen magic do that before," Skarlyt whispers.

"What do you mean?"

"It's like it has an awareness and understood what you were asking," she responds.

"Isn't that how magic normally is? When we reach inside and ask it to help?" I ask looking between both of them.

"Kind of. But normally that awareness stops once it leaves our body. This is different."

"Maybe because the vines are alive?" I supply.

"Maybe," Skarlyt responds, still looking at the wall in confusion.

We need to work on a strategy, so we run back to our friends, pumping our legs and arms as fast as they will go. I call the air to me, raising me up from the ground and torpedoing myself faster, not knowing why I wasn't doing this in the first place. Hearing some loud growls, I look to my right and see the vines open and allow several jaguars through. I panic at first before realizing they're not attacking anyone. They must be here to help, so our message worked.

"We're ready," Alaric says, coming to stand by Sebastyn, Skarlyt, and I once we land. "Can you open a section so we can see them?"

I nod and walk up to the vines. "Okay. We need to see who we're fighting against. Open a small section please."

As the vines open up, I see the fuckface of the century. "Where is she?" Koto screams.

"Where is who?" I snap back. A week ago, I would never have dreamed of speaking to a man like him in this way, but now, I know that I'm not alone anymore. I have a family and friends who will stand by my side, and I have more power in my little finger than this man has in his entire body.

"You know exactly who I'm talking about. Where is she?" he calls out once again.

"Here," Blaze says, walking up beside me, flames licking up her arms.

Koto lunges forward so fast none of us even have a chance to stop him and grabs her by the arms. He screams as her flames burn his hands, but he doesn't let go.

"You will be coming with me," he growls out. As soon as the words are out of his mouth, he's tackled from the side by a large jaguar, forcing both him and Blaze to the ground. The shifted jaguar bites down on his arm and begins to pull him away from her, and she rolls away, scuttling back to her feet.

Koto shifts smoothly into his sleek black jaguar form, and the two circle each other. I reach to bring Blaze back next to me, but her body seems to take an involuntary step forward. Just as I get my arms around her, the two jaguars lunge at each other, clashing together with claws and teeth.

I push Blaze behind me and raise my hands, ready for an opening to attack. "Wait," Alaric says, stepping up beside me. "It's now a challenge. That's Kenji," he says, pointing to one of the jaguars. How he can tell them apart, I have no clue, but I trust Alaric. As the thought pops into my mind, I realise that's something I would never have said a week ago: that I trust a man. I glance around and recognize that he's not the only one either. I trust all the men in our group, including Calder, and that has me awe-struck.

One of the cats gets a good hold on the other's neck and lets off a yowl in pain. To my surprise, Blaze ignites, her flames going higher and hotter and the beginning of wings are sprouting from her back. She screams out a screech, floating toward the two. In their shock, the one releases the other's neck, and she steps between them.

"You will not harm my mate," she screams again, and her

flames answer her call, creating a barrier around her and the fallen jaguar.

We all suck in a breath. "Mate?" I whisper to Alaric.

"It seems this just got more interesting," he whispers back. Sophia and Phoebe both shift at her declaration and join her in protecting her mate, and Sebastyn rushes to the shifter's side. As he shifts back, I realize this must be Kenji. He looks similar to Koto but different enough to tell the difference. Both have dark skin, long, pitch black hair and chocolate brown eyes. Kenji, though, has a long scar running down his chest.

Sebastyn helps Kenji to his feet, and he goes to stand beside Blaze, clasping his hand in hers. Her flames lick up his body, but rather than burning him, they caress him and repair his wounds. That's new. I've never seen that happen with Phoebe and Alaric or Darren and Sophia. But then again, I also haven't seen them injured with their mates.

"You will not win, brother. Once again, you've proven that you're corrupted by power. You are trying to take what the Mother has granted another, but this time I will not step aside. I do not want to kill you, but if you insist on trying to claim my mate, I will have no choice," Kenji growls out to his brother.

Koto shifts back with a disgusted look on his face. "Why would I care what the Mother wants? She's obviously stupid, pairing someone as weak as you with a powerful phoenix. She is not yours; she is mine. I challenge you for the right to be her mate."

"No!" Blaze screams. Kenji turns to her, placing her face in his hands gently.

"It's okay, love. I was not trying before. I had, and still have, no desire to hurt my brother, but for you, I will. I will not lose. I promise you," he says, and he places a soft kiss on her forehead. She claws at him, trying to keep him near her. It takes both Phoebe and Sophia to pull her back to the group.

She rushes to me, wrapping her arms around me, burying her face in my neck. "He can't die," she sobs.

I rub her back and smooth her hair away from her face. "He won't. But I don't understand how you know he's your mate," I whisper.

"I turned eighteen today. Everyone seems to have forgotten, but as soon as I saw him, I knew. He can't die, Sarah. He just can't," she sobs again.

I continue to rub her back as I watch. Kenji was right. He really wasn't trying before. Within a few seconds, he gets a good hold on the back of his brother's neck, and they both freeze. Everyone seems to hold their breath as we watch. I know Kenji does not want to kill his brother, but anyone with a brain can see that if he doesn't, he will never stop coming for Blaze. Koto begins to thrash around, trying and failing to get his claws at his brother, and Kenji clamps his mouth down. You can hear an audible crunch with the snapping of his neck, and everyone lets out the air they were holding in their lungs.

Kenji shifts back at the same time as his brother tenderly lays him on the ground and closes Koto's eyes. When he turns toward us, I can see the tears brimming, but he blinks them away as his gaze lands on Blaze in my arms. I give a nod and watch him relax as Alaric steps up to offer him some pants. Where Alaric keeps getting these pairs of pants and shorts from, I haven't a clue. It's like he's pulling them out of thin air. I incline my head towards Alaric in thanks; Blaze may be used to jungle life and now be eighteen, but I'm sure she doesn't need to see her mate in all his naked glory for the first time in front of a large audience.

Once dressed, he rushes over to us. She tries to bury herself further into me until he speaks. "My love?" she twists her head and throws herself into his arms, continuing to sob. He rubs her back and brushes her hair with his fingers, all the while telling her over and over that he's okay, that she's okay, and that nothing is going to separate them ever again.

It's the most beautiful thing to watch, and when their lips meet for the first time, I turn away to give them privacy. If I'm being honest, I want to hold my own mate in my arms. This wasn't the battle that we were expecting, but it still could've gone differently. We could've lost one another tonight. He seems to have been thinking the same thing as our eyes lock together, and we rush toward one another.

We are still holding onto one another when Kenji speaks loudly, addressing all the jaguars present. "We will no longer be two prides, but one. If you do not wish to follow me as your alpha, then you will be exiled from the jungle. For too long, we have fought amongst each other and for what? For my brother's sick idea that what the Mother has granted us was not enough?" Blaze stands beside him, looking like the queen she was meant to be. Or more accurately, half of the alpha pair she was meant to be. "I will give you two days to pledge your allegiance to me or leave. There will be no second chances," Kenji finishes and most of the jaguars in the forest come forward, bending the knee to their new alpha pair. There are a few I watch leave, but it's a lot less than anyone expected, I'm sure.

As Kenji and Blaze turn and walk toward us, I get this over-whelming feeling that everything is going to be okay. That this was the Mother's plan all along. To unite the shifters in the jungle and around the world. Not only did we stop a war between clans in the jungle, but we have now created allies across continents. It brings my thoughts back to Andres and his talk about some prophecy. Is that the reason all of this is happening now? And if so, what does it mean?

Our even larger group heads back into the clearing where the barbequed food is, and the grill is fired back up. We eat and cele-brate throughout the night until Phoebe and Alaric head home, then Skarlyt and Lennox. Sebastyn and I discuss it, and we decide to head back to his home as well, promising to return the next morning for Sophia, Darren, Samara, and Trevan. I just really want to start our new life, besides I've yet to see where Sebastyn lives.

Popping into a massive home completely filled to the brim with books is not what I expected. I look around, and it almost feels like a reoccurring nightmare I used to have. There are books on shelves, books on the floor, on tables and chairs. It's so cluttered it's hard to find a single clear surface, and my chest starts to constrict. "I know it's not much but..." Sebastyn says.

I shake my head no. It's not the lack of anything that is causing my heart to race; it is the sheer amount of everything. "It's perfect. Well, it will be when we organize everything," I tell him.

He sucks in a breath and places his hand over his heart. "I know where everything is," he says.

"I'm sure you do. But I can't live in a home like this," I say. To my surprise, he takes my hand and together we walk out of the room and into a pristine kitchen and dining room. There is not a speck of dust on anything and nothing out of place. "I don't understand."

"I knew you wouldn't be comfortable living in a home with my disorganized self, so I've spent any time we had apart getting it ready for you. I forgot that I didn't finish the living room when we popped in there," he says, setting my mind at ease.

"Thank you. But as a compromise, you can keep the living room however you want it. It can be your space," I tell him. He gushes, sweeping me up into a bridal hold and carrying me to his bedroom.

That night, we christened every room in the house, including the living room on top of all the books. It has been the best night of my life so far, and the beginning of the greatest adventure.

Chapter Twenty-Three

Sebastyn

Waking up in my own bed, next to my mate, is out of this world. Something I never thought I would want. Something I ran from for a very long time. But the second I heard her name, my life changed. She came in like a Trojan horse and stole my heart, wrapping it around her beautiful fingers and claiming it for her own.

I roll over, give her a soft kiss on her head and climb out of bed as quietly as possible so I don't disturb her. There are some things I need to do before she wakes up. After quickly going through my morning routine, I teleport to my mom's house.

"Mom?" I call out, already standing in her kitchen.

"Sebastyn? What are you doing here so early?" She says with a yawn, wrapping her robe around her as she leaves her bedroom.

"I was hoping to get help from you and Rita with something. Can you get dressed and start coffee while I pop over and get her?" I don't wait for an answer, instead teleporting to Rita's front porch.

I raise my hand to knock, but Rita pulls the door open quickly. "Is everything okay? Is it Sarah?" She asks, looking anxious.

"Everything is fine. Better than fine. We're back from the

Amazon. Everything is figured out there. We didn't end up needing to fight because the prides handled it on their own."

"Oh, good," she says, visibly relaxing. "Wait, then why are you here so early?"

I chuckle at the similarities between her and my mom. "I wanted to get you and my mom to help me with something for Sarah before she wakes up."

"Of course. Come in. I'll just grab my shoes," she says, pulling the door open farther and disappearing inside. She comes back a few minutes later, and we both step onto the porch before I clasp her hand in mine, popping us both into my mom's kitchen.

"Good morning, Constance," Rita says, greeting my now dressed mother who is pouring a third cup of coffee.

"Good morning, Rita. He didn't wake you, did he?"

"Oh, no. I've been up for hours. I didn't know when things were going to happen in the Amazon, so I've been sleeping fully clothed, just in case." She gives me a pointed look and I feel a pang of guilt. We did promise to get her before anything happened.

"Sorry about that. Everything happened really fast, and we didn't need to fight at all. Although your daughter is amazing, you should see what she did," I say, smiling.

"Why? What did she do?"

"Do you want me to tell you or show you?" I ask with a smirk. It will only take me a few minutes to take them both to the coven and back. Besides, Sarah is sure to sleep for a while after how much magic she used yesterday. And our late-night antics christening the house.

"Show us," my mom says. I clasp both of their hands. With the boost in my magic after mating with Sarah, I'm able to take them both at the same time.

We land directly in front of the wall, and both women clutch at their chests. "She did this?" Rita asks, immediately seeing the wall. My mom's brows furrow with confusion, not knowing that it wasn't here twenty-four hours before.

"Yes. She got the idea from the huts you built over the benches in the clearing. She got the rest of the coven members here to help her."

My mom reaches out and touches the wall, and it begins to move under her touch, growing and twirling tighter together. "This is incredible."

"It is."

"It's almost like it has a mind of its own, growing stronger when I push against it," my mom says, poking and prodding it in different spots.

"I noticed that, too," Rita says doing the same. "I wonder how she did that?"

I shrug my shoulders. "I honestly don't know. She talked to it after, asked it to let our allies in and keep the rest out, and it listened. Then she asked it to make a hole big enough for us to get through, and it listened again."

"Incredible," my mom whispers.

"We can come back with Sarah another time so you can see it in action. Right now, I need your help with something," I say to them both. I don't bother listening to their protests and pop us back into my mother's kitchen.

Rita seems to be the first one to snap out of her awe-struck state. "Okay, so what do you want our help with?"

"I want to make Sarah a ring. But not just any ring. I want it to have a moon stone in the center with storm magic running through it so that, when you look directly into it, you can see the lightning. That's why I need you here, Rita. Mom has the moonstone, but you have the magic. Mom, I need your help making the setting. I want the metal to be titanium with a crescent moon shape on top with the stone in the center."

"That sounds beautiful, Sebastyn," my mom says, coming over to give me a hug.

"It does," Rita agrees.

Together, the three of us finish our coffees and head to the work room. My mom passes Rita the moonstone, and I see her close her eyes, holding it tightly in her hands, imbedding her magic within. My mom quickly slips out a small nugget of titanium and places it in a cast iron pot over a burner to melt.

"Here, Sebastyn, you can forge the mold," my mom says, passing me a stone mold. I pull up the vision I have in my head of what I want the ring to look like and close my eyes. I place my hands on the smooth stone, urging it to change to what I need it to. By the time I open my eyes, it's done, and the metal is ready to be poured.

A quick gust of cool air later, and I'm pulling out the exact setting I envisioned for Sarah. It has a band that looks like three vines entwining together going around with a crescent moon on the top and an empty space for the large moon stone to slip in.

"All done," Rita says, passing me the stone. I look down at it in my hand and watch as lightning bolts streak across the smooth black surface.

"It's perfect!" I exclaim, setting it in and closing my eyes once more, bending the metal around it to keep it in place.

I show both moms the finished product with them both oohing and awing over it. "Thank you both," I say, giving them each a hug before teleporting back into my bedroom.

Goddess, I hope she likes it. I walk over to her on the bed and slide the ring gently on her ring finger. It fits perfectly. I place a gentle kiss on her cheek. "Good morning, my love."

Her eyes flutter open, and she smiles. "Good morning." She stretches her arms above her head, and I hold my breath, waiting for her to realize what's on her hand.

She freezes mid-stretch, bringing her left hand back down and staring at the ring. "What the ...?"

"Do you like it?" I whisper, wiping my super sweaty palms on my pants.

"You gave me this?" She asks, not taking her eyes off the ring but turning her hand to look at it from every angle.

"Yes, our moms helped me make it."

"You made this?" I nod. "It's beautiful."

I wipe the stray tears from her eyes, and she finally looks up at me. "We don't do engagement or wedding rings, normally, but I thought that maybe you would. But if you don't like it, we can always pick..."

She cuts me off placing her lips on mine. "I absolutely love it. Thank you."

"You're welcome."

"What type of stone is this? It looks like there's lighting in it."

"There is. It's a moonstone, but your mom infused it with Storm magic, making the storms appear inside when you look directly at it."

"I didn't think you could get any more perfect, Sebastyn Moon."

"I'm far from perfect, sweetheart, but I'll never stop trying to be perfect for you." I give her another kiss. "And as much as I would love nothing more than to spend the day in this bed with you, I am supposed to head to the academy to sign the employment papers before we head back to the Amazon to get Sophia, Darren, Samara and Trev."

"Can I come with you?" She asks.

"Of course, you can. I assumed you would be. We can leave as soon as I get back from the academy. Take your time getting ready. I won't be long."

"No, I meant I want to come with you to the academy. Darren

asked me to teach, too. I'm thinking that maybe now that I'm feeling more confident in myself, I should give it a shot."

"Oh. Of course. We'll head over there after you get dressed so that we can spend the day exploring in the Amazon."

She gives me a quick kiss on the cheek before jumping out of bed and rushing through her morning routine. We have enough time to stop at the diner on pack land and grab a couple muffins before heading over to Westwood Academy.

"Sebastyn, Sarah. I didn't expect you two to be here." Phoebe says, standing on the front steps with the boys next to her and Aurora in her arms.

"Sarah's decided to take Darren up on his offer and teach along with me," I tell her as my mate walks up and quickly steals Aurora from her mother's arms, snuggling her. I can't wait to see her do that with our children. She's going to be the most amazing mother.

"Really?" Phoebe exclaims, wrapping Sarah in a hug at her nod. "That's great. Alaric is in there now with the rest of the alphas, and Skarlyt is trying to figure out who can teach a class so the boys can start this year. Come on. Let's go tell them." She clasps Sarah's hand, pulling her inside while the boys and I shrug and follow them in.

We can hear loud voices before we get to the board room, but it quiets down as we walk in. "I found our solution," Phoebe announces, pulling Sarah forward.

"What do you mean?" Axel demands while Trixie raises a brow in question, but Alaric and Skarlyt both smile.

"Are you up for it, Sarah?" Skarlyt asks, coming around to stand in front of her.

Sarah looks down at Aurora and then at the boys before nodding. "I think so. I was going to be a teacher before Joe stopped me from going to university. I may have to brush up on some things, but I'm sure that I can teach the younger kids everything they would learn in a regular school." Her voice is confident and sure, two things I wondered if I would ever hear coming from her. Gone is the meek, shy woman I met. In her place is this gorgeous goddess of a woman. My mate. I'm the luckiest man in the world because she's all mine.

A short discussion and a whole lot of papers to sign later, and we finally walk out of the academy, saying goodbye to our friends and heading back to the Amazon.

Chapter Twenty-Four

Sarah

After spending an amazing day in the Amazon and saying our extremely emotional goodbyes, we all leave, heading back to Phoebe's and Alaric's to celebrate. But as we get there, we find an empty house and a note saying, 'Meet us at Supernatural'. "What's that all about?" I ask Trev. He shrugs his shoulders with a smirk, making me not believe him for a second. They're up to something. All of them.

Sebastyn clasps Darren's and Sophia's hands while Samara, Trev, and I wait. I've never been to Supernatural before so I have no idea how to teleport there. Trev would probably have a picture that would help me, but I haven't practiced doing that yet, and honestly, I don't think I'm ready to.

Sebastyn comes back, taking Trev with him, leaving Samara and I alone. "What is going on?" I pin her with a 'you better tell me' look.

She shrugs her shoulders, "I don't know."

I put my hands on my hips. "Don't you lie to me, missy." I demand and watch her face fall. Just as she's about to cave, Sebastyn pops back in front of us and whisks us away.

The next thing I know, we're landing in the middle of the most beautiful room I've ever seen. There's a large tree in the middle, with a huge trunk growing up to the ceiling, and there are branches running along the ceiling and down the walls, sporting thick green vines and beautiful purple berries. There is a bar on one side that looks like it's made out of vines but with a shiny top. There are booths along the other side, also made out vines. At the far end of the room is a dance floor full of my friends and a bunch of others that I don't recognize.

I turn to Sebastyn, "What's going on?"

"This is our joint bachelor and bachelorette party, apparently." He says, putting his arm around my shoulders while Samara gives me a wink and walks behind the bar with her mate.

"Come on, Sarah. Let's do some shots!" Sophia says, grabbing my hand and pulling me over to the bar with shot after shot lined up. All the girls come up, grabbing a shot and encircling me.

"To Sarah," Phoebe cheers, and we all clink our glasses together and down the liquid. I expected a burn that usually accompanies taking a shot, but it goes down smooth and leaves a fruity aftertaste.

"Thanks, ladies!" I giggle, quickly followed by a hiccup.

"Sarah, I'd like you to meet Drusilla and Rayne," Skarlyt says, pulling two of the most beautiful women I've ever seen toward me.

The beautiful blond sticks out her hand. "You can call me Dru. Everyone does." She gives me a smile but there's something in her eyes that almost seem haunted, like she's got some demons in her past. I clasp her hand in mine and get a flash. It's of her and the girl next to her, but younger and dirtier. It's gone so quickly I'm not even sure what I saw. I smile and release her hand.

"Sarah. It's nice to meet you."

The bombshell brunette steps forward next, and I immediately feel intimidated. She has an aura of power around her; though it doesn't feel like magic but something more.

"I'm Rayne. Thank you for letting us crash your party. I needed to get out tonight," she says with a wink, sticking her hand out to mine again. I hesitate for a moment, worried that I may get another flash vision, but luckily, I don't. Instead, there is a tingle that runs up my arms at her touch. There's something about these two women that I just can't put my finger on. Something important.

"Sarah. But you already know that," I chuckle, and she joins in while stepping back.

We turn back to the bar, finding another line of shots waiting for us. I turn and search out Sebastyn, finding him in a similar predicament, surrounded by our guy friends. He smiles and waves at me. I blow him a kiss before turning back to the girls. We down our shots before I'm being pulled onto the dance floor. As soon as I step onto the tiles outlining where the dance floor begins, the music begins pounding loudly, as if I just walked through a bubble that was keeping the noise down throughout the rest of the bar. I lose myself in the music, moving my body to the beat while surrounded by my girls. I've never experienced something like this. Never being allowed to go out dancing when I was younger and then once I married Joe. Well, let's just say this-- where a bunch of girlfriends go out to a club, dancing, drinking, and having a good time—is something I'd only seen in movies.

After a few songs, sweat is pouring off my body, my muscles are burning in a good way, and I slip away to grab myself a bottle of water. I sit at one of the stools at the bar, grabbing the waiting bottle from Trev with a smile and wink.

"You, okay?" Skarlyt asks, coming up to sit beside me.

I nod with a smile. "Better than ever." I tell her honestly. I hear the song Sexy Bitch by David Guetta and Akon come over the speakers, and while it's dulled for me because of the bubble, it is obviously loud for those on the dance floor if the energy of the women is anything to go by. My eyes are drawn to Rayne and Dru;

they're moving like they were born to do this. I notice Rayne glancing over at a booth and follow her gaze, finding Drake sitting there with a scowl on his face. I turn back to Rayne and find her with a sinister smile, increasing her movements, like she is doing a seductive dance only for him, and I raise a brow.

"What's up with that?" I ask.

"What?" Skarlyt says, following my gaze.

"Drake and Rayne."

"Well..." Skarlyt says, rubbing her hands together like she's going to tell me a big secret, leaning over in my ear. "So Dru is Drake's baby sister, and she was captured by hunters when she was sixteen. She spent years with them until another hunter set her free."

My mouth drops open in shock. So that's what the haunted look is about. "But that doesn't explain..."

"I wasn't finished." Skarlyt chuckles. "The hunter that helped her escape was Rayne." Once again, my mouth opens so wide it could catch flies in it, but I don't say anything, not wanting to interrupt Skarlyt again. "Turns out that Rayne was with the hunters and mages when Darren was captured, and Phoebe saved her. After that, Rayne knew she couldn't be part of what they were doing anymore and set out looking for Phoebe, hoping to get help to disappear. Fast forward a little and it turns out that she and Drake bumped uglies but once he found out she was a hunter... Well, you can just imagine. But if I'm right.."

She pauses and I grip her arm, not able to handle the suspense. "If you're right about what?"

She leans over dramatically and whispers in my ear. "I think they're mates."

"No?" My hand flies to my mouth. I can't see Drake being too happy with having a hunter as a mate. He's not a very pleasant guy to begin with. I've met him half a dozen times and have yet to see his lips tip up in a smile.

She nods, smirking. "It's going to make life very interesting for a little while."

"I guess so." I chug the rest of my water and turn back to her. "I've been meaning to talk to you."

"You have?" she asks, and I dip my chin.

"I wanted to apologize."

"Apologize?" She asks, confused. "For what?"

I take a deep breath. "For not remembering you. My mom told me that you and I were close when we were younger and that you didn't handle my..." I pause not knowing what to say, "'death' very well."

Her eyes soften and she wraps her arms around me. "You don't need to apologize. I'm just happy to have you back." She pulls back a little. "Plus, now you're my sister; there's no getting rid of me."

I chuckle at her. "I won't ever want to get rid of you."

She waves her hand before downing her drink and rushing back to the dance floor. I drink the rest of my water as Sophia walks up. I need to talk to her, too. No time like the present.

"Sophia?"

"Yes?" She says, turning to me as she twists the cap off her water bottle.

I twist my hands together anxiously, worried about how she will react. "I have to tell you something," I say, glancing up at her eyes.

She places her hand on my shoulder. "You can tell me anything." The way she says it almost makes me want to keep it to myself. What if she hates me?

"It's about Joe... he was..." I begin but can't force the words out.

"Devin's nephew?" She supplies and my shoulders relax.

"You knew?"

She nods. "I suspected. Devin used to talk about his nephew Joe who lived in Ontario. I assumed that they were the same

231

person after you told me your story but wanted to wait for you to tell me."

"So, you don't hate me?" I ask. She smiles and wraps her arms around me.

"Of course, I don't hate you. You didn't choose him and even if you did, just because they were related doesn't mean you did any of those things to me. If anything, it means we understand each other's experiences even more," she says, and I pull her back to me. I don't know why I didn't realize this is how she would react. I grab her hand, pulling her to the dance floor with me. I purposely try to keep my eyes off Rayne and Drake but don't miss the death glare she gets from Drake when a large shifter begins dancing behind her.

If Skarlyt is right, tonight is definitely going to get interesting. Before I can watch the scene unfold, strong arms circle around my midsection. I don't need to turn to know that it's Sebastyn. I'd know him anywhere.

"Ready to go, love?" He whispers, blowing on my neck and placing kisses up and down it.

I barely bob my head in agreement before we're landing in the middle of our bedroom.

"As fun as tonight was, I need my mate," he says huskily, and I turn, stripping off my clothes and walking to the bathroom.

"Where are you going?"

"I'm sweaty and need a shower. Are you coming?" I call out, turning on the water and stepping into the glass doors.

Within seconds, a very naked Sebastyn is popping in front of me, lifting me instantly so I wrap my legs around his waist. He wastes no time, sinking deep into me and I cry out with a moan. His mouth meets mine, clashing together, our tongues instantly seeking out one another, dancing sensually.

I brace my hands on his shoulders, lifting my body in time with his thrusts, each time, his cock hitting the spot inside me that has me crying out his name with my release. I'm still shaking when he lowers me down, sitting on the bench and spinning me so that I'm sitting on his lap, thrusting back up into me. I arch as his fingers find my clit, and I try to focus on going up and down on his cock but his skilled fingers make that very difficult. He uses his other hand to grip my hips, helping me create a rhythm that has us both crying out.

"I love you, Sarah Storm."

"And I love you, Sebastyn Moon."

We wash up quickly and collapse in our bed, falling into a peaceful sleep quickly. Goddess, my new life is amazing. An amazing mate, an amazing job, incredible friends and family, and best of all I don't need to be anything but me anymore. I know that each person in my life will love me just for being me no matter what.

Chapter Twenty-Five

Sarah

It's been a few days, and although it was hard to say goodbye to Blaze and the rest of her family, it was with a promise that we will see each other again. As it turns out, it's sooner than I expected. Today is the day Sebastyn and I chose for our mating ceremony, and I wake up to a very excited Blaze jumping on my bed.

"Sarah!" she exclaims. Still half asleep, I jump up.

"What happened?" I question, my purple magic at the ready.

She giggles. "Nothing, silly. We came for your mating ceremony. Sebastyn wanted it to be a surprise."

"It is most definitely a surprise," I tell her, wiping the sleep out of my eyes before throwing my arms around her.

"Constance got me and Fyre a dress each and everything. You should see them. They're the most beautiful dresses I've ever seen," she says, bouncing up and down on the bed.

"Come on, sleepy head. Time to get ready," Skarlyt says, popping her head in the room.

"I'm coming," I respond, stretching out the kinks from my night's sleep. As I walk down the stairs, I notice the house is full of all the women in my life, and my heart skips a beat. Never in my wildest dreams did I think this would be my life. I never dared to dream of having one friend, let alone a house full of them. When I see my mom walking through the door carrying a large garment bag, I place my hand on my chest to keep my heart from bursting out.

"We didn't have much time to go dress shopping, but this was my mother's mating dress, and her mother before her. I altered it a bit to be more in style. I hope you like it," my mom says, walking over to me. I don't care what the dress looks like, just the fact that I have my mom here with me today is more than I ever could have dreamed.

"I'm sure I'm going to love it," I tell her, wrapping my arms around her. I consider telling her my plans for later but decide to keep my mouth shut. It wouldn't be much of a surprise if I did. At this point, I'm not even sure if it's going to be a good surprise or a bad one, but it's something I think we both need in order to move on with our lives.

The day is filled with laughter and fun. Constance made us a giant feast while Skarlyt and Opal set up the clearing. We had gone back and forth about doing it on pack land or here, but after talking with Skarlyt and Alaric, we decided on the clearing. Sebastyn and I also suggested doubling it as the announcement for the merging of pack and coven. It just feels right. It was Phoebe and Alaric who saved me, and Skarlyt and Sebastyn who gave me a home. She argued saying that she didn't want to take any of the spotlight off me as she put it, but after I told her that it would make me happy, she readily agreed.

Everyone else but my mom and Constance leave to get to the clearing on time and I go upstairs to get dressed. I unzip the bag and suck in a breath. It is a beautiful princess style white dress with a sweetheart neckline and large white tooling. As I look closer at the bottom of the dress, I see small purple and green rhinestones embedded into it. Tears form in my eyes.

"The purple and green represent you and Sebastyn," my mom says from the doorway.

I don't trust my voice, so I nod, turning and rushing into her open arms. I let the tears slip down my face. "It's more than I ever expected," I whisper.

"I know my sweet girl, but it's still not as much as you deserve," she raises my chin so my eyes meet hers. "You deserve every bit of happiness that you have coming your way. It will never take away the hardships you dealt with in your previous life, but you've proven already that you didn't allow the hand you were dealt to break you. You have grown into a beautiful, caring woman who I am so proud to call my daughter."

The tears flow faster at my mom's declaration. "But now we need to get you ready. That mate of yours is going to start getting worried if we don't get there soon," she says, wiping my tears first, before her own.

We get me in my dress, and I leave my long brown hair flowing down my back. Constance pins some small flowers and jewels throughout, after placing a flower crown over my head. The dress fits like a dream, like it was made exactly for me, because I guess it was.

As we step into the clearing, I look around in awe. They have obviously done a lot of work, and Skarlyt must've taken what I showed her back in the Amazon and put it to use, because there are pews made of vines along the aisle with a large vine archway covered in flowers at the end. Sebastyn is standing just under it at the end of the aisle, waiting for me. He is wearing a pair of linen pants and a button-down shirt, looking like a god in human form. The sun is even shining brightly down on him, providing a halo of sorts.

I reach him, place my hands in his, and turn to face both Skarlyt and Alaric. "Welcome everyone. I'm sure you're all wondering why Alaric is up here with me." Murmurs go through the crowd, and she pauses momentarily before continuing. "Well, after a lot of consideration, we have decided to merge the pack and coven, becoming the Moon-Westwood Alliance rather than the Westwood Pack and the Coven of the Moon." People begin to murmur louder now, but Skarlyt raises her hand to silence them. "It is no secret that I am mated to a wolf, and with more and more of us finding our mates within other supernatural species, it makes sense that we merge. Everything will remain as it has been, the only difference being that if I am unavailable for whatever reason, Alaric can now be contacted for help, as well as Sebastyn and Sarah as the next in line as High Priest and Priestess."

People start talking louder now, obviously shocked by this decision. Alaric speaks up, "Listen, everyone. You know me. You know the pack. We have been allies for centuries. Nothing will change. Skarlyt is right, though; this is the most logical move. I will never overstep my station, I recognize Skarlyt as the coven leader, and I have no desire to take over any of her duties. The only thing that will change is that, rather than having Phoebe and myself making decisions solely for the pack and Skarlyt and Lennox deciding for the coven, we will discuss all decisions amongst the four of us to ensure that it is in the best interest of everyone."

"But that still makes more shifters in charge than witches," one of the coven members speaks up.

To my surprise, it's Opal who stands up next. "If you think that any of the shifters or the Moons will take advantage of us, then you haven't lived in the same coven I have. Really, this is the way it has been for years. It's just now become official. When was the last time Constance made a big decision without first consulting the pack?" she asks, looking around. Everyone seems to shake their heads, not able to come up with an example. "Exactly. They are our friends, some are our mates, and some are our family.

This changes nothing except our name." Opal finishes and sits back down with a nod at us.

"Thank you, Opal," Skarlyt begins. "If you are truly not in agreement, we will not go forward. But we all believe this is the best course of action." I look out at the members present and notice the changes on their faces. Where they were unhappy with the change, they now seem content.

Skarlyt and Alaric both visibly relax as we turn back toward them. "Let's continue. We have been brought together today in front of the Mother to join these two together as a mated pair," Skarlyt says loudly.

"Do you Sebastyn Moon take Alexandra Sarah Storm as your mate?" Skarlyt asks, and Sebastyn's eyes go wide at the use of my birth name.

"I do," he says.

"And do you pledge your allegiance to me, Skarlyt Moon, as your coven leader as well as Alaric Westwood?" she asks.

"I do," he repeats.

"And do you, Alexandra Sarah Storm, take Sebastyn Moon as your mate?" Alaric asks.

"I do," I respond, looking into Sebastyn's eyes.

"Do you pledge your allegiance to me and Skarlyt Moon as the leaders of the coven and pack?" he asks. Now that sounds better, Skarlyt should use those words instead.

"I do," I reply once more.

"Then, before the Mother and these witnesses, we declare you a mated pair," Skarlyt says, clapping her hands together. I throw myself into Sebastyn's arms.

Cheers sound off from the crowd as we kiss. Reluctantly, we separate and turn to face our friends and family, who clap as we make our way back down the aisle. We were mates before. There was no doubt about that; the ceremony just makes it official.

We eat and dance for a few hours before it's time to enact my plan. "Are you sure you want to do this?" Phoebe asks, coming to stand beside me.

"I am. I need to do this," I tell her, and she nods, giving me a hug.

"And you're sure you don't want me to come with?" She asks. I shake my head *no*, knowing I need to do this with my mom, Skarlyt, and my mate. My family. "Okay. I'm here if you need me," she says, walking back toward Alaric.

"Are you ready, love?" Sebastyn asks as he and Skarlyt walk up.

"As I'll ever be. We just need my mom," I say.

The three of us walk over to my mom, and I pull her aside. "Mom. I have to do something, and I'd like you to be there. I was going to call it a surprise, but I'm not sure if it really is," I ramble, and she bobs her head along with a concerned look on her face. "I am going to see dad. I need to stand up to him if I'm going to start this new life right," I see the fury on her face at the mention of my dad. But I also see the determination set in. She needs this as much as I do.

"Okay," she says, walking up to Skarlyt and holding her hand. I had teleported into the backyard with Skarlyt the other day so that she would know where to bring my mom.

We blink away, and seconds later we arrive in the backyard of the home I grew up in. For a second, I don't think anyone is home, but then the light turns on in the kitchen, and I see my dad's silhouette. I walk up to the back door and knock, leaving the rest of my group in the yard.

"Sarah. Good, you came to your senses," he says with a sneer as he opens up the door.

"No, Dad. I didn't. I came to tell you that I will never be coming back. And that I forgive you," I state to him as I hear breaths suck in behind me. I hadn't told them my plan to forgive him, but I have thought about it a lot. Holding onto all that hate and rage toward him isn't going to do me any good. If I want to be able to move forward with my life, I need to be able to let go of my past and forgiving him is the first step.

"Well, I don't," my mom calls out as thunder begins to roll. My dad's face turns from shock to complete and utter terror as he realizes who just spoke.

"Rita," he whispers.

"Don't you 'Rita' me. You stole my daughter from me. You made me believe that you were both dead for twenty-five years. There is no excuse that you could give me that would make any of that better," she spits, poking him in the chest.

"You don't understand," he pleads.

"No, I don't, and I don't want to. There is literally nothing you can say to excuse your actions," as she speaks, the lightning begins to come in more frequently and the rolls of thunder boom louder. "I, Rita Storm, reject you, Robert McKay as my mate," she spits and my dad falls to the ground, clutching his chest.

I wrap my arm around my mom, seeing that she is also in pain, with tears streaming down her face. I understand her reasoning for it, but I'm not too sure if I would have been able to do the same thing.

"Dad. You will never see either of us again. If you have anything to say, now's your chance," I tell him.

"You will regret this" is the only thing that comes out of his mouth as his blue magic starts to form on his hands.

My own purple magic flares up surrounding me, and he stops, shock registering on his face. "Oh yeah. I also have a lot of magic. Like a lot. Way more than you led me to believe. But I guess that was just one more thing you lied to me about."

"You will still regret this. I am a part of something bigger than you will ever understand. You just wait and see," as my dad finishes, I hear something very large land behind me, but not wanting to take my attention away from my dad—and trusting that

Sebastyn and Skarlyt will be able to handle anything–I don't turn.

"No. You will be the one to regret your choices, mage," a familiar voice calls out.

Everyone stares in shock at Andres, except Sebastyn and me. "I didn't know how you would find us," I say to him.

"You know this dragon?" my mom asks.

"Yeah... about that. Sebastyn and I kind of met Andres while we were in the Amazon," I tell them.

"And you didn't think to tell us?" Skarlyt asks, her jaw so wide it might as well be on the floor.

"Well, we weren't sure if he would be able to find us, plus we had a lot of other things to deal with," Sebastyn reasons.

Mom and Skarlyt both nod, with my dad shaking in fear on the step where he is still crouching. "Goodbye, Dad," I tell him, walking back over to Sebastyn. "Andres, can you fly to meet us, or do you want Sebastyn to come back and teleport you?" I ask.

"I will fly. I have never enjoyed teleporting," he replies, shifting and taking to the sky.

"You two have so much explaining to do," Skarlyt says angrily and then she gets a grin on her face. "Just wait until Phoebe, Sophia, and Samara find out you've kept this secret," she says with an evil laugh.

"Oh shit," I whisper to Sebastyn.

"It will be okay, love. They'll understand. Besides, I will have Alaric and Darren to deal with, too," he says with a kiss on my forehead, and we teleport back into the clearing.

Oh great. They can't interrogate us on the night of our mating ceremony. Right?

To my surprise, Andres is already waiting for us in the clearing, surrounded by all of our friends and family. Although they initially seem upset about us not telling them, they take it in stride, understanding that we had slightly more pressing issues to deal with.

But the prophecy is a different situation entirely. It has every single one of us worried as Andres recites it:

"When the daughter of the storm and the son of the moon
become one;
A hunter and her prey put aside their differences;
The lost daughter of air mates the first son born of magic and fire;
A son and daughter of fire join together;
The dual natured son and the dawn cement their bond;
A new age arrives where Supernatural beings will need to come out
of the shadows as a new enemy awakens."

That's not ominous at all. A storm seems to be brewing in the supernatural world. Two parts of the prophecy have already started, assuming that Andres is right and I am the daughter of storm and Sebastyn being the son of the moon. Not to mention if what Skarlyt says is true, and the hunter Rayne is truly the mate of Drake, the vampire. Now we just need to figure out the rest before this new enemy comes to light.

Epilogue

Drake

After leading my coven through the woods behind Alaric and his pack, we spread out in the trees, waiting. I take my spot at the very back of the group, hoping to stop anyone from sneaking up behind us should the barrier fail.

Soon after, there's a big commotion at the front, and Phoebe's phoenix is flying high with a screech that has me covering my ears. Things must not be going the way they want it to. I rush toward them, seeing everyone fighting. And from the looks of it, with the mountain lions, bears, wolves, witches, and my coven, we're winning. I don't pause, quickly jumping into the fray. I don't give two shits about the mages; there are others here that have more beef with them than I do so I leave them to be picked off. But the hunters? Well, that's another story.

I'm leaping from tree to tree, focusing only on the hunters. I don't know if these are the same assholes that took my sister years ago, but it doesn't matter. They're all entitled pricks who think that they're better than everyone simply because they are 'normal'. They think there's nothing special about them, and to them that's a good thing; not to me. I know that the pure hunter bloodlines are descended from the Norse gods and are, in fact, more supernatural than human. But you can never tell any of them that. In reality, they're not much different from us. Yet they call us monsters. Yes, we drink blood, but vampires, as a species, haven't practiced source feeding in years–other than from willing donors.

I wish Dru was here to tell me if these fuckers are the ones, but then I'm also glad she isn't because we've made so much progress with her mentally. I don't know if this would set her back again. She escaped ten years ago, but she still frequently wakes up with nightmares and hasn't left our compound since.

As I'm taking out the most recent hunter to cross my path, I catch a whiff of the most amazing scent. Whoever's blood that is, it is making my mouth water to the point that I actually feel saliva drip onto my lips. Something that hasn't happened in years. I haven't felt true bloodlust like this in... I try to think back to a time where I have felt like this and come up blank. Even in my teenage years when I had trouble controlling my thirst, I've never lost control like this. Never. I finish my task quickly and go in search of that arousing aroma.

I search for hours after the battle but never find the source. The only explanation is that the scent is coming from the one person I wasn't in a hurry to find. I was never too worried about finding my mate, but after tonight, one thought consumes me; I need to find her.

* * *

Want more from the Westwood Pack?
Of course, you do!
Information on Book 5, Hunter's Heart here:
https://fdfairauthor.wixsite.com/website

About the Author

F.D. Fair is the author of the Westwood Pack Series. As an avid reader of Paranormal Romance Novels for the past 20 years, she turned her love of everything paranormal into steamy True Mate novels with a twist.

F.D. Fair lives and works in southern Ontario, Canada and

spends her time when she is not working or writing with the loves of her life—Her husband and 3 boys.

She is as weird as they come but is proud of it. Embracing her weirdness makes for some great stories.

Sign up for FD Fair's Newsletter:
https://dashboard.mailerlite.com/forms/76323/5809623843156931o/share

Make sure to stalk her...

Instagram:
https://www.instagram.com/f.d.fairauthor
Facebook:
https://www.facebook.com/profile.php?id=100071688648516
Goodreads:
https://www.goodreads.com/author/show/21734156.F_D_Fair
Twitter:
https://twitter.com/FdFair
Bookbub:
https://www.bookbub.com/authors/f-d-fair

More from Foundations

Witch Trial Legacy by Katherine Eddinger Smits

GET IT HERE: https://katherineeddingersmits.weebly.com/witch-trial-legacy.html

Sybilla Sanborn must break a centuries old curse before everything she cares about goes up in smoke.

Sybilla is a nurse gifted with the ability to heal with her touch but cursed with visions of future tragedies she cannot prevent because no one heeds her warnings. With help from the mediums of the spiritualist town of Cassadaga, Florida, she learns she is descended from both the first person executed for witchcraft in this country and the man who accused her.

Conn Ahern is an Iraq war vet dealing with pain and PTSD while working as a paramedic and struggling to save the ranch his grandmother founded. He's an atheist who wants nothing to do with the people of the town.

When Conn and Sybilla meet, sparks fly, but not always in a good way, and their relationship fans the flames of jealousy and revenge in someone who doesn't want them to work things out.

During a séance, her ancestor's spirit reveals how Sybilla can rid herself of the curse and save Conn, but the price may be too high.

Foundations Book Publishing

Our mission is to exceed the expectations of our authors and the reading community with an uncompromising commitment to quality, individualism and personal pride. We measure our success one book at a time.

You can find more great works in multiple genres including Romance, Literary Fictions, Thrillers, Suspense, Young Adult, and more!

Visit us at FoundationsBooks.net